TIME CALL

By Wendy Lupo

Publisher's Note: This is a work of fiction. Names, characters, places, and incidents either are the product of the author's imagination or are used fictitiously, and any resemblance to actual persons, living or dead, business establishments, events, or locales is entirely coincidental.

ISBN-13: 978-0615430836 (Chamberlain Hill Press)
ISBN-10: 061543083X

- For Mom -

One

I always found it odd to sit on the opposite facing seat on a train and experience the sensation of moving backward. Not being able to see where I was going, only where I had been, had always been a little disturbing to me. The reverse motion never felt quite right and traveling alone only added to my uneasy feeling.

It had been three weeks since Laura and I broke up, this time for good. It had been a roller coaster ride that lasted three years, off and on. I recall that during our last fight she screamed in my face that she had wasted the last three years of her life with a man who did not love her and never would. I didn't do anything but stand there and take it. What was there for me to say anyway? She was right and I knew it.

Laura continued her rant about how I would never fight for her — or for us — and added that I stayed with her simply for the convenience of it. "I was far too easy a conquest for you, Joseph Eaton! You didn't have to do a thing to gain my affections. Don't you have anything at all to say? Anything?" Nothing, I said absolutely nothing. My lack of words told her all that she needed to know. She stormed out and that was the last that I saw of her.

"What's wrong with me?" I said to myself once I realized that I had been staring out the window of the train but seeing only the images that were in my head.

The conductor announced that Valley View would be the next stop and I realized that my sister had been right. The train ride from Philadelphia to Valley View *would* be a short one.

I was really looking forward to seeing Margo again. We had not seen each other at all in the two years since our mother's funeral. She had always been the wild one in the family and would do or try just about anything. I, on the other hand, would only be uninhibited after consuming large amounts of alcohol. Unfortunately much of my early twenties was spent being uninhibited.

As the train rolled along, I wondered what kind of trouble Margo may have gotten herself into over the past two years. It didn't really matter though. She was always smart enough to get herself out of trouble too. I always envied her boldness and how any mistake she would make would just roll right off of her like water off a freshly waxed car.

Margo had moved to Valley View, Long Island shortly after our mother's death. Mom had described Valley View, her childhood home, as the perfect environment in which to grow up. Thinking about it now, maybe Margo had moved there so that *she* could finally grow up. After her rebellious teen years, Margo had made many attempts to get closer to our mother. Perhaps her move to Valley View was Margo's final attempt to try to understand what made our mother into the cold hard person she was. This coldness, in my view, was the cause of the strained relationship we both shared with our mother. I'm sure that Margo felt as I did and regretted that the bond between mother and child had never been repaired.

My mother's family had been Valley View residents since my great-grandparents relocated there from Brooklyn in 1913. Whenever Mom had a chance to tell us how wonderful the town was she didn't let the opportunity get away. If Valley View was so great, I often wondered, why did she ever leave? I was born and raised only a few short hours away by car, why did Mom never take me to see this utopia?

The train slowed to a stop and I exited. The Valley View train station was certainly nothing to write home about. The place was run-down, worn out, and was permeated with the persistent aroma of urine.

"Hey, baby bro!!!" someone yelled. I turned around to see my sister Margo approaching. She was in her early thirties but still looked like a high school girl. Her hair was jet black and straight as a pin. I noticed that she still carried that little bit of baby fat on her short frame.

"Margo!" I replied, "You look great!" We hugged and I knew that Margo could tell something was wrong.

"What's going on, Little Joey? Why'd you come alone?" Little Joey! Yuck! I hated it when she called me that. Since Margo was older than me by two years, she had often played the big sister card, but only when it suited her to do so.

"I told you over the phone that Laura and I broke up, didn't I?"

"Yeah, but you didn't tell me why. What happened, Little Joey?"

3

"I wish I knew," I lied. "I guess I have commitment issues or something."

"That's a bunch of crap," Margo declared, "You probably just haven't met the right one yet, that's all. I've got a friend here in town that'd be perfect for you. I'll call her right now." Before I could mount any sort of protest, Margo had whipped open her cell phone and had reached her friend.

"... Great. Then we'll see you tonight? Yeah, come around nine. Okay, see you later, Stacy."

Just like that, I had been set-up by Margo the Matchmaker. As we made our way toward Margo's car I sighed, "Does *she* know that it's going to be a set-up?"

She unlocked her tiny car and shrugged, "Yeah, she knows."

"You know, I was hoping to spend time with my sister when I got here, not go on a blind date," I muttered as I made sure not to hit my head on the ceiling of Margo's sub-compact.

Margo smiled sweetly as she turned the ignition key and started the drive toward her home. "C'mon, Little Joey, just meet her. She's really pretty and she's funny too. You'll like her!"

"All right ... all right, just stop with the Little Joey crap when she comes over okay?"

"Okay," Margo repeated with all seriousness and then she giggled in the same manner as she did when she was a teenager.

***

It was warmer than expected for an early June afternoon. The strong sun and high humidity gave the day more of a mid-July feel. As Margo drove us up Franklin Avenue toward her residence, I noticed that this area of town was almost as run-down as it was near the train station, but it looked as though it may have been nice at one time. The street was lined with grand old oak trees that guarded proud brick homes that had valiantly stood the test of time.

After a few turns off of Franklin, we arrived at Margo's house, a vintage white Victorian that appeared to have three floors and an attic. The large surrounding lawn, about an acre and a half, was kept neatly manicured. "Home sweet home," said Margo with a flourish, "I rent on the ground floor."

"Wow, what a great place! How old is it?"

"It is gorgeous, isn't it? My landlord said it was built in the 1890s. His family has lived in the house next door for four generations." Margo quickly glanced over my shoulder. "Oh, no, speak of the devil."

"Margo, hello" said a voice belonging to a jolly, short, and balding man who was striding over to us at an accelerated pace. "Hi, this must be your brother." He extended his hand. "I'm Charles Manning, call me Chuck."

I was a bit startled by the man's overt friendliness, but I shyly extended my hand in return, "I'm Joseph, nice to meet you, Chuck."

"Margo says you'll be staying here for a few days. You're in from Philly, right?"

"Yeah, I'll probably just be here till after the weekend."

Chuck studied me for a moment and said, "Then you're going back?"

I thought his last question somewhat strange, but before I could relay a good reply, Margo shouted, "Come on, I don't have all day!" and she started toward the door. I shrugged my shoulders at Chuck and grabbed my suitcase. Chuck returned the shrug as I walked away to join my sister.

When I caught up to her I said, "That wasn't so nice."

"I did you a favor, Little Joey. He would have talked your ear off."

"Still, he seems like a nice guy. You should be nicer to your neighbors," I advised.

Margo replied with laughter, "He's such a busybody. When I told him that you were coming for a visit, he wanted to know your whole freaking life story. You know, I didn't think he would be so friendly to you. The lady upstairs says he only rents to women so I figured he doesn't like other men." She turned the key to her apartment door and proclaimed, "Mi casa es su casa."

She opened her front door and it led directly to her living room. I noticed that the room contained pictures, trinkets, and even furnishings that were very familiar. The entire apartment looked as though it had been decorated entirely from items that originally belonged to my parents and grandparents. The Victorian-style table lamp with its pink flowers and white doily were from my paternal grandmother's apartment in New Jersey. The ugly, red swivel chair came from the house in which we grew up and it seemed odd and out of place without my father's rear end attached to it. On the wall was the painting of a meadow that my mother had labored over for years until she believed it to be "artistically correct," whatever that meant. On an antique-looking oak telephone table that I did not recognize, stood statuettes that I believed had belonged to my great-grandmother. The tiny statues were of well-to-do ladies in various poses and dresses. Margo had managed to produce — either intentionally, or unintentionally — a shrine to our family. "Nice place," was all I could think of to say.

"Your room is on the right. Sorry it's such a mess. I keep meaning to put some of the boxes in the attic but I haven't gotten around to it yet."

I was almost relieved to see such a mess. This was more akin to the sister I remembered. She had always been the sloppy child in the family. I have a permanent and vivid image of how her bedroom floor usually looked when we were kids; a chaotic orchestra of clothes, candy wrappers, teen magazines, and failed homework assignments. This room, though not quite as much of a disaster as her childhood bedroom, was in a state of disarray and was in stark contrast to the pristine conditions of the living room. I was probably the only other living person besides Margo to have entered this room since she moved in.

"There's a couch that opens up under those boxes over there," Margo pointed to a mountain of boxes, "And I emptied a drawer in the dresser for you."

Clumsy me banged into one of the boxes with my foot and nearly tripped. "Sorry. Where's the dresser?" I said, only half joking. "Oh, there it is." It was hidden behind an oriental-patterned room divider. "This will be fine," I said.

After I unpacked, I used Margo's bathroom to clean myself up a bit. Her bathroom was filled with frilly excesses ranging from the pink petal wallpaper to the lacey shower curtain. I never knew my sister to be such a girly-girl.

As I washed my hands, I took a long hard look at myself in the mirror. Another breakup had taken its toll on my mind but I hoped that it had left my body alone. I checked for gray hairs but none had mixed in with my dark brown curly locks. After further inspection I decided that I still looked relatively young — after all, I was only twenty-nine years old — but I did feel a little older and beaten down. I had always been considered rather good looking, but now I wasn't so sure. There were a few faint lines forming on my long, thin face that I had not noticed before. "Great," I said to myself. "I got a blind date with a young chick and I feel like an old man."

Stacy, my date, arrived nearly an hour late, a fact that went unnoticed by Margo and apparently by Stacy herself. I had planned to have a beer or two before Stacy's arrival to alleviate my nervousness. Since she arrived late, I had consumed three more bottles of beer than I had originally planned and was now feeling a bit buzzed. As far back as I can remember I was always shy in the presence of girls that I didn't know, that is, when I wasn't intoxicated, and I never knew what I was supposed to say or do. Laura was forced to make the first move with me when she and I first met.

Margo offered introductions. "This is my friend Stacy. Stacy, this is my little brother Joey, uh ... I mean

Joseph." Stacy was certainly as attractive as Margo said she would be. She had long slender legs that peeked out below her clinging violet patterned dress. Her hair was blonde but her dark eyebrows gave away her true hair color.

Stacy attempted a joke with, "For a little brother, you're awfully tall." I pretended to laugh, and barely got out a "nice to meet you" before Stacy began to chatter away with Margo.

It was a very long night. I was unable, or perhaps unwilling, to keep up with the fast-paced conversation, so I decided to drink away the rest of the evening. While Margo and Stacy babbled on and on, I drank beer after beer and tinkled away on Margo's upright piano, the same old Baldwin we both had lessons on as children. I played both classical and contemporary tunes. With each contemporary song I played, I could hear my mother's voice in my head saying, "Playing that nonsense will get you nowhere, Joseph." She would have preferred that I stick with the great masters like Mozart or Bach but I preferred more contemporary masters like Lennon-McCartney or Elton John. Mom had great aspirations for me to become a famous concert pianist but, needless to say, I had proven to be a big disappointment.

Nine bottles of beer later, I decided it was time to say good night to my sister and my "date," so I went to bed to sleep off my intoxication and my growing despair.

As I drifted off to sleep, unclear images began to appear in my mind's eye. It was as though I was being shown an old photo album. I could see that the album was made up of black and white pictures, but that was all I was able to determine. I was unable to focus clearly on any of the photos. I tried harder and harder to focus, but all of the images remained blurry. I gave it another try, and with complete effort one of the images suddenly became clear enough for me to see. It was a photo of me, smiling wide, standing beside a beautiful young woman that I did not recognize. Pleasant dream, I thought to myself. Then, at that moment, I was awakened by the sound of Margo banging on my bedroom door.

"Do you want to get up? It's nearly 10 a.m."

"Yeah, yeah, I'm up," I muttered.

Margo and I sat down at the kitchen table quietly sipping our coffee. I rubbed my forehead and broke the silence by saying, "Sleep well?"

Margo replied through a yawn, "Yeah, okay. How about you?"

"Good! I haven't slept that long in years. I haven't had that much to drink in quite a while either."

"So?" Margo said as she gave me a sideways look.

"So, what?"

"So, do you like her?"

"Who, Stacy?" As if I had no idea who she was talking about.

"Yeah Stacy, you idiot. She liked you."

"You're kidding me, right? I barely spoke two words to her all night."

"She wants you to call her to make plans to take her out tonight."

I laughed, "You're not going to come along with us, are you?"

"What do you mean, Little Joey? Did I monopolize her too much last night?"

"No. It wasn't your fault. I was just too shy with her," I admitted. "Besides, I don't know if I'm exactly ready to date yet anyway. She is very pretty though ..." I weighed my options and didn't think I had much to lose by going out on a harmless date. "All right, I'll give her a call and take her out somewhere nice for dinner. Okay?"

Margo seemed satisfied. "Okay."

"What did you want to do today? Did you have anything planned?" I inquired.

"Not really," she answered.

"Good. How about we clean up my room and put some of those damn boxes up in the attic?"

***

To gain access to the attic, I had to go up to the hallway on the third floor of the house and pull down a ladder that folded neatly into the ceiling. Victorian homes like this one usually had a stairway that led to the attic but the stairway was likely removed and replaced with the pull ladder when the house was renovated for apartments.

"You're sure you're allowed to store things up there?" I asked. After an assuring nod from Margo, I began my ascent. I climbed up the ladder while my teeth clenched a string with a flashlight attached to it. When I was high enough that I could see inside, I turned the flashlight on and peered just above the attic entrance. It was as dark and musty as I expected it to be. After I had climbed up the rest of the way and was

11

inside the attic, I was surprised that I was almost able to stand all the way up without hitting my head on the ceiling. I pointed the light and moved it slowly around to see what sort of items were stored there. To my left were stacked boxes that appeared as though they hadn't been touched in years. Further back I saw an old sewing machine that, if operational, was probably worth a small fortune. To my right were three old large trunks stacked one upon the other that I assumed contained vintage clothing or bedding. Behind the trunks there was dusty walnut wood furniture from another era, an old Victrola with old records to match, and hand-cranked kitchen appliances that appeared older than the ones Margo displayed above her kitchen cabinets.

"You should see what's up here," I shouted down.

"Any dead bodies?" Margo joked.

"Not quite. Get another flashlight and come up and take a look at this stuff. You'll love it."

With a flashlight in hand, Margo started her climb and I helped her up the rest of the way. After she scanned the attic with her flashlight she squealed with delight, "Wow, look at this stuff! I wonder if Chuck knows what's up here."

While Margo was busy admiring the old furniture and then the kitchen gadgets, I headed toward the Victrola. I clumsily banged my foot into a trunk that I didn't see and the impact must have loosened the trunk's latch because it slowly began to open. Flashing the light inside the trunk, I saw it was filled with old clothes, black and white photographs, and an old-style telephone. I disregarded the clothes and the photos and concentrated my attention on the telephone. Tinkering with electronics and stereo equipment had always been a hobby of mine, one of the few hobbies I was allowed to have as a child, and I wanted to bring the old phone and Victrola down from the attic to see if they worked.

The phone was tall and thin and mahogany in color. It had a rotary down by its base and its receiver attached to a hook that protruded from its stem.

"Hey, Margo, take a look at this old phone," I implored, but she didn't take her eyes off of the old hand mixer she was inspecting. "You think your landlord would mind if I take some of this stuff down?"

"I doubt he even knows what's up here. When I asked him if I could store some of my things in the attic, he didn't seem to care. Maybe you'd better ask him just in case."

"Me?" I asked.

"I try to avoid talking with him as much as possible. Besides," she said as she cringed," I think he has a *thing* for me."

"All right, I'll ask him myself."

***

With the guest room pleasantly clean, I sat on the pull-out couch and let out a contented sigh. I felt good about all of the work I put in storing the boxes, dusting, straightening up, and vacuuming. Margo was happy about it too. Now that there was room for it, her computer was released from its internment in the guest room closet and, thanks to me, in running condition.

I called Stacy to arrange our date, and then upon her recommendation I made 8 p.m. reservations at a local Italian restaurant. Even with the time it would take to shower, get dressed, and pick up Stacy, I still had over an hour to kill. It was as good a time as any to ask Chuck, Margo's landlord, for permission to bring the Victrola and the old telephone down from the attic.

The heat and humidity from the early afternoon gave way to a nice ocean breeze and a clear and dry early evening. Chuck Manning was in his yard trimming the privacy bushes that shielded his large front bay window. He did not seem to notice my approach, so I cleared my throat to gain his attention. Chuck turned to look at me and immediately stopped his trimming.

"Hello, hello. What can I do for you?" he said in a friendly voice.

"Hi, Chuck. I hope it was okay. I put some of my sister's things in the attic for storage."

He removed his work gloves and brushed off his pants. "Yes, yes, I told her she could use the attic if she wished."

"Okay. Good." I nodded my head up and down a few times. "While I was up there I couldn't help but notice some interesting items."

"What do you mean by *interesting items*?" said the jolly-faced man.

"Well, there's old furniture, and there's this amazing Victrola, and ..."

"Oh, those old things," Chuck interrupted. "Yes, they've been up there for years. I've always meant to try and restore them but I have never quite found the time to do it."

"Well, maybe I can help," I proudly replied. "I'm kind of a hobbyist in a way. I like to know what makes things work and I am pretty good at fixing them. I wouldn't mind a crack at the Victrola and the old telephone."

"Telephone? I didn't know there was a telephone up there. How old is it? Where was it?"

"It was in a trunk that I ... accidentally opened." I flashed Chuck a wry smile and hoped that he didn't mind me going through the trunk. "I don't know how old it is but it looks like it could be from the 1920s or 1930s"

"And you say that you think you can restore some of these things, do you?" Chuck inquired with genuine interest.

"I think so. I'm not looking for any money or anything like that."

He smiled and said, "How about we work on them together?"

***

Stacy and I sat across from each other sipping red wine in a restaurant booth at Cammeratta's. We had just finished our fine Italian meals and I was waiting for what seemed like an eternity for the waiter to bring the check. Stacy was talking a mile a minute but I wasn't listening. I had tuned her out much earlier in the evening. I was adding nothing to the conversation, not that Stacy needed any help in carrying it all by herself. It was not my shyness that kept me from talking. It was simply that I was not interested in her. She was very attractive, there was no doubt about that, but she seemed to have no substance whatsoever. There was nothing terribly interesting about her. My former girlfriend Laura, as un-captivating as she was, at least had a love of animals that made her somewhat interesting.

While Stacy talked seemingly without end about wandering through the Valley View Mall, my mind wandered toward the old telephone and Victrola. Chuck and I had made plans to work on them the next day and I was really looking forward to it. Now, I thought to myself, how do I bring this evening to a graceful end?

The bill finally arrived. I paid it in cash and left a nice tip for the waiter. Stacy then slid out of the booth and cheerfully exhorted, "Where to now?"

My head was in overdrive trying to quickly come up with an excuse to end the date. Despite searching all quadrants of my brain, all I came up with was, "I don't know. I think the wine went straight to my head. Would you mind if I just took you home?"

Stacy looked slighted and replied with a decidedly dejected tone, "If that's what you really want."

Realizing that I may have hurt her feelings, I responded with all of the false sincerity I could muster. "No, really, I've got a bit of a headache, that's all," but judging by her long face I knew the damage was done. The last thing I wanted to do was to hurt her feelings, but I had done so anyway.

The drive back to Stacy's apartment was a quiet one. When we arrived, I parked Margo's car at the curb but kept my seat belt on and the engine running. I had no intention of walking Stacy to her door and risk being put in a position where a good night kiss would be in order. A warm handshake from the driver's seat was all I would offer.

As I drove back to Margo's place I damned her for talking me into the date in the first place. I banged on the top of the steering wheel with the flat side of my fist and screamed one obscenity after another. When I finally began to calm down, I took some stock in myself. While stopped at a traffic light, I peered in the rear view mirror and asked the man who peered back, "What the hell is wrong with you? You're out on a date with a pretty girl and all you can think of is how best to get rid of her!" At that point I decided I would never date again.

***

It was nine o'clock Sunday morning. Margo had left a note next to the coffee pot that said she was leaving for church and that she didn't want to disturb me. "When did *she* become so devout," I wondered aloud as I poured the murky remains of the coffee into a fine bone china cup that used to belong to my mother.

I had another fairly good night's sleep, except for being awakened at four a.m. after another wacky dream. It was almost the same dream I had experienced the previous night. Again, I was being shown an old photo album and, at first, I was unable to focus on any of the pictures. After trying my hardest, the photos eventually became more clear and easier to see. They were, perhaps, even more bright and in focus than they were in the first dream. Once more, I saw the photo of myself beside the beautiful young woman and

I noticed that same young woman was in a great majority of the photos. In some of the snapshots she was posing alongside me. In others, she was with a different man. I shook my head and smiled as I wondered if these strange dreams had any meaning. I had originally dismissed my first dream experience as a product of too much beer, but my wine consumption the previous night was not enough to produce the headache I faked, let alone manufacture crazy dreams. It was almost time for Chuck to arrive so I swigged down the rest of my coffee and got myself ready for the day, but I knew I wouldn't be able to shake off those dreams.

***

Chuck Manning was all smiles when I greeted him at the door. He arrived with a set of small tools in hand and was dressed ready to work, wearing blue jeans with a plain white t-shirt and an old Brooklyn Dodgers baseball cap that covered his balding head. He appeared to be as anxious to start as I had been.

The two of us climbed up the attic stairs and we carefully brought down the Victrola which was much heavier than we had anticipated. "I guess things weighed more when they weren't all made of plastic," Chuck remarked smartly.

We went back up to the attic again and I led Chuck to the trunk where the old telephone was located. He pulled the phone out of the trunk which caused a cascade of items to shift toward the space the removed phone had previously occupied.

As Chuck studied the phone, I noticed what appeared to be an old book peeking out slightly from underneath a neatly folded dress. I pulled the book out of the trunk, opened it, and soon realized that it wasn't a book after all. It was an album that contained black and white photographs that looked very familiar. I soon realized that I recognized some of the pictures because I had seen them in my dreams. I turned a few pages and had to catch my breath when I saw a photo of a man, who looked an awful lot like me, standing next to a beautiful young woman. Just as in my dreams. The photos of this same woman with the other man were in the album as well. I didn't recall finding this photo album the day before when I found the phone, but I figured that I must have taken a quick look at it, at the very least. That would explain my dreams to a certain extent. A photo of someone that could pass as their twin next to a beautiful woman would stick in any man's self conscious, I thought. But then, if I had seen the album the day before, why was it so neatly tucked underneath the dress? I knew that I wouldn't have put it back in the trunk with such care. I wondered if maybe Margo had done so, but dismissed the notion knowing that my sloppy sister would never have taken the time to put it away so neatly. I was intrigued to say the least, but I didn't want to mention my dream to Chuck. Instead, I decided to ask him about the woman. Maybe he might have known her or one of the men in the photographs with her. I handed him the album and said, "Do you know any of these people?"

Chuck studied the photographs, looked up as though he was about to speak, and then studied them in more detail. Finally, he said, "I believe that gentleman there was my Uncle Freddy," he pointed to the man that I did not resemble. He then went on to tell me about his uncle, Frederick York, who was once a real big shot in the town. His Uncle Freddy had died bitter and nearly penniless but no one quite knew why.

Chuck was telling me that his uncle liked to drive around town in his hot car when I impatiently interrupted. "The woman in the picture with your uncle, is she your aunt?"

The jolly, red-faced man again studied the photo. "I don't know who the woman is. Uncle Freddy never married, but he did have many lady friends. She must have been one of his admirers."

Chuck continued to speak of his uncle and his uncle's many girlfriends as he handed me back the album. I interrupted him once more. "Do you know anything about this guy here?" I asked as I pointed to the man in the photo who could have passed as my twin.

"Hmm ... I don't know who he is either," Chuck said with a laugh, "but he looks an awful lot like you! Your mother's family grew up in town, right?"

"That's right."

"Well, maybe he's one of your long lost relatives."

"Maybe. When do you think these pictures were taken?" I inquired.

"My Uncle Freddy looked very young ..." He stopped and I could tell he was doing the math in his head. "Well, sometime in the 1930s, I suppose."

"How old would you say *my twin* is in this picture?"

"Well, I'd say about the same age as you are now. Maybe it's your grandfather?"

"I don't know. I'll have to ask Margo about it. She's the keeper of the family heirlooms and photographs. She would know if it's my grandfather."

Chuck snapped his fingers and offered, "I could ask my mother, she knew practically the whole town when she lived here. Poor Mom's in a nursing home now. She has her good days and bad days. Give me the photo album and I'll ask her."

"I'd rather wait until I speak to Margo. She has other photos of my grandfather and I'd like to see if any of them match up."

"Suit yourself," Chuck replied. "Now, how about we get to work?"

We brought the phone down to Margo's apartment, as well as a few of the kitchen gadgets. My interest in the Victrola and any of the other items had waned. The telephone had my entire focus. After all, it was in the same trunk as the mystery photo album and that made it much more intriguing to me. I cleaned the surface of the phone as best as I could without using any harsh chemicals.

While Chuck cleaned up the old Victrola, I used Margo's computer to get more information on the telephone and turned up a great deal of material on the Internet. I found that the phone was a model 51AL candlestick telephone made by Western Electric and was originally manufactured in the late 1920s to the early 1930s. I even found a complete schematic which I hoped would help me bring the phone back to working order, assuming that it wasn't already. One website recommended that I purchase a special adaptor if I planned on plugging the phone into a modern phone jack.

"Hey, look at this!" exclaimed Chuck as scratchy sounding jazz music played on the Victrola, "The old thing still works! They don't make 'em like this anymore."

"Wow, that's great. What did you have to do to get it to play?"

"Nothing much really, just an adjustment here and there. How are you doing on the phone?"

I explained that I would have to go to an electronics store to get the adaptor that was needed to plug the phone in. Only then would I be able to determine if the phone was operational. If it wasn't, I explained further, I would then use the schematic I downloaded to try and repair it.

"Okay, then," said Chuck with a broad grin. "Let's take a ride."

***

To my surprise, Chuck pulled out of his garage in a vintage Plymouth convertible. He rolled down the window and yelped, "Hop in!"

"This was my Uncle Freddy's at one time," Chuck explained as he drove. "He used to love to drive it around town in the hopes of impressing the ladies," he said with a wink. He paused and then continued, "Uncle Freddy sold it to my father when he was in dire straits. My father gave it to me just before he died. A beauty, isn't she?"

"She sure is!" I exclaimed, "Do you know how much this car is worth? It's got to be worth ... my God,

I don't know how much, for one in such good working condition."

"It doesn't matter. I wouldn't sell her for any amount of money. I never had a family of my own, Joseph, so, in a way she is my child, my pride and joy. I take her out once in a while and I knew you'd get a kick out of it."

"That's putting it mildly!" I said excitedly.

It took a while, but I eventually found the adaptor in the electronics store that Chuck had brought us to. On the way back, Chuck gave me a history lesson on the area. We passed Fireman's Field, where every major sporting event that ever took place in the town was held. We also drove by the Blessed Mother Roman Catholic Church where the Manning family, and most of the town, had gone to worship for many years. Driving down the main strip on Rockaway Avenue, we passed Mitchell's – the world's best diner according to Chuck.

As soon as we arrived back, Chuck announced that he would have to leave. "It's Sunday afternoon, that's when I visit my mother at the nursing home." He dropped me off in front of Margo's house and said, "Good luck with the phone and I'll see you later." As he drove away he hollered out the car window, "Say hello to Margo for me!"

I waived goodbye, and as I walked toward Margo's front door I realized that I actually enjoyed spending the morning with Chuck and that I found his stories interesting. I was glad to have found myself a friend.

Margo was undressing in her bedroom when I entered her apartment. "Is that you, Little Joey?" she shouted.

"Yeah, it's me," I shouted back and I kept on walking until I reached the kitchen hoping to scrounge up something to eat. Margo followed me in shortly after. "Church?" I inquired while giving her a sideways look.

"So, what's wrong with church?" she snapped back.

"Nothing's wrong with church. I just never heard of one with you in it! The only thing that could get you to church early on a Sunday morning would be a swarm of locusts or … a guy!" "That's it, isn't it? You have your next guy lined up and he goes to church on Sunday."

"That's not completely true," she said as she flipped her hair into a ponytail and held her nose slightly upward. "Sometimes he goes to mass on *Saturday* evening."

"Please tell me he isn't a priest," I chuckled.

"No, he's not a priest … at least not anymore," she replied in almost a whisper.

"Oh, my God, my sister is dating a priest!"

"Well, we haven't actually gone out on a date yet, but if it's okay with you, he asked me out for tonight and I'd like to go. I know you're leaving on Tuesday and we haven't spent a whole lot of time together."

"Actually," I said, "I was hoping you wouldn't mind if I stayed a little longer. This morning Chuck and I worked on restoring some of the stuff from the attic and I would really like to spend some more time on the old telephone I found. I don't actually have to be back at work until the end of the week. Oh, yeah, by the way, Chuck says hello."

"You can stay as long as you want, Little Joey, you know that!"

"Then if you don't mind me staying longer, I don't mind you going out tonight with your priest ... I mean ex-priest. Besides, I can spend the night working on the phone."

Margo changed the subject and snickered, "I can't believe you spent an entire morning with Chuck and you didn't want to kill him!"

"C'mon, he's not such a bad guy," I retorted. "Yeah, he talks a lot but at least he's saying something when he talks. He doesn't just babble on and on like *some* people I know. He also knows a great deal of the history of this town. And besides ..." I added sheepishly, "he drives a hot car!"

"Sounds like I should have set you up with Chuck instead of Stacy!" she joked.

"Oh, I've got something really weird to show you." I walked into the living room and retrieved the old photo album. I then held open the page that displayed the picture of the man that looked so much like me. "Is this our grandfather or some other relative?"

Margo scratched her head and mused, "I don't know ... It's definitely not Pops. He was a short, fat guy from what I remember. It doesn't look like any of the pictures I have of him. This guy looks tall and thin and, I might add, a lot like you! Where did you find this?"

"It was in the attic, in the same trunk as the old telephone. Chuck thinks the photos were taken sometime in the 1930s." I looked at the photo again and squawked, "It really *does* look like me, doesn't it? Chuck thought so too!" "What about Dad's father? Do you think this could be him?"

"I doubt it," Margo replied, "He would have been a teenager then and the man in this photo is definitely not a teenager."

"Well," I sighed, "whoever he is, he looks happier than *I've* ever been. Have you ever seen *me* smile like that?"

Margo gave me a look of pity and shook her head. "Unfortunately, no, Little Joey."

Two

It was just beginning to get dark outside and storm clouds appeared as though they would take over the sky before the moon would get a chance to glow. After polishing it up to the best of my ability, I was ready to test the old telephone. I moved my great-grandmother's statuettes to a safer location and set the phone down in what I believed to be its rightful place — on top of the antique oak telephone table in Margo's living room. I connected the newly purchased adaptor into a nearby unused phone jack and then plugged the phone into the adaptor. I listened closely but heard nothing, "Damn!" I cried out, "No dial tone."

"Just don't blow up my apartment," Margo screeched from her bedroom as she was getting ready for her date with the ex-priest. I ignored her and began to take the old phone's receiver apart.

The receiver didn't appear to contain many parts, but the parts it did have were hardly recognizable. They only barely resembled the type of electronic components that I was used to seeing. There were copper coil windings, copper wires, and very old resistors. I noticed that one of the copper wires appeared to be corroded, or perhaps burned, so I carefully removed the wire and soldered a new one in its place. "That should do it!" I put the receiver back together, plugged the phone back in to the adaptor, and again listened for a dial tone. I cursed loudly when there wasn't one.

Margo strolled out of her bedroom wearing a very low-cut red mini-dress. "Is that what priests are into these days?" I asked sarcastically.

"I told you he's not a priest anymore. Besides, I figured he wouldn't mind seeing a little skin now that he's no longer married to God."

"You're despicable," I spat out, Daffy Duck-style.

"Any luck with the phone?" she asked feigning interest.

"No. Not yet. I'll get it to work though."

"Why is it so important to you to get that old phone to work anyway?"

"It's not *that* important. I don't know ... I guess because it was in the same trunk as the pictures," I admitted, "I figure the phone is somehow related to the guy who looks like me and the pretty girl standing next to him."

Margo's short attention span had reached its end. "Okay, whatever, I've gotta go." With a wink she said, "Don't wait up for me, Little Joey."

"Don't wait up? It's Sunday night! You have to work tomorrow morning and I expect your date does too. Does this guy know what he's getting himself into?" I asked with all sincerity.

"Let's hope not!" she replied cutely as she closed the door behind her.

Margo was gone and I had the whole place to myself. I could finally work without any distractions. With a printed version of the schematic that I had found on the Internet at hand, I began to look deeper into what troubled the old telephone. The rhythm of the pouring rain and the occasional thunderbolt did not deter my intense concentration. Only when the power was lost for a few moments was I distracted in any way, and then I just laughed out loud thinking about Margo getting soaking wet on her date.

Once the power was restored, I used an electronic meter and other tools that I had borrowed from Chuck to find that another wire had become burned, this time in the base of the phone. I carefully replaced the wire, reassembled the phone, and was ready for another test. I was just about to plug it back in when a very close lightning strike made me practically jump across the room. Fearing that the lightning could cause damage to the phone that I wouldn't be able to repair, I decided the next test could wait until the storm passed.

While waiting for the storm to subside, I studied the photo album and especially the picture of the man whom I so closely resembled. I noticed a very small speck on the man's face below his lower lip on the left side of his face. Using a magnifying glass from the box of tools that Chuck had let me borrow, I examined this speck more closely. I tried to flick it off, but then realized it was part of the photo. It looked as though the man in the photo may have had a mole or a beauty mark. "Well," I said to no one but myself, "it's definitely not me in the photo. I don't have a mark like that under my lip."

The storm had mostly passed and I was ready to test the old phone once again. I plugged the phone in to the adaptor, picked up the receiver, and hoped for the best. Unfortunately, there was still no dial tone. I pressed and released the receiver's hook a few times hoping to make something happen, but it was to no avail. I just couldn't get a dial tone. I had started to think that maybe repairing the old telephone was simply out of my league when suddenly another very close lightning strike occurred. The crackle and crash of the thunder startled me and I accidentally knocked the phone off of the table. It dropped hard onto the floor and the receiver fell off its hook. I thought that I had just destroyed any chance of the phone ever working but as I bent down to pick it up, I heard a very familiar sound. It was a beautiful sound. It was the hum of a dial tone.

I wondered who would be best to call to test the phone further and decided the smart thing to do would be to call my cell phone. First, I made sure that my cell phone was on and set to ring. Then I put my index finger in the dialer and dialed my cell phone number. I could hear the ringing in the old phone's receiver, but, to my surprise, I did not hear my cell phone ring.

Just as I was about ready to hang up, the call was answered. "Hello?" said a young soft female voice.

"Hi. I'm sorry, I was trying to call my cell phone and I must have dialed your number by mistake."

"Oh, that's okay. I often dial a wrong number myself. What is a *sale* phone? Are you some kind of salesman? Do you call people on the telephone and try to sell your merchandise? I really don't think it's proper for a salesman to ring my home! Knock on my door if you must, but ..."

"No. No. I tried to call my *cell*, C-E-L-L."

"I don't understand," said the young woman. "Were you trying to ring someone who is in jail?"

Thinking that the woman was flirting with me, I responded with a hint of laughter, "Now, ma'am, do you think I am the kind of man who spends his evenings calling criminals in their cells trying to sell them striped pajamas?"

"I should certainly hope not, sir." Now she *was* flirting. "I should think that these criminals have enough to worry about, breaking up rocks and all, without being pestered by a charlatan like you," she giggled.

What a sweet giggle it was. I compared her laugh to Stacy's annoying whine of a laugh. Even Laura's laugh was not this engaging. This woman seemed to have a good sense of humor and a nice mix of intelligence with a dash of innocence. I tried to think of something else funny to say, but drew a blank. All I could come up with was, "Well, it was nice talking with you. Once again, I'm sorry for the wrong number. Goodbye."

"Good … bye," her voice sounded as if she was surprised that I was ending the call.

I hung the receiver on its hook and cursed myself. It was a rare occurrence when I had a connection with a woman like the one I just had, and I let the moment get away far too easily. I never even thought to ask her name, let alone what the number I actually dialed was. I thought about trying to call her back, but decided against it as I had no idea which digit, or digits, I dialed incorrectly to reach her in the first place.

Thoughts of Laura went through my head saying, "You would never go the extra mile for me or for us." Maybe she was right after all. At the time, my idea of a perfect relationship was one where everything was easy and nothing would be the slightest bit difficult. If it's too tough to get things started, I used to think, then it just wasn't meant to be. Maybe I had been all wrong, but what were the odds of finding the right phone number to reach this unknown woman again?

Deciding to score my experience with the woman on the phone as a lesson learned, I moved on with the testing of the old telephone. This time I slowly and carefully dialed my cell phone number. I made sure to dial "1" first for a long distance call, as my cell had a Philadelphia phone number. I then dialed my area code and then the rest of my cell phone number. Once again, I heard the ringing in the receiver, but my cell phone was curiously quiet.

"Hello?"

It was her again! I was sure I had dialed the number correctly this time, but reached her again anyway. I thought that maybe I was unable to reach my cell phone because, for some reason or another, the old phone couldn't handle a long distance call. Whatever the reason was that I reached her again, it didn't matter. I was given a second chance and I didn't want to blow it this time. I decided it would be charming to speak somewhat mechanically. "Hi. We just spoke a few minutes ago. I don't know why I keep calling your phone by mistake. Anyway, my name is Joseph Eaton. I'm a college dropout who is underemployed, but I am not a salesman of any kind. I enjoyed speaking with you before and I am *not* sorry I accidentally called you again."

She responded with her own mechanical version. "Hello. I'm Katherine Whitney, and I too am not sorry that you have difficulty dialing a telephone. I was upset when you abruptly ended our earlier conversation."

"Where are you from Katherine Whitney?" I asked hoping that my sister had an inexpensive long distance service.

"I live in Valley View. Where do you live Mr. Eaton?"

My thoughts about the phone not being able to dial long distance may have been correct. "Actually, I live in Philadelphia but I am visiting my sister who lives in Valley View."

"What do you think of our beautiful town Mr. Eaton?"

Valley View was nice, I thought, but hardly beautiful. It was a little run-down in some areas though other parts of town were very well kept, including the block my sister lived on. I decided to be tactful and said, "Just lovely, Miss Whitney." I used the formality that she started and hoped she would not correct "Miss Whitney" to "Mrs. Whitney."

"How long are you in town for, Mr. Eaton?"

I noticed no correction. "Just until the end of the week and then it's back to work."

"What do you do for a living?"

"I'm an account representative for a paper company in Philadelphia. We sell in large quantities to large corporations. It's not exactly my dream job, but it pays the bills."

"Sounds like you're a salesman to me!" Katherine asserted.

"Well ... I guess I am in a way, except I don't call them, they call me. In my book that makes me a glorified order taker, not a salesman. What do you do for a living?"

"Me? Well, I work part-time at a law firm. I wanted to go to college, but Father doesn't think that a young woman should, as he would say, *waste the time and money on an education.*"

"Wow, he sounds extremely old-fashioned," I said.

"He is, isn't he?"

"What would you study if you could go to college?"

"I love to read books of all kinds, so I would probably study English Literature."

I turned the topic of conversation to Ernest Hemingway, my favorite author. It seemed odd that Katherine had heard of him, but was only familiar with his earliest work. Her favorite authors were Emily Bronte, Jane Austen, and F. Scott Fitzgerald. Apparently, she too was fond of the classics.

The conversation flowed easily and before I realized it, we had been speaking for almost an hour and a half. In that time, Katherine revealed much about her family. She told me that she was the youngest of five children. Her two older brothers had attended Ivy League schools and were both very successful in their fields of business. Her two older sisters were both homemakers and never had the desire to be anything else. The whole Whitney family story seemed to come from an earlier America. Jack

Whitney, Katherine's father, came across as a very hard man who was old fashioned to a fault. Ellen Whitney, Katherine's mother, sounded like a very good soul who was a good buffer between her children and her gruff husband. I discovered that the Whitneys all attended the local Catholic Church on a regular basis. I told Katherine about my Catholic upbringing and added that I hadn't attended church since I was a teenager. I spoke about my childhood, most of which was spent sitting on a piano bench, and failing to fulfill my mother's dream for me to become a great concert pianist. We both talked about life and what we wanted out of it and happiness seemed to be a common theme. It was, hands down, the most enjoyable and meaningful conversation that I ever had. Recalling my vow from only the previous day to never date again, I laughed at myself. I was ready to try again with Katherine and I did what I could do to get something to materialize. Somewhere in our conversation, the formalities of Mr. Eaton and Miss Whitney were dropped. We were now simply Joseph and Katherine.

A male voice, that I assumed belonged to Katherine's father, could be heard in the background telling her that she shouldn't spend so much time talking on the telephone. "I guess we have been talking for a long time," I agreed. "Can I meet you? I mean in person. Is there someplace in town where we can meet?"

There was a long pause, too long for my comfort. Finally she replied, "Do you like ice cream?"

"Of course. Who doesn't?"

"How about Teddy's on Rockaway Avenue?"

I wrote *Teddy's* on a piece of paper. "That sounds good. How about we meet there at noon tomorrow. Would that be okay?"

"Okay, noon it is. I'll meet you inside. I'll be wearing a blue dress."

"You know, I don't even know what number I dialed. Can I have your phone number?" I wrote down her phone number and thought it strange that she would use two letters followed by five numbers. "Okay, it was wonderful talking to you. Good night, Katherine and I'll see you tomorrow." I hung up the old phone and was ready to burst from excitement and anticipation. I couldn't wait until the next day.

I decided to take Margo's advice and not wait up for her. I thought it would be best to go to bed early so that I could get an early start the next day. My list of things to do included renting a car to get around town with, get a haircut, and buy some new clothes so I would look presentable for my date with Katherine.

When I drifted off to sleep, I started to have the dream again. Once more I was shown the photos in the album, but this time the still black and white pictures slowly started to move. It was as if I was being shown a home movie. It appeared that the mystery couple from the photograph, my look-alike and the beautiful young woman, were the stars of the film. They were smiling and hugging each other and they were even doing a little kissing. They were obviously two people in love. At first the only sound I could hear was the ticking sound of a movie projector. Then slowly, the sound of a woman's voice morphed with the sound of the projector. The voice sounded very far away and it echoed a great deal. I couldn't quite understand what she was saying, but her voice had a familiar tone to it. Just as her words were almost becoming understandable, the annoying beeping sound of my travel alarm clock woke me. As I shut off the alarm, I realized immediately that I had the dream again, though it was different this time. Why was I dreaming about these people? What did it mean, if it meant anything at all?

I got up out of bed and walked by Margo's bedroom to see if she had ever made it home the night before. She was there lying in her bed under a heavy mixture of sheets, blankets, and the outfits that she had tried on for her date with the ex-priest but didn't make the cut. I banged on her door that was left ajar. "You want me to make the coffee?" Margo moaned something that sounded like an affirmative response, so I slowly walked to the kitchen.

When the aroma of the coffee had made it to her bedroom, my slightly comatose sister dragged herself out of bed and into the kitchen. "Good morning, Sunshine," I teased as I poured her a cup. "I must warn you, I make it very strong."

She took a sip and exclaimed, "Whoa, talk about your eye openers! This stuff would wake the dead! What did you put in, double the amount?"

"Good, you're awake now. Now you can tell me about your date with Father Lucky."

Through a yawn she said, "I had a nice time. We went to the movies and then to Mitchell's afterwards for dessert."

"You mean he didn't have you for dessert?" I joked.

"C'mon, Little Joey, it was a perfectly respectable date. We laughed, we talked, and we walked. Nothing else happened. It was nice."

"Wow! Sister Mary Margo the Respectable," I said in my best Irish brogue.

"What did you do all night, Lonely Joe?" she asked sarcastically.

"I got the old phone to work and, quite by mistake, I called a very nice young woman … twice. I have a date with her this afternoon," I said smartly.

"Look at you. I wondered why you were all smiles this morning. What's the unfortunate girl's name?" she jawed back.

"Katherine. Katherine Whitney. She lives here in Valley View. You know her? Please say no!"

"Nope. Don't know anyone by that name. Well, at least you won't be able to blame this impending disaster on me!"

This kind of sarcastic banter was the same manner of communication we used when we were kids. Even though I missed this kind of teasing, I dropped the lighthearted attitude and said in all seriousness, "I've got a good feeling about this one. I really do."

"Oh, my God!" Margo cried. "You're really serious, aren't you? And you only spoke with her on the phone? What does she say she looks like?"

"She didn't, and I didn't ask."

"And you're going out with her anyway? She could be a real bow-wow for all you know. She could be as big as a house."

I calmly answered, "I guess she could, but, like I said, I've got a good feeling about this one."

"Wow! I never thought my baby brother could be such a romantic. Incredible! Totally freaking incredible!"

I asked Margo if she could drop me off somewhere where I could rent a car on her way to work and she agreed. She gave me advice on where I could go for a good haircut and where to get nice clothes at a reasonable price. There was one problem though, I couldn't find a listing for Teddy's in the phone book and Margo had never heard of it. I did an Internet search and found that there was a place named Teddy's many years ago on Rockaway Avenue, but now a different ice cream parlor was at the address where Teddy's once was. I figured that maybe the locals never stopped using the old name of the place and decided that must be where she wanted us to meet.

As we walked out of the house toward Margo's car, Chuck spotted us and hurriedly headed toward us shouting, "Good morning! Good morning!"

Margo, out of the side of her mouth, said to me, "What the hell does *he* want so early in the morning?"

I replied quietly to my sister, "Be kind." When Chuck was in normal hearing distance we said in unison and with cheery faces, "Good Morning!"

Now huffing and puffing from his sprint across the lawn, Chuck said, "I just wanted to know how Joseph made out with the old telephone? Did you get it to work?"

"Yeah, I did. I don't think it can call long distance for some strange reason, but I made a few local test calls and it worked."

"What are you doing today?" Chuck asked.

I explained about my date and that Margo was dropping me off at the car rental place.

"Would you like some company? I could drive you to the mall; I could use a few things there myself. After, I'll take you to get a haircut and then drop you off at the car rental place. Do you mind?"

"Of course not, Chuck ... and thanks." I turned to Margo and said, "I guess you can go." I got out of the car, tapped its roof twice and shouted, "Thanks anyway for offering." As she drove away I could see her shaking her head, and I knew she was wondering why her brother was allowing someone who she thought was such a jerk become his friend.

"Shall we go?" I said as I motioned toward Chuck's garage.

"The mall doesn't open for another hour and a half. How about we stop for breakfast first? I could go for some eggs and home fries. How about you, Joseph, are you hungry?" Chuck rubbed his round tummy and said, "I'll take you to the world's best diner."

It was an offer I couldn't refuse.

***

"Tell me about your young lady. She a local?" Chuck said between mouthfuls of rye toast.

"Yes, she is." I explained how I accidentally called her and that we had struck up an engaging conversation. I told Chuck that I had no idea what she looked like and that we were to meet at Teddy's or "whatever the place was called now."

40

Chuck said with astonishment, "Teddy's! Teddy's? You're telling me that she wants to meet you at Teddy's?"

"Yeah, that's what she called it. I know it's not called that anymore, but I figured that's what the locals still call it. Is that not the case?"

"You see that ice cream parlor right over there?" Chuck pointed across the street. "It used to be called Teddy's many years ago. In fact, it hasn't been called Teddy's since probably before the war."

"Which war?" I asked.

"Doubleya doubleya two, the big one. In fact, the man that used to own Teddy's started the diner we are sitting in right now."

"So no one calls it Teddy's as far as you know?"

"Not in fifty or sixty years."

"Oh, great! Now I don't know where to meet her." I was annoyed and a little embarrassed at the same time. "Excuse me. I have to make a phone call." I got up from the diner booth and went outside to use my cell phone to call Katherine. I dialed "1," then the area code, then the numbers that corresponded with the two letters she gave me to start her phone number, and then the rest of the number. A recording answered and said that the number wasn't in service. I dialed the number again to be sure and got the same result. In anger, I flipped my cell closed as hard as I could and marched back into the diner.

Complaining to Chuck I said, "The number she gave me is not in service. She gave me a fake number! I can't believe it! I really thought we hit it off!" I was really agitated at this point and I slammed the side of my fist on the table prompting looks from employees and other patrons.

Chuck tried to calm me down. "Take it easy, Joseph. Maybe you just wrote the wrong number down. I'll call information and get the correct number for you. What is the young lady's name?"

Still upset, I barked, "Katherine Whitney!"

Chuck took out his own cell phone and called information. There were many Whitneys in the local area. He wrote down as many phone numbers as he could on a napkin and then tore it down the middle. Handing me half of the list he said, "You call those numbers and I'll call these."

The two of us made call after call but could not find a Katherine Whitney in Valley View. Finally, Chuck suggested that I just go to the ice cream parlor at noon and see, maybe she would show up. Since I couldn't think of anything else better to do, I agreed and decided to continue with the rest of the morning plan.

We went to the local shopping mall where I bought a nice pair of cuffed tan khaki slacks and a blue pullover shirt with a Polo emblem. I decided to wear my new clothes out of the store.

In the mall parking lot on the way to Chuck's car, I noticed that Chuck was empty handed. "I thought you needed to get a few things?"

Chuck averted his eyes from me and replied, "Well, I was looking at some shirts, but they didn't have my size." He let out a sigh that did not seem sincere and said, "Oh well, maybe they'll be better stocked some other time." He nervously fumbled the keys to his Volvo as he attempted to remove them from his pocket and they fell to the pavement. His knees cracked as he crouched down to pick them up and he made a loud "Ooooomph" sound. Then he said, "I'm getting so out of shape I can't even pick things up anymore." He made another "Ooooomph" on his way back up.

I wasn't really sure why Chuck wanted to come with me, but decided that he was just a lonely man who was looking for a little companionship. "I'm sorry I made you take me here and you didn't find anything for yourself," I said and then smiled, "but I was glad for the company."

"Think nothing of it my friend, nothing at all. Now, let's get your hair looking nice for your girl, shall we?"

***

I got my curly brown hair cut relatively short and the hair stylist worked in a little gel to give it a more finished look. It was then on to the car rental place where, after much thought, I decided to rent a mid-sized four-door sedan. The car was a bluish-black color and I thought that would portray a little class without breaking the bank. I rolled down the window of my rental and waited for Chuck to pull up alongside me. "It's about twenty minutes to noon so I'm going to go straight to the ice cream parlor. Thanks for everything today. Maybe I'll see you later?"

"Hey, good luck with your date. Ring my bell later and let me know how it all went."

"Okay, will do. Bye." I put the car in gear and began to drive. "What a nice man," I said to myself,

"Margo is such an idiot." I then started to focus on my date, hoping there was going to be one. I went over our phone conversation in my head and tried to detect any deceit in her voice but was unable to do so. She seemed so sweet and genuine. "She's gotta show!"

I arrived at the ice cream parlor at five minutes to noon. Other than the young man behind the counter, there was no one else in the place. I asked the man if anyone had ever called the place Teddy's. He just shrugged as if he had no idea.

There were three small booths in the establishment and I sat in one of them while waiting for Katherine. Ten minutes went by and not a soul entered. Finally a young woman came in, but she was accompanying a small boy. I didn't think that she would be Katherine, but I asked her anyway. She was not. An old lady entered shortly after that. I decided not to ask her if she was Katherine.

I got up from the booth and looked around outside for her and noticed a Volvo that looked a lot like Chuck's going up the street. If it was Chuck, what was he doing? Did the guy want to make sure that my date was going well? Was he spying on me for some reason? Maybe, I thought, he had some other business to attend to in this part of town. Just then, a very attractive young woman walked toward the ice cream parlor. I was about to ask her if she was Katherine, but she walked right on by and entered the health food store that was a few doors down. I looked at my watch, it was 12:15, and I decided I would give her until 12:30 to show. As I turned to go back inside, I noticed that same Volvo coming back down the street. I tried to get a better look at the car and its driver, but just when the car was in close sight, a dirty white box truck drove by in the other direction and blocked my view.

I went back inside the ice cream parlor and waited there for another fifteen minutes. At around 12:30, a heavyset young woman came into the store and I asked her if she was Katherine. She wasn't so I decided I had enough and left.

I stopped and grabbed lunch at a fast food place on the way back to Margo's. I thought about the Volvo I saw on Rockaway Avenue and, if it was Chuck that kept driving by, I wanted to ask him why he was spying on me.

Still eating my greasy French fries, I rang Chuck's doorbell. "Back so soon?" he asked. "I guess you got stood up."

"Were you driving up and down Rockaway Avenue?" I accused.

"I was," he stated sharply, slightly put off by my harsh tone. "I had some errands to run near the ice cream parlor. I thought I would pass by to see if your young lady arrived. I guess she never did."

"No, she didn't," I resigned.

"I'm so sorry, Joseph."

"Aw, it's no big deal. It's not the first time I've been stood up and it probably won't be the last."

"Hey, you want to take a ride with me? I've got to go back to the nursing home and drop off some things for my mother. She loves her candy and they won't allow her to have any there, so I sneak them in for her. What do you say?"

Needless to say, I hesitated as the thought of spending the afternoon at a nursing home hardly seemed like a fun adventure. Chuck added, "C'mon, it beats staying home with a broken heart. I promise I won't stay long."

"Well … Okay. You promise you won't stay too long?"

"Promise. I'll even take the old Plymouth out of the garage again for the trip."

***

Sacred Heart Nursing Care Facility had a pleasant, but very sterile, environment. They were well staffed, and the patients appeared to be well cared for, but it just looked too much like a hospital for my taste. I followed Chuck to room 136 where he suddenly stopped before opening the door.

He turned toward me and said quietly, "Now, she has her good days and bad days. Hopefully this will be one of the good days."

"What is she like on her bad days?" I asked.

"She sleeps most of the day and doesn't eat, and she gets confused very easily."

Chuck handed me the bag he was holding and opened the door. I could see that Mrs. Manning was sleeping, or at least resting comfortably. She was hooked up to some kind of machine that made an awful breathing-like sound. The room was filled with flowers that I suspected had been picked from Chuck's home garden. "Mother? Wake up, Mother," Chuck said as he gently nudged the elderly woman.

Mrs. Manning let out a light snort and then awakened. "Hello, Dear," she said to her son.

"Mother, I brought a friend with me today. I'd like you to meet Joseph Eaton. He's staying in the house next door with his sister Margo." He then turned to me and said, "This is my mother, Alice Manning."

"How do you do, ma'am," I said as politely as possible.

The old woman perked up immediately upon the sight of me and exclaimed, "Joseph? Joseph! My God, how have you been?"

I wasn't sure why she was so excited to meet me, but I continued to be polite. "I'm fine, ma'am. I hope they're treating you well here."

"It has been so long since we last spoke." Alice Manning then eyed the bag that I was holding under my arm and said in a whisper, "And I see you brought me more Life Savers."

Still puzzled by her enthusiasm toward me, I said, "I'm sorry, ma'am, I don't believe we've met before today." I handed her the bag that indeed contained Life Savers candy.

"Don't you remember, Joseph? You and Katherine stayed with me when my parents … went … out." Her sentence slowed when she realized how ridiculous it must have sounded. "Please forgive an old fool. It's just that you look so much like someone I knew long ago."

"Did you say Katherine?" I started to get excited myself.

She was about to answer when Chuck intervened and said, "I think we should go now and let you rest, Mother. I'll be back on the weekend to see you. Don't let the staff find the candy." He kissed his mother's forehead and left the room, ushering me ahead of him. I wasn't even given the chance to say goodbye.

When the door was closed he whispered, "This is not one of her good days. She was starting to get confused. I think it is best to let her rest when she gets that way."

I whispered back, "Who is this Katherine she was starting to tell me about?"

We headed toward the lobby and the whispers were dropped. "Probably someone from her past. When she gets confused like that, the past and the present sort of become one to her."

"She told me I looked like someone she knew. Do you think it may have been the man in the old photograph? Was his name Joseph too?" I had so many questions.

"Maybe, I don't know. As I said, she gets confused very easily. Even though I just introduced you, it may have seemed to her that she had been introduced to you long ago. Her past and present are fused in a way." Chuck joined his left hand with his right hand and shook the result to accentuate his point.

As we left the facility Chuck asked, "So, what would you like to do now, my friend? You want to work on the old phone or play some more of those old records on the Victrola?"

I paused and studied Chuck suspiciously for a moment and I really wasn't sure what to make of him. Was he just a lonely man who was trying to make a friend, or was there something more, something possibly a little devious? "I think I would just like to go back and take a nap. I was up very early and I didn't sleep all that well. Maybe we can get together later, after dinner?"

"Okay, that's fine. I'll take us home and we'll get together after dinner. Shall I knock on your sister's door?"

"Yeah, that sounds like a plan."

***

I peered out the window to see if Chuck was still watching me. We had arrived back from the nursing home approximately an hour before and I was supposed to be napping. Chuck was in his front yard watering his flower beds but looked up toward my window every few moments. I slowly closed the curtain and thought about what I could do to escape.

There was an urgent need inside of me to visit with his mother alone, so I needed to sneak out without him seeing me. I had to find out more about the Katherine that Chuck's mother was getting ready to speak of before he stopped her. Was this Katherine somehow related to the Katherine that stood me up? I planned to bring the photo album that I had been dreaming about with me in the hope that she could identify the people in the photographs and maybe put a stop to the dreams. Chuck couldn't know what I was planning to do because there was a good chance that this would make his mother upset and confused and I knew he wouldn't allow that for very long.

Once more, I checked outside the window. This time the coast was clear, so I decided to make a break for it. I got out the front door and closed it slowly and quietly. I glanced left and then right and there was no sign of Chuck. I took a few more steps into the driveway, peeked around once again, and then I saw him. He was in his backyard doing some sort of yard work with a giant clipper. I didn't think that he noticed me, so I ran the rest of the way toward the curb where my rental was parked. I made it. I was free.

***

I opted to not sign the guest register at Sacred Heart Nursing Care Facility. The woman at the reception desk was deep in conversation in what appeared to be a personal call, so I nonchalantly walked right past. I really didn't want any record of my being there anyway, especially if I had to lie about it later.

Alice Manning was lying on her bed watching TV and sucking on the Life Savers that had been brought to her earlier in the day. I softly knocked on the door to her room that was left halfway open. She didn't seem to hear it, so I knocked much louder hoping it would be at a higher volume than the din of the television.

"Yes?" She slowly turned in her bed and squinted. "Can I help you, young man?"

"Hello, Mrs. Manning," I shouted, much louder than I would have liked. "I am a friend of your son Chuck. I'm Joseph Eaton, we met earlier, remember?"

"Who?" She turned down the volume of her TV.

"Joseph Eaton, ma'am," I said at a more normal level. "Earlier today you were going to tell me about someone who looked a lot like me and also a woman named Katherine." She stared back at me blankly. I started to get a little frustrated and sighed, "Do you remember *any* of our previous conversation?"

"Come closer, young man, so I can see you better."

I stepped toward the bedbound woman until I was right next to her.

She studied me for a moment and then suddenly smiled. "Sit down, Joseph. We have a lot of catching up to do."

I pulled a chair as close to the old woman's bed as possible and sat. Instead of reminding her that we had only just met for the first time earlier in the day, I decided to let her do the talking.

"How is Katherine?" she asked.

I didn't expect her to start off with a question but decided to play along. "She's fine. She sends her best." A light bulb turned on above my head and I continued, "In fact, just the other day Katherine and I were talking about how we met. Do you remember that story?"

Alice responded with laughter, "Of course. I remember Katherine telling me that you just popped in on her one day. She said that you scared her half to death but you both eventually fell in love. You were smitten with her right from the start, though. I remember when you both sat for me when my parents went to the theater. Boy did I have fun with the two of you." Then she looked around to make sure no one else was listening and whispered, "That is until you disappeared."

Wanting more answers, I pressed on. "Mrs. Manning, I have a photo album with me. Do you think you could tell me who the people in the photos are?" I opened the album to the page that contained the photo of my look-alike and the beautiful young woman, and showed it to her.

"Give me a minute. I have to put on my reading glasses." She reached into the drawer of the night table next to her bed and produced a pair of filthy glasses.

"Let me, ma'am." I took the glasses from her and wiped them as best as I could with a tissue and then handed them back. "Here you go. Now, can you tell me who they are?"

Alice put on the glasses. "Now let me see. Oh, *you* know who that is, Joseph."

"Humor me, ma'am. Who are they?"

"That's you and Katherine, silly."

"Do you remember Katherine's last name?" I inquired.

She thought for a moment and then said, "Whitney. The Whitneys were our next door neighbors for many years."

I was not completely shocked by her answer. Then I asked, "Humor me again, ma'am. What is the last name of the man next to her in the photo?"

"Now you're starting to sound like the doctors here, asking such obvious questions."

"Please, Mrs. Manning, the last name of this man?" I tapped the picture with my index finger for emphasis.

She looked at me very closely, as if she were studying the contours of my face. Then, with a deadpan expression, she declared, "Eaton. The last name of this man," she tapped the photo with *her* index finger for her *own* emphasis, "is Eaton."

Still, I was not completely shocked, but I was absolutely amazed. Was that really me in the picture?

Could the beautiful Katherine in the photo and the Katherine I spoke to on the old telephone be one and the same? If so, how could it be? How could I have been in this picture that was taken so long ago?

I had more questions for Alice. "Who is this man in these other pictures with Katherine? Chuck seemed to think it was his Uncle Freddy who I guess would be your older brother."

"Ah, yes, that's Freddy. He was always much more style than substance. He loved Katherine too. Well, at least he thought he did. I always thought that he just wanted to possess the prettiest girl in town. I don't think she ever really cared for him, though."

"Did they used to date?" I asked.

"Well, Freddy would drive by in his car to show off to her. I think he asked her out so many times that she just finally gave in and went out with him. I believe her father also pressured her into it because he thought Freddy had money. When you showed up and she chose you over Freddy, he became obsessed with her. Later on, he even bought the Whitneys' house after Katherine's parents moved away."

"Chuck said that he died penniless?"

"Damn near," Alice replied. "He put everything he had into buying the Whitney house. He sold everything he owned to buy it; everything, that is, except for his car. He was eventually forced to sell the car to my husband much later on, but I think that he loved his car at least as much as he loved Katherine. The funny thing is, he never lived in the Whitney house after he bought it."

I could sense that the old woman was starting to tire, but I had one more question to ask. "Do you know what year the pictures were taken, Mrs. Manning?"

"Oh ... I would say sometime around 1935."

I leaned over Alice's bed and said, "Thank you so much, Mrs. Manning. You've been a real help. I'll be back to bring you more candy some other time." I kissed her forehead and left. I may have left with more questions than when I came in, but I felt, maybe for the first time in my life, a real sense of purpose. I was going to find the answers.

Three

The drive back from the nursing home was one filled with emotions. I was starting to believe that maybe I *was* the man in the photo with Katherine Whitney, but I was still not completely convinced. The man in the photo seemed to have a mole of which I did not possess. And of course there was the logistics involved. How did a man from my time end up in a photograph from 1935? I decided I should do more research into the life of Katherine Whitney and see where that would lead me. I also thought about calling her from the old phone again to see if I could still connect to her.

As I parked my rental in front of Margo's house, a chubby, 60ish man was running toward me and I realized that my first order of business was going to be to deal with Chuck.

"I …<huff> … thought … <huff> … that you … <huff puff> … were taking a nap?" said an overexerted Chuck.

As I got out of the car I replied, "I decided to take a ride around town." Being a good liar was never a strong asset of mine, but I didn't think it would be a good idea to tell Chuck about visiting his mother in the nursing home. I also decided that I shouldn't tell him about the dreams I was having or how the photo album, the old telephone, his mother, and Katherine Whitney were all tied together in some way.

"It's nearly suppertime. Would you like to go get something to eat? How about some steaks?" Chuck rubbed his tummy and apparently didn't detect my lie.

"No. I think I'll pass on that. Besides, Margo will be getting home soon and I wanted to spend some time with my sister this week before I go home on Thursday." Not a total lie.

"Thursday? I thought you were leaving tomorrow?"

"Oh, I guess I didn't tell you. Yeah, I decided to stay a little longer than I originally planned. I don't have to be back at work until Friday. Anyway, I thought it would be nice to spend at least one night alone with my sister. That okay?" I felt bad for the guy, but I wasn't totally lying about wanting to spend time with Margo. I also knew I wouldn't feel comfortable in Chuck's presence so soon after going to see his mother behind his back.

"Yes. I understand. You want to spend time with your dear sister. Perhaps we can do something tomorrow morning or afternoon?"

I could sense that Chuck was at least slightly put off by the rejection of his dinner invitation. I wanted to end the conversation on a positive note. "Yes. That would be fine. I'll be looking forward to it, really."

***

Margo was due to arrive home shortly and I wanted to get a call in to Katherine before then. I decided to try to call her using my cell phone one more time, but the call still wouldn't go through. I then picked up the receiver of the old telephone and noticed that there was, once again, no dial tone. "Damn. How am I going to call her now?" After fiddling with a few wires and shaking the receiver a few times, I remembered that I didn't get a dial tone the previous night until I accidentally knocked the phone to the floor. "Should I?" After a moment to think about it, I purposely knocked the phone to the floor. After it landed with a thud, I once again heard a dial tone. I bent over to pick up the phone and dialed the number that Katherine gave me.

After a few rings, a man answered. "Yes. Who is it?" the man said curtly.

"Is Katherine there?"

"Katherine? Young man, do you make it your practice to telephone people at home during their mealtime?"

"Oh, I'm sorry. I didn't mean to disturb your dinner, sir. May I speak with Katherine?"

"She is eating now with her family. If you tell me who is calling, I will give her the message and you can call back in an hour."

I thought about leaving Margo's phone number for Katherine to call back, but I wasn't sure if these calls through time would work from past to present. I also figured that it wasn't considered proper for a young woman to call a man in those days, so I decided that I would try to call her back later. "Can you please tell her that Joseph Eaton called and that I look forward to speaking with her in one hour?"

"Eaton? Yes, I will deliver your message. Good evening."

I realized that I must have been speaking to Katherine's father and I tried to show him proper respect by wishing him a good evening as well. "Good evening to ... <Click>". He hung up on me before I could get all of my words out.

I hung up the receiver and started to worry. What if the phone didn't have a dial tone in an hour? Would I have to bang the phone on the floor again, and how many more times would that make the phone work before it caused permanent damage? I checked every few minutes to see if I was still getting a dial tone. In the meantime, I did an Internet search on Katherine Whitney but found out very little about her. There was really no way for me to know if it was the same Katherine Whitney, but *a* Katherine Whitney married a Naval Captain named Samuel Barnard in 1941. That would have made her nearly 30 years old when she got married, very old to get married for her time. Captain Barnard died in battle aboard his vessel in the Pacific theater in WWII in 1943 and was buried at sea. There was no mention of them having had any children and, assuming she had passed on, no mention of where she may have been buried. The chilling thought that Katherine had died and may have been dead for many years went through me like a knife. I wondered why Mrs. Manning didn't mention any of this. Maybe it was a different Katherine Whitney.

Margo arrived home just as I had finished with my research. Once she was settled, I told her everything that had been going on. I told her about the dreams, the calls with the old phone, the meeting with Chuck's mother, everything.

She didn't believe me at first and thought I was playing some kind of joke on her. I explained it all again to her and, though she still didn't believe my story, she started to at least believe that *I* believed it. "You worry me, Little Joey. I think you're starting to crack up. Maybe you'd be better off going home and getting back to work."

I tried to stay calm. "Listen, I know it all sounds crazy. I thought that you would think that all of this was really cool."

"Oh, I do. It just doesn't seem right coming from you. I mean, even on your worst day, you were still the sensible one in the family. It sounds more like ... like me!"

"Well, Margo, if it *was* you, what would you do?"

"Hmmm," she wondered, "I guess I would pay my spiritualist a visit, Madame Byzanski."

"Madame Byzanski? Your spiritualist?" I said with sarcasm.

"Yes. She's helped me with a lot of issues. My men issues, my mother issues, job issues ..."

"Let's see now, you're single, dating an ex-priest, you moved to the town where our mother grew up for some odd reason or another, and you barely make enough money to make ends meet. Yeah, Madame Byzanski sounds *very* helpful."

Margo didn't appreciate my continued sarcasm and fired back, "Well, she *has* been. She has really helped me put perspective on my life and she only charges me what I can afford to pay."

Still astounded by my sister's naivety I said, "Cash only, right?"

"Let me call her and make an appointment. You'll see! She's the real deal."

"What does she do, speak to the dead? Or does she just feel," I put my fingers out like quotation marks, *"psychic vibrations."*

"Yes, she channels the deceased. I've spoken to Mom on a few occasions through Madame Byzanski. It was all very enlightening."

"How come you never told me this before?" I insisted.

"Well, you've never seemed to be open to this kind of thing until today. I'm gonna call her and make an appointment for tonight. This is so cool!"

"Well, okay. When you are finished calling Madame Whatshername, I'll need to plug the old phone back in to call Katherine."

"It's Byzanski! So you think you can only talk to your girlfriend using that old telephone? You're adorable, Little Joey!"

"What if your spiritualist believes me? Then will you? I'll bet if she said to jump off a bridge you would?"

Not wanting me to have the last word, she waltzed slowly past me and, while twirling her index finger near her head she said, "You're C-R-A-Z-Y."

Margo made the appointment for later that evening with Madame Byzanski. It had been an hour since I had called Katherine and I was hoping to speak with her before seeing the spiritualist. The phone didn't need to be "dropped" this time as I got a dial tone right away. I was glad when Katherine answered, as I didn't want to have to talk to her father again. I decided that I would covertly ask Katherine questions to see if she really was receiving the call in 1935.

"Hi, Katherine, this is Joseph Eaton. I'm really sorry we missed each other today."

"What happened to you?" Apparently, she did show up for our date after all and thought that *she* was the one who had been stood up.

She sounded upset, so I felt that I'd better offer up some kind of fake excuse. "I'm sorry, you see my sister took ill and I had to take her to the hospital," I lied.

"Oh! Is she going to be okay?"

"Yes. The doctor said she will be fine in a few days. I hope you didn't wait too long for me?"

"Well, I *did* wait, for almost an hour. Mr. Dapple felt so bad for me he gave me a free ice cream."

I desperately tried to tie in the ice cream topic with one of my time test questions without sounding like an idiot. "You know what I like? I like to have ice cream at a baseball game. Maybe we can go to a baseball game sometime. I'm from out of town, you know, so what's the nearest major league ballpark?"

"That would be Ebbets Field in Brooklyn. My brothers and I go to a few Dodgers games a year. I'd love to go with you. That would be real fun!"

I scribbled down *Ebbets Field* and *Brooklyn Dodgers* on a piece of paper and continued with the baseball theme. "Yeah, we could go to a ball game. Maybe the President will throw out the first pitch. What's his name again?"

"You mean you don't know the name of our President?" She sounded shocked.

"Crazy, isn't it? I forget names sometimes and now it's going to bother me all day! Please, what's his name again?"

"You mean Franklin Roosevelt?" Katherine replied.

"Yes, that's it, Franklin Delano Roosevelt." I said nervously and wrote down *F.D.R., President,* on the piece of paper. I motioned for Margo to come over and see. Margo looked at the paper, then at me and shrugged her shoulders as if to say "So, what?"

"Are you feeling okay, Joseph? You sound kind of strange. Do you think you may have caught whatever ails your sister?"

I realized that I had done a poor job on my covert operation, but tried to play it cool. "Oh, I'm fine … I … I just get excited talking about baseball." It was a dumb thing to say and I knew it, but I kept going with my unorthodox interrogation. "Did you lose any family in World War I?" I knew that World War I was referred to as the Great War before there was a World War II and I figured she would correct me if it was before 1941.

"Pardon? Do you mean the Great War?" she replied.

I mouthed "BINGO" to Margo and wrote down *The Great War.* I had narrowed down Katherine's time to between the two world wars and during the Franklin Roosevelt administration. Again Margo was not impressed. "Oh, yes, the Great War? Did your family lose anyone?"

"Well, that was quite a while ago. I think we did lose a great uncle or something like that. Did your family lose anyone?"

"No, we managed to escape unscathed." I let out a fake chuckle.

"Are you sure you're all right? Perhaps your sister's illness has shaken you up more than you would like to admit."

"Perhaps," I replied. I then realized that I had lied to her repeatedly during our conversation and it wasn't sitting right in my stomach. I debated telling her the truth but was afraid she would think I was crazy. Instead, I decided to try to show more sincerity without revealing the time I was calling from. "Katherine, I know I sound very strange tonight and my jumping around from topic to topic sounds absurd, but I really want to meet you in person. I just don't know how or when we can get together. Please don't give up on me." Then I thought about what Chuck's mother had said about how Katherine and I met. "I may just pop in on you one day, out of the clear blue."

"I would really like to meet you in person, as well, Joseph. Call me when you can and tell your sister that I wish her well."

We exchanged goodbyes and I hung up the phone. I was a little melancholy about not being able to see her and still felt guilty about lying to her. I began to think about how this time travel thing would work and when it would take place so that we could finally meet in person. Was this something that would just happen by itself or was there something that I should be doing to make it happen? This was not something I had really considered before. Should I be trying to build some kind of time machine to make this meeting take place? If fate says that Katherine Whitney and I are to meet, then would fate provide the means of transportation?

I shook my head and told Margo, "I hope Madame Byzanski isn't a fake." I once again showed her the piece of paper that I had scribbled my notes on and barked, "Did you really look at this?"

"What? I don't get it, what's the big deal?" she replied.

"Umm, only that Franklin Roosevelt hasn't been President for nearly seventy years, and she says he is the President now! Also, Ebbets Field was torn down long ago and the Dodgers left Brooklyn longer ago than that! And she has never heard of World War II!"

"I don't know," said Margo. "Maybe she's just uninformed … or maybe she's just nuts!"

***

"Let me see your hands, Joseph," said a toothless, saggy-faced old woman. Her grey-streaked hair looked like it hadn't been shampooed in a month and her body smelled like newly cracked soft boiled eggs. The stench from her breath was as wretched as the rest of her. I tried in vain not to breathe in Madame Byzanski's pungent odors. "You have a very strange life line. Do you see how it breaks off here into two separate paths? This path here," she pointed to the left line on my left palm, "shows a long life filled with love and joy. This path," she then pointed to the right line, "shows a short and miserable life. You are nearly at that fork in your life's road now."

Madame Byzanski then motioned toward an old oval wood table with a single candle in the middle of it.

All of the chairs that surrounded the table looked like they originally came from different sets. Every window in the room was covered by heavy black curtains and all light fixtures seemed to have been purposely removed. Candlelight was the only illumination in the room. "Margo, Joseph, let us sit at the table and we shall see if the spirits wish to speak with us this evening." Margo and I sat across from each other with the spiritualist on my left. "Let us hold hands." We formed a chain of hands held together. "Spirits! Spirits, do you hear me? We have a young man with many questions; can you answer him, spirits?" Madame Byzanski then jerked her head backward and let out a howl that would rival any a wolf could make. As her eyes rolled around in her head, the candle began to flicker.

I flashed a "you're kidding me, right?" look toward Margo. Then I remembered my own situation and thought that if I could travel in time, it wouldn't be out of the realm of possibility that the old woman could channel the dead. I decided to try to keep an open mind.

The spiritualist continued to howl and moan with her head tilted back until finally she slowly brought her head back up. She looked around the room with her eyes partially turned around in her head and said in a female voice that was not her own, "Is Joseph Eaton among you?" The voice sounded faintly familiar to me.

Margo waited for me to answer. When I didn't, she kicked me under the table. Finally I said, "Yes, Yes, I am Joseph Eaton."

The possessed woman then turned her entire body in one motion toward where I was sitting. She took in a breath and then again as if she hadn't breathed for a very long time. "Why have you not come to see me, Joseph?"

"I don't understand, Madame Byzanski. I am here to see you now," I replied.

"No, Little Joey, she's not Madame Byzanski," Margo chirped. "She's someone else now."

"If you are not Madame Byzanski, then who are you?" I demanded.

"I think you know who I am, Joseph," said the spirit voice.

"Say your name and then maybe I will believe you!" I commanded.

"My name is Katherine. Katherine Whitney."

I then flashed another look toward Margo as if to say, "You told her everything, didn't you?" Margo flashed back her own look, one of innocence, followed by an expression of wonder.

"Why have you not yet come to me, Joseph?"

"I don't know how! I'm sorry, but if you are Katherine, I don't know how to reach you. Is there something I need to do? Some place I need to be?"

"All you need is to believe, my love, and we will be together. Just believe and it will all happen the way it is supposed to happen. Just believe, believe, believe …" The spirit voice began to get softer and softer until, eventually, it could no longer be heard.

Madame Byzanski slowly came out of her trance. She appeared somewhat flustered and almost embarrassed. She broke the chain of hands and got up from the table to get a sip of water. "I hope you received the answers to your questions. The spirits have had their say." When she had completely caught her breath and regained her wits, she said with a toothless grin, "That will be seventy-five dollars cash."

***

"Was that a crock or what?" I said to Margo as we drove back from Madame Byzanski's.

"I don't know. It seemed real to me. I think I believe you now."

"And you didn't say anything to her about why I was there?"

"No," Margo insisted. "All I told her was your name and that you were my brother. That's all."

"Hmm ... Maybe there was really something to it, then. Tell me this, though. How do I do it? Travel back to 1935, I mean. She didn't tell me how to do it."

"Yes, she did, Little Joey. She said all you have to do is believe and it will happen."

"Believe what?"

"Believe that it is possible. Believe in your destiny. Believe that not everything in life is black and white and to look for the gray areas."

With that I smiled and took one hand off the steering wheel and affectionately messed up my older sister's hair.

***

That night I had the dream again. The pictures were in motion as in the previous night's dream, but this time the black and white images became filled with color. The sound became crisper and cleaner and soon it was as if I was actually in the movie. The young woman's voice, Katherine's voice, was easier to understand now. As she spoke, her voice was doubled by what sounded like her voice as a much older woman, much like the voice of the possessed Madame Byzanski. Young Katherine and old Katherine spoke as one to encourage me to continue my quest. "Don't give up, Joseph, you are very close now. Continue to believe and we will be together."

"Please, please show me how! I don't know how to reach you! I want to reach you with all of my heart, but I don't know how! Show me how! Please, show me how!" my dream self pleaded.

Suddenly, I was awakened by the sound of the Tuesday morning garbage pickup. The loud warning beep of the reverse gear of the garbage truck was just too much for me to take. I thought that I had actually made it to her. My dream was so vivid and filled with color that I thought I was there in 1935 with Katherine Whitney. I sat up in the bed and, in disgust, threw my pillow across the room. When I got out of bed to pick it up, I could hear the sound of Margo taking her morning shower, so I decided to stay out of bed and get ready for the day.

I slumped in my chair at the kitchen table and sipped my coffee. Margo came in shortly after and greeted me with a rare morning smile. "Good morning, Little Joey! Sleep well?"

"Yeah, until the world's loudest garbage truck woke me up! Why are you so chipper this morning?"

"Oh, I have a lunch date today with my honey. What are your plans today?"

I replied with sarcastic anger, "Oh, I don't know, maybe make breakfast, get the paper, travel to 1935!"

"Why are we being so hostile this morning?" said an unwaveringly happy Margo.

"I'm sorry. I thought that I made my journey to 1935 while I was sleeping only to wake up to the garbage truck. I don't know what to do. Am I supposed to just sit around and wait for it to happen? Should I just go about my business as usual? What am I supposed to do? I wasn't given any kind of time table. It could happen today or it can happen next year for all I know, or maybe this is all nonsense and it won't happen at all. The more I think about it, the more ridiculous it all sounds anyway."

"Why don't you try to do more research today, maybe go to the library? That would be constructive. Get Chuck to go with you. I'm sure he would love to give you another history lesson."

"I don't know about Chuck anymore. I think he's been spying on me for some reason. I also don't want to tell him that I went to see his mother behind his back."

Margo stood near the kitchen table and drank down the rest of her coffee. "I've gotta get to work. Go hang out with Chuck. He's a jerk, but he's no spy. Tell him everything and I'll bet he will help you. See ya."

I decided to take my sister's advice and seek out Chuck's help. After showering, I got dressed and walked across the dewy grass to Chuck's house. It was a sunny morning, but dark clouds loomed on the horizon. Just as I was about to ring the bell, Chuck opened the door. "Joseph! I thought it was you walking on the lawn. Come in, come in. Did you and your sister have a nice night?"

Chuck's house looked like a bigger version of Margo's apartment with furnishings and decorations from a time gone by. I surmised that the house was preserved exactly as Mrs. Manning had left it before entering the nursing home. "Yes, we had ... an interesting night. We went to see a psychic. Can we sit somewhere and talk?"

Chuck directed me to a beautiful sitting room with white lace curtains on the windows and silk roses in crystal vases. We sat on a couch that faced a window with a nice view of Chuck's backyard. "You went to a psychic? Why in heaven's name would you waste your time and money with a psychic?"

Explaining the mysticism of what had been going on to Chuck was going to be difficult, I thought. I decided on a different starting point. "Chuck, please don't get mad. Yesterday when I said I was just out for a ride, I actually went to visit your mother in the nursing home."

He became very upset and started to shake with anger. "Why would you disturb my mother like that? I told you that she has difficulty distinguishing between past and present events. The more you placate her about it, the more upset she gets when she realizes her errors!"

"Look, I'm sorry, but I had to talk with her again. I think her past may be tied in with my future!" I pleaded.

"What in the world is that supposed to mean?"

"You remember the old photo album and the man that I closely resemble? Well, I believe that I *am*

70

the man in the pictures. The reason that I look so much like that man is because I *am* that man!"

"That's impossible. That would make you about a hundred years old. I'm sorry, but you look no more than thirty," Chuck said doubtfully.

"Well, I haven't been there yet, though I expect it to happen soon," I said, thinking I was making perfect sense.

"What?"

I took a deep breath to try to gain my composure. "According to your mother, Katherine Whitney and I become quite close. Katherine and her family lived in the house next door to you, the house where I am staying!" I paused to study Chuck and thought I detected deceit in his eyes. "You didn't know that? Why didn't you know that? You seem to know everything else about the neighborhood and the town, but you didn't know that Katherine Whitney lived right next door? You *did* know, didn't you? At the diner you acted like you never heard the name before."

Chuck slowly began to smile and then eventually let out a booming laugh. "Joseph, calm down. I know all about it. At least I think I do."

"What do you mean?" I inquired.

"I know all about Katherine Whitney and her mystery man, although I don't think I ever really believed the story until now."

"What story did you hear?"

"My Uncle Freddy told me about a man who would come out of nowhere and take away the affections of his girl. The girl was Katherine Whitney and the man's name was Joseph, Joseph Eaton."

"That's it? Is there more to the story?"

"Oh yes, a lot more. My uncle believed that this Joseph Eaton had come from the future with the sole intent to take Katherine away from him. I always thought it was just the musings of a drunken madman — you know that later in his life, Uncle Freddy would freely hit the bottle. Anyway, he thought that this man from the future had completely ruined his life. I'm not sure how he knew that the man from the future occupied the house next door, but he believed in it so firmly that he purchased the house with what little money he had left, and in his will he left strict instructions that no male may ever occupy it. I don't know if you noticed, but all of the renters are female."

"Yes, I have noticed," I said. "Margo thought that you were afraid of other men for some reason."

"I do not rent to men simply because if I did, the house would be turned over to the state. Anyway, Uncle Freddy died in 1955 with only the shirt on his back, the Whitney house, and the change in his pocket to his name. I was eight years old. Two weeks before he died, he told me the story and said if I promised to help him, he would leave me the Whitney house in his will."

"So you promised you would never let a male live in the house?"

Chuck stood up and began to pace back and forth in front of the couch as he spoke. "Yes, but that was only part of the promise. I also pledged that I would be on the lookout for this so-called man from the future. When your sister contacted me about renting the apartment and I saw that her last name was Eaton, I began to wonder about my uncle's story. When Margo told me that her brother would be staying with her for a few days and that his name was Joseph, I thought a little bit more about my uncle's story and decided that I better keep tabs on you. Then, when you showed me the photo I was completely thrown for a loop! And then, when you told me you had a date with a Katherine Whitney, I really started to wonder and began to consider the possibility that the story was all true. I still didn't completely believe it, though, and figured that your date must be with another Katherine Whitney. Now, well … I guess the man from the future really is you. Now, the thing is, what do I do with you?"

"What do you mean?" I said somberly.

Chuck stopped his pacing and stood right in front of me. "Well, I'm supposed to try and stop you from ruining my uncle's life. That's what I promised."

I got up from the couch and stood up right next to Chuck and was at least a half of a foot taller. I looked down toward him and said as menacingly as I could, "And just how do you propose to do that?"

He put his head down and walked quickly away from me toward a small chest of drawers. He opened the top drawer, pulled out a revolver, and proceeded to point it directly at me. The gun, like everything else in the house, was at least fifty years old. His hands shook nervously while he said, "I really don't want to have to shoot you. Please, just go back to Philadelphia and everything will be fine."

I slowly and calmly crept toward him. "Now c'mon, Chuck. I know you don't want to do anything you will regret later. I know you're not going to shoot me." I smiled and added, "You're just too nice of a guy."

Chuck's hands began to shake even more and sweat started to roll down his brow. "I will shoot you if I have to! Just go! Leave! Go back where you came from!" he said in a nervous and desperate voice.

"You and I both know you're not capable of hurting a fly and you're not going to shoot me." I said as I inched closer and closer to him. I firmly believed what I had said and couldn't really imagine Chuck being the kind of man that could intentionally hurt someone.

"Yes, I will!!!"

"No, you won't."

I lunged toward the hand that held the gun and Chuck's grip on it loosened. As we wrestled for possession, we knocked into the furniture. Then, suddenly, I heard a loud bang.

I lay sprawled on the floor holding my face. Dazed himself, Chuck dropped the gun and came to see how I was. "You shot me!! I can't believe you freaking shot me!!!" I yelled.

"I didn't shoot you, Joseph. The gun wasn't even loaded. I was just trying to scare you into going home."

"Then what was that loud bang and why am I bleeding?"

"The bang was the sound of the coffee table flipping over. I'm not sure why you're bleeding, but I think I may have scraped your face with my watch."

After checking myself, I realized that he was probably right. He somehow managed to rip off a sizeable chunk of my skin with his watch while we grappled. Even though I was bleeding, I was glad to discover that, at least, I hadn't been shot.

"Are you hurt badly? Should I call 911?"

"No, it's just a cut." I wiped the blood off of my lower lip on the left side of my face. "It's not that bad."

"Let me see." Chuck studied the wound. "I think it will be okay. Let's go wash it off in the bathroom. I'm so sorry, Joseph. I really didn't want to hurt you."

I looked at myself in the bathroom mirror and then realized why I sported a mole in the old photograph. It wasn't a mole at all. It was a wound from my scrap with Chuck. A smile came over my face as I wondered if being in possession of that bloody gash was an indication that I would be making my journey soon after. I still couldn't believe that Chuck would pull a gun on me, even an unloaded one. I shook my head and said, "Why the hell did you flash a gun at me, Chuck? What were you thinking?"

"Here, put some iodine on it." Chuck handed me the bottle and a cotton ball. "I'm sorry, Joseph. I didn't want to, but I didn't know what else to do. My uncle said that you would be an evil, vile man. I am so confused. You are not evil. In fact, you are one of nicest men I have ever met. Yet I am supposed to stop you from ruining my uncle's life."

"Did it ever occur to you that Katherine had very little interest in your Uncle Freddy? Your mother told me that Katherine only dated him because her father made her. Her father thought that your Uncle Freddy had a lot of money. Your uncle was so persistent that she finally gave in and went out with him a few times."

"Then you really didn't destroy his life?"

"I don't think so. Maybe I became a scapegoat for him. Maybe it was easier for him to blame it all on me than for him to accept that Katherine didn't have feelings for him. I'm sure after a while he truly began to believe it and made me out to be someone sent from hell."

"You're probably right, Joseph. Again, I am so sorry."

"You are not going to try and stop me anymore, are you?"

Chuck nodded his head from right to left. "No, sir, but I am worried about one thing?"

"What is that?"

"I am worried that you will change history somehow and that I will no longer exist."

I put my right arm around the man's shoulders. "Chuck, I apparently was already there. It all happens or it did happen over seventy years ago. I would think that if I had changed the future and you didn't exist, then you wouldn't be here now."

Chuck seemed confused at first, but then an expression of understanding enveloped his face. "I see, I see. Joseph, please accept my apologies for being such a detriment to you. Is there any way I can help you now? I really mean it. I want to help."

"I don't know. I don't really know what kind of help I would need. I was told that if I believe, that it will all just happen. Well, I believe, but I don't know if I believe enough. Maybe if you can think of some way that would totally convince me beyond a shadow of a doubt that I was here in 1935, that would help."

Chuck contemplated for a while and then snapped his fingers. "I got it!"

***

I looked up and down at the large oak tree in the backyard of the house where my sister lived. "I don't get it. Explain it to me one more time."

"When you get to 1935, dig a hole near this tree and bury a penny from that year in a mason jar," Chuck explained.

"And what will that do again?"

"Well, if you make sure that you do it, then we should be able to dig it up right now. There should be a mason jar with a 1935 penny in it right down below. If there is, that should convince you completely that you traveled to 1935."

"Okay, I see. If I pick the spot now, when I get to 1935 I just have to make sure that I bury it in that same exact spot. That's easy! Okay, let me see ..." I lined up the tree with the house and marked it in my mind so that I could do the same thing when I got to 1935. I walked what I thought might be about ten feet on an imaginary line that ran from the trunk of the grand old tree to the kitchen window of the house and declared, "The jar with the penny should be right here! Hand me the shovel, good man!" Chuck gave me the shovel and I began to dig. "How far down do you think I should go?"

"I don't know. How far down do you think you would dig to bury it?"

"Well ... I guess about two or three feet." I continued to dig until there was a hole about two and a half feet deep. "There is nothing here." Just then I heard a loud bang of thunder and I looked up at an ominous sky. "It looks like rain, should I keep digging?"

"Yes. Meanwhile, I'll get another spade and I'll dig around the area too." Chuck left to get another shovel out of his garage.

I kept on digging and digging. The rain started to come down, but I continued on. I moved a few feet to the left of the hole and started to dig a new one. When I didn't find anything I dug another hole over a few feet to the right of the original. I still found nothing. I was starting to doubt the whole idea, but kept thinking of Katherine and said to myself, "Believe, believe, believe ..."

Chuck arrived back with another shovel and started to dig around the areas that I had missed. He wasn't able to find anything either. Then on a whim, I started to dig in an area that was a little closer to the house than my original hole. I repeated to myself, "Believe, believe, believe ..." Mother Nature responded with a bolt of lightning that made both of us jump, but we kept on digging. Shortly thereafter, I heard a "clink" when I dug into the earth. Carefully, I removed the dirt around the object and with my hand I pulled out a very old mason jar. "I've got it!!!" I yelled out. "It was about three feet down, but I got it!!"

Chuck put down his shovel and turned to see what I had found. He handed me a rag that had become wet from the rain and said, "Wipe it off, but do it carefully." I wiped off the old jar and could see that there was something inside it. I started to gently shake the jar and it made a clinky, rattling sound. "Now, open it very slowly," Chuck directed. Another close bolt of lightning with accompanying loud thunder scared us both, but we continued on.

I had slight difficulty opening the jar, but with a little added muscle I was able to do it. I poured the contents of the jar in my hand and held it up. "It's a penny!!!" I proclaimed.

An equally excited Chuck said, "What is the year on the coin? Can you read it?"

I picked up the wet rag again and wiped the coin as hard as I could until I was able to read the year. As soon as the year was legible, my eyes bugged out. I held the coin up over my head as if I had won a major sports trophy and with the rain pouring down on me I screamed at the top of my lungs, "1935!!!!"

Four

Three hours had passed since I found the penny and I was still drying off from being in the storm outside. Chuck had an errand to run, so I was alone in Margo's apartment waiting to travel to 1935. I didn't know when it was going to occur, but I felt it would be soon. I had changed out of my wet clothes and was now wearing my old blue drawstring sweatpants with a hole near the left knee and a plain white undershirt. The thunder and lightning still persisted and I couldn't figure out what to do to keep myself occupied. I started to pace back and forth until I nearly wore a hole in the carpet. The wound on my face was still raw and occasionally dripped a little blood which I wiped away with a tissue.

While glancing at Margo's CD collection, I saw the Beatles' *White Album* and decided to give it a play. Trying to relax a little, I danced and sang along with *Back in the U.S.S.R.* only I playfully changed the words to *I'm back in 1935. I'm so glad to be alive, yeah.*

The music helped ease my tension a little, but I decided to see if Margo had any beer left in her refrigerator to help me relax a little further. Unfortunately, there was none left. I tried the freezer and found a bottle of vodka. I took out the orange juice from the fridge and mixed myself a very strong screwdriver. It wasn't my cocktail of choice, but would do in a pinch.

As John Lennon and I sang *Bungalow Bill*, the glass was empty and I was ready for my second drink. By the time Ringo finished singing *Don't Pass Me By*, I was ready for my third screwdriver. I was feeling no pain at all when I belted out *Sexy Sadie* out of rhythm with the actual song.

A new wave of storms approached and I knew the electricity would soon be gone. I was worried that I wouldn't be able to find any candles, but quickly realized that Margo had scented candles all over her apartment. Midway through *Helter Skelter* the power went out. There was sudden silence followed by very close lightning and then by deafening thunder. The thick cloud cover had made a late spring mid-afternoon look like midnight.

I lit a candle and sat Indian style in the middle of the living room floor. As I breathed in the scent of the candle, Spring Cherry Blossom, I wondered if Katherine Whitney had ever sat in the same spot where I was in what used to be her family's house.

I then imagined myself in the past and wondered if a modern-day man would stand out like a sore thumb in 1935. Would Katherine consider my differences to the other men of her time a good or a bad attribute? It was then when I realized that I had no real plan of what to do if and when I arrived in 1935. Should I just walk up to Katherine's house and ring the bell? Should I lay low for a while until I got a feel for the people and the time? I thought about how happy I looked in the old photos so I decided to put trust in both fate and myself and just wing it.

The power had been out for nearly a half-hour and I began to get restless. I had finished all of the vodka and was now just drinking plain orange juice. I wasn't totally drunk, but I wasn't completely sober either. The sky was still and black as night, but there hadn't been any close lightning strikes for about fifteen minutes. During most power outages the telephone lines are still operational, so I figured it was a good time to call Katherine again. I had nothing else to do anyway.

I picked up the old phone, was pleased that I got a dial tone, and laughed as I dialed 1-800-MATTRES. I knew that the call wouldn't be routed to the mattress company. If my suspicions were correct, it would dial Katherine Whitney's phone in 1935, the same phone that I was holding in my hands. It didn't matter what number I dialed, the end result would be the same.

"Hello?" said a sweet voice from the past.

"Hi, Katherine, this is Joseph Eaton. I hope I'm not disturbing you."

"Oh no, I just arrived home from work and I was going to help Mother with dinner in a short while. It's good to hear your voice again, Joseph."

"It's good to hear yours, as well, Katherine. So ..." I don't know why, but I had difficulty coming up with something to talk about. I blurted out the first thing that came to mind. "So, what are you making for dinner?"

"We are making Father's favorite, roast beef with mashed potatoes and squash. Shall I set another plate?"

I quickly answered, "Oh no, as much as I'd love to join you for dinner, I won't be able to make it, but thank you."

"Are you sure you wouldn't like to join us? We have plenty. It wouldn't be any bother to ..."

"No, no" I interrupted. "Anyway, would you really want our first face-to-face meeting to be with your family present? Besides, it has been so stormy out today that I would probably get soaked on the way there." As soon as the words came out of my mouth, I wished I could have swallowed them back in. For all I knew it may have been a beautiful spring day in 1935 without a cloud in the sky.

To my surprise and delight Katherine replied, "Yes, it certainly has been a rainy day. The lightning has been frightful and you are right, our first real meeting should not involve my parents. But when are we going to meet, Joseph? I would love to have a face to match the voice. I'm sure you would too."

"I just know you are lovely, Katherine. I don't need to see you to know that," I said, knowing full well what she looked like.

"I understand that you need to tend to your sister's health right now, but I would really like to see you."

It took a few moments for me to remember the lie I told her about Margo's illness. "Yes, I must attend to my dear sister, but she is getting much better. We will meet soon, Katherine. I'm sure of it." Then a very close lightning strike occurred followed by ear-splitting thunder. I thought I heard the same sound from the phone receiver, as well, so I figured there must have been a similar storm on that day in 1935. "Wow, did you hear that?" I asked.

"Yes, you would have to be deaf not to. A few more of those and I may yet lose my hearing or my sight from ..."

Suddenly, I could no longer hear anything from the receiver. "Katherine? Katherine, are you there?" I pressed and released the phone's hook a few times. "Katherine? Katherine? ... Damn it!" I screamed and tried the hook a few more times. There was nothing. No dial tone or anything. The phone was completely dead. I then tried the "drop the phone on the floor" trick hoping that would make it work again. It did not. As I held the receiver in my hands, I shook it inside my fist and cursed. I looked to the ceiling and yelled, "How the hell am I supposed to do this! What am I supposed to do now?"

The reply to my question was another close lightning strike, and then another, and then another even closer than that. Before I could even hear the thunder of the last strike, everything went black. After a while, I realized all was black because my eyes were closed. I felt as though I was in an automobile speeding backward on the highway. I tried to open my eyes but couldn't. It was as if there was some kind of G-force keeping them closed. I caught a quick glimpse of streaking light, but that was all. My arms and legs were completely immobilized. I had no idea what was happening to me. Had I been struck by lightning and was I in an ambulance speeding toward the hospital? Maybe, I thought, this is how it feels to be dead. Suddenly I felt lighter than air and I was able to slowly open my eyes. What I saw was unreal or maybe it was just surreal. I was in the vacuum of space and galaxies were being born and dying right before my eyes. Stars would spring to life and then go supernova within what felt like seconds. All the while I could still feel the old telephone's receiver in my hand, but I couldn't move my head into the right position to see if it was really still there. I thought that maybe this was what the journey to heaven might be like.

Slowly, I stopped in space and I regained the ability to move my head and observe my surroundings. I became distressed that I could not see my own arms or legs or any other part of my body. I thought I saw an angel and was convinced that I must be dead and on my way to heaven and maybe I had stopped because I had arrived.

Suddenly, I felt as though whatever was holding me up had been removed and I began to free fall. I began to think that maybe it wasn't heaven I was going to after all, but that other place. As I fell, I could feel myself scream even though I wasn't sure if I possessed the necessary vocal chords, or even a throat, to accomplish it. I was heading down at an unimaginable speed and I wondered what, if anything at all, would break my fall. Was this to be a free fall for all eternity? I imagined other beings such as myself free falling all over this place. The more awful a person you were when you were alive, the faster your free fall would be. I must have done something very wrong to be falling at such an astonishing pace — maybe the way I hurt Laura?

I was relieved when my free-falling pace gradually slowed into more of a hover, as if I were a bird's feather floating down from the sky. I floated down for what seemed like hours and hours, just waiting to land on something, something soft I hoped. A pillow factory or a foam manufacturing plant would be nice, I thought. The clouds were now above me and I could make out mostly tall buildings to my left and much smaller buildings to my right. As I got closer to the ground I could see that everything appeared to be from an older time. The cars, the buildings, the streetlights, even the few people I could distinguish, seemed to be different. Afraid that my path was going to take me right onto a roof of a house, I closed my eyes and braced for impact, but felt no collision when I ceased falling.

I opened my eyes and I found myself in a dark and strange, yet somehow familiar, place. I was not on the roof. Somehow I had made it indoors. The only light in the room was a soft glow from the moonlight. I realized that my body was once again intact and I could see that I was still holding the old telephone's receiver. The phone didn't look quite as old and worn as it had the last time I saw it. It looked relatively new and it glinted in the light of the moon.

There was a newspaper on a nearby chair and when I saw that it was dated Thursday, June 6, 1935, I began to shake violently. My body felt as cold as deep space and when the receiver fell from my icy hands, it landed on the floor with a loud thud. The noise prompted a light to be turned on in what appeared to be an upstairs hallway. I could hear the sound of footsteps coming down the stairs. Someone was coming and they were heading directly toward me. I continued to shake and didn't know what to do.

"Who's there?" I heard someone whisper. I managed to get low to the floor and hid in a crouched position next to a china cabinet. Unfortunately, I was still shaking and each shake sent a vibration through the china cabinet and the resulting rattling sound gave my hiding spot away. I could see that the whisperer was a young woman who appeared vaguely familiar in the dark. Slowly, I got out of my crouched position and stood up next to the china cabinet. As the woman got closer, I leaped toward her and put my hands over her mouth to keep her expected screams from being heard by any others.

"Who are you and what do you want?" she asked in a muffled voice.

"I-I-I a-a-a-m-m J-J-oseph Eat-t-t-on" I struggled to say through chattering teeth. "I d-d-don't wan-t-t t-t-o h-hurt you."

Using a twisting motion, she easily broke away from my frosty grasp. "Joseph Eaton? Did you say you are Joseph Eaton?" she whispered. Instead of trying to speak again, I found it easier to nod my head. "Joseph, what are you doing here in the middle of the night and why are you shivering?" She turned on the kitchen light and looked down at my shabby sweatpants and t-shirt. Not knowing what to make of my clothing she paused and said, "And why are you wearing only your underwear?"

In the light, I could finally see who I was speaking to. It was the woman from the photographs, Katherine Whitney, my Katherine Whitney. It wasn't heaven or hell, it was 1935 and I was with Katherine. The black and white photos had not done her justice as she was even more beautiful in person and in living color. Her blonde hair had light reddish-brown highlights that draped down her cherry colored cheeks and extended to her long, elegant neck. Her lips were full and pouty and her eyes were the loveliest shade of emerald green that I had ever seen. She was a genuine beauty and I stood there before her shaking and speechless. She was so beautiful that I was afraid if I stared at her too long, I would go blind.

"Come on, then, follow me to the cellar. There's a trunk down there with some of my brothers' old clothes. While you look for something to fit you, I'll make some tea to warm you up. And keep quiet, the last thing we want to do is wake my father." We both crept quietly down to the basement and Katherine showed me the trunk. When she left to make the tea, I watched her ascend the basement steps and tried to imagine what her figure might look like without her cumbersome robe. She was tall for a woman of her time and she was thin, probably considered too thin by her peers.

All of the clothing in the trunk smelled strongly of moth balls. I found a pair of thick corduroy pants that would be too big on my waist and way too short for my legs. Katherine's brothers must have both been short and stocky, as I could find nothing else in the trunk that would come close to my size. Anything would surely be considered better than my ripped up sweats, so I decided to wear the corduroy pants and also put on a thick wool sweater that had a small cigarette burn. I was hoping this ensemble would at least help warm me up.

Why I was so cold and shaking I didn't know, but I assumed it had something to do with traveling through time. I wondered if other time travelers had the same cold sensation, if other time travelers even existed. It was then that the reality of my situation truly hit me. I had traveled in time. Just about everyone that I had known in the world had not yet been born. It was 1935 and I was with Katherine Whitney. I closed the trunk and managed a smile when I realized that this was probably the very trunk that I found, or would find in about seventy years, in the attic of Margo's house; the trunk that would start me on this journey.

There was a quiet knock on the other side of the basement door. "Are you decent?" Katherine whispered.

I caught a glimpse of myself in an old dusty mirror and decided that I looked like a real nerd in the odd-fitting clothing. I turned to my left and looked at a side view of myself and laughed back, "I guess so." I was starting to calm down and was no longer shaking as violently as I did when I first arrived.

Katherine walked down the basement steps and expertly balanced two cups of tea in her hands. "I took the liberty of putting in cream and sugar. I hope that's how you like it?"

"Yes, that will be fine, thank you." I reached for the cup that she offered and lightly touched her hand in the exchange. Her hand was soft as silk, yet electrifying at the same time. Despite the fact that I was still shaking a little, I managed to grasp the cup without spilling a drop. I tried to focus on the tea but could only think about touching her hand again.

"So, Joseph, what brings you here in the middle of the night?" she asked sternly. I continued to shake and wondered if I should continue to lie to her. Before I could come up with an answer, she asked, "Are you ill? Have you caught whatever has made your sister so ill? Do you need a doctor?"

I continued to try to figure out how I should proceed. If I told her the truth, that I was from the future, she would probably think me to be mad and scream for her father. Her father would then call the police, and the police would probably send me to a mental institution and they would do God only knows what to me there. It was 1935 and I didn't know a soul except for this lovely woman. With no family, no job, and no place to stay, half-truths seemed to be in order along with quick thinking. "I think I'm okay now. I guess I was just out in the elements too long today. My sister's health has improved, but she has permanently left town. Unfortunately, that has left me with no place to stay. The only other person in town I know is you."

"But how did you know where to find me? I don't remember telling you my address."

Thinking quick, I said, "I ran into the gentleman from the ice cream parlor and he told me where you lived." I looked innocently up at Katherine and hoped that the man at the ice cream shop would have known where Katherine's family resided.

"Why the middle of the night, and why didn't you at least ring the bell?"

I rolled my eyes. I was thankful that she didn't question me further about the ice cream parlor owner, but I had a new round of impossible questions to answer. "I didn't realize that it was so late. I had been walking around town since my sister left, not knowing what to do or where to go. I guess I just wasn't thinking when I didn't ring the doorbell."

"I don't know about Philadelphia, Mr. Eaton, but here we do not enter other people's houses without being invited in and certainly not in the middle of the night!" She said with anger.

"I am so sorry, Katherine. Please forgive me. I'm lost here and I don't know what to do."

"You are forgiven, Mr. Eaton" she said, though the tone of her voice suggested otherwise. "You will find my heart a generous one. Do not take it for granted."

"No, ma'am, I will not. Thank you."

"Now, what do we do with you for the rest of the night? You can't sleep on the living room couch because if my father finds you he will skin you alive."

"Can you sneak me up to your room?" I asked innocently.

"Certainly not! Maybe in Philadelphia young women entertain their gentleman friends in their rooms, but not here, Mr. Eaton."

"Oh, I didn't mean to …"

"No, you will have to stay down here in the cellar for the remainder of the night. I will bring you a pillow and a blanket and you can hide out here until morning." Katherine left to get the pillow and blanket and when she came back she said, "The cellar door will be locked so you will not be able to go anywhere until I come to see you in the morning. Will you be okay by yourself?"

I wanted to say so much but all that came out was "Yes, ma'am, I'll be fine."

"I will be the first one up in the morning so don't worry. Don't try to go out the outside exit of the cellar. Father chained it up years ago after Mother got hit on the head with the door. Good night, Joseph."

Envisioning Katherine's mother getting hit on the head with the cellar door made me chuckle as I said, "Good night, Katherine." She turned off the light and locked the door, and that was the end of it. It was my first night in 1935 and I was going to be spending it alone in a damp and dark basement. There was nothing but darkness to keep me company and nothing at all for me to do except try to sleep. I lay down on the makeshift bed that I created out of the blanket Katherine gave me and the old clothes in the trunk. The concrete floor didn't help my comfort any, but at least I was somewhat warm. The severe cold that I felt when I first arrived in this time had subsided.

As I lay there, I wondered what the next day would have in store for me and then began to worry that I might not still be in 1935 the next day. If I were to fall asleep, would I wake up back in my own time? If I did, Katherine would question how I got out of this locked tomb. It would have been considered quite a Houdini act. Did she even know who Harry Houdini was? I started to shake again, but this time it was more out of fear of an unknown place and time than from being cold. "I will not disappear in my sleep," I reasoned out loud. "Why would I be sent here to only barely meet Katherine and then go back? It doesn't make any sense. I will not disappear in my sleep!" With a firm belief in my reasoning, I settled down and eventually fell asleep.

That night I had a very different dream. I was on a big swing going back and forth. I climbed higher and higher and when I thought I couldn't go any higher, I jumped off. On my way down I passed people that I knew from the life I had left behind. As I passed my sister Margo she said, "You made it, Little Joey. I can't believe my little brother is a time traveler. Look!" She showed off her left hand and there was an engagement ring on her finger. Then I passed Chuck Manning and he said, "Way to go, Joseph! You get that girl!" I was getting closer to the ground and when I landed, Katherine was there to greet me. We then walked away, together, hand-in-hand. The sky was blue, the park was clean and tidy, and all was right with the world until I was awakened by the sound of a dog barking and scratching. As I rubbed Mr. Sandman from my eyes, the barking got louder and deeper. I realized that I was no longer sleeping and I was still in the place I had been the night before, Katherine's basement. Thank God I hadn't traveled back, I thought.

There was only a sliver of light that came from the gap between the bottom of the basement door and the floor of the kitchen and it was intermittently being blocked by the barking dog who was trying to press his nose up against the bottom of the door to get a good sniff. The dog smelled something unfamiliar behind the door — me. He sniffed and sniffed and then started to bark again. I figured if he looked anything like his bark, then he must have been the world's largest dog. An image of Katherine posing for a photo with her humongous pooch for the Guinness Book of World Records popped into my head. I was surprised that he didn't bark when I had arrived the night before. He must have been in a deep sleep or maybe the Whitneys kept him outside for the night.

"What is it baby? Is there a mouse down there?" I heard a voice say that I assumed came from Katherine's mother. "Do you want to go down and see?"

"Oh, no!!!" I whispered to myself. Katherine had told me that she would be the first one up in the morning! Where was she? The door opened and down came a gigantic St. Bernard dog that was almost as large as I had imagined. I had to think quick as the dog moved closer to me.

"Good morning, Katie dear," I could hear Katherine's mother say to her daughter.

"Good morning, Mother," Katherine responded. She must have heard the dog barking and carrying on and asked with a panic-stricken voice, "What is King doing in the cellar?" I tried to send her a telepathic S.O.S. but there was probably no need. I'm sure she knew I needed help.

"Oh, he's got a mouse or something. I'll go down and get him."

"No, no ... I'll get him, Mother." Katherine crept down the basement steps and looked around for me. The dog was barking at the trunk of old clothes, but all of the clothes were scattered on the floor. "Joseph?" she whispered.

"In here," I whispered back. I opened the trunk a crack, stuck out a finger, and wiggled it a little for her to see. With that, the dog started barking more vigorously and started to ram the trunk with his tremendous head.

"C'mon, boy, let's go outside. C'mon, King."
The dog paid no attention to her. "I'll be right back"
she whispered.

"Hurry!" I half-whispered back.

Within a minute, Katherine returned with a
large bone and got the dog's attention with it. "Let's go
outside, King, c'mon." She started toward the stairs
and King the dog reluctantly followed. He then
stopped and turned toward the trunk and let out one
last mean growl as if to tell me that we had some
unfinished business.

All became quiet in the basement, but I was still
afraid to leave the safety of the trunk. I heard
Katherine and her mother talking in the kitchen.

"Who were you whispering to in the cellar?"

Katherine replied, "Just the dog, Mother."

"Was there anything down there or did King get
all frenzied over nothing at all?"

"There were no mice that I could find down
there. Sometimes I think that dog is just off his nut! I
put him outside, maybe he can find some field mice to
play with out there." Katherine started to walk toward
the basement again.

"Where are you going, dear?" her mother asked.

"Umm ... King made a real mess in the cellar, so
I'm going down there to clean it up," Katherine replied
slickly.

She started down the steps and closed the door
behind her. I popped open the lid of the trunk and
gushed, "Thanks for getting rid of that dog. My God,
could he get any bigger?"

"Shhh, Mother will hear you and my father will
be up any minute now."

From the floor above we could hear a male voice yell, "Katherine!"

"Oh, applesauce!" Katherine whispered. "He's awake! I was hoping to get you out of the house before he woke up. Now you're going to have to stay hidden until he leaves for work."

"What about your mother?"

"Don't worry about her. I can handle her. Just stay hidden and quiet until I get back."

"How much longer do I have to hide?"

"I don't know, perhaps an hour. I'll be back later." She kissed her finger and touched me on the check with the same digit. Then she left and locked the basement door behind her.

The voices were muffled a little, but I could still hear the upstairs conversation. "Good morning, Father!"

"Good morning, my dear. What was all that ruckus with King?"

"He thought there was a mouse in the cellar," Katherine's mother said before Katherine could answer.

"A mouse in the cellar? Did he find one, Ellen?"

This time Katherine interrupted, "No, Father, there was nothing down there, nothing at all."

"Nothing at all? Well, maybe I should go down and take a look. There are probably all kinds of nasty vermin down there this time of year."

"No, Father, everything is fine down there, I just looked," Katherine said with a controlled but frantic voice.

"Oh, *you* looked," Katherine's father smirked in a derogatory manner, as if her ability to check the basement for rodents was based solely on her gender.

"You're going to be late for work, Jack," Ellen Whitney said, sensing her daughter's discomfort. "You can check the cellar when you get home tonight. Now, have some eggs and toast or you'll be in a bad mood all day."

The aroma of the Whitneys' breakfast was just making it down to me. It had taken it a while to break through the invisible moth ball barrier. The food smelled great, but what I really wanted was a cup of coffee. I didn't imagine that there were any Starbucks around in 1935 or even an automatic-drip coffee maker. Without either, I just lay in the trunk empty-handed and listened to the Whitneys' breakfast conversation.

"Now remember, Jack, that the Wilkersons are coming tonight for cards," Mrs. Whitney said to her husband who was making a rustling sound, probably thumbing through his morning paper and paying more attention to it than to his loyal and faithful wife.

Mr. Whitney turned the page. "Huh, cards tonight? Oh Ellen, I'm going fishing early tomorrow morning with that nice young Freddy York from next door. Cancel the Wilkersons. I need to get to sleep early tonight."

"We canceled on them two times last month. We are not canceling again," she said sternly. She then softened her approach, "I'll make sure that they leave early enough for you to get enough sleep for your fishing outing with Freddy. Besides, I think Freddy is sweet on our Katie. Maybe he will be asking you for your permission for something?"

"Oh, Mother!" Katherine smirked.

"You would do well to marry a young man like Freddy York!" Katherine's father interjected. "He must be doing well to afford that contraption he drives around town."

Her mother added, "You know, you are not getting any younger, dear. Don't you want a family like your sisters have? You can't work part-time for that law firm forever."

"I wouldn't marry Freddy if he were the last man on earth! He thinks he's the cat's pajamas. When we went to the picture show last month his behavior was quite appalling!"

"Oh, don't overreact, dear," Ellen Whitney said. "Freddy York is a perfectly nice young man. You should really give him another chance."

"I would rather die. He may act like a nice young man to you two, but when we are alone all he ever wants to do is kiss me. I will not subject myself to that again." Katherine walked out of the kitchen in a huff while her parents laughed at her resolve. She had gotten so angry at her parents for trying to push Freddy York on her that she almost forgot about me hiding out in the basement. I hoped that her father would be leaving soon and that she had been trying to figure out how best to distract her mother long enough for me to escape the house. She quietly unlocked the basement door, turned on the light, and softly walked down the steps.

I opened the trunk to stick my head out and was about to speak when Katherine put her index finger to her lips. "Shhh. My father will be leaving soon. When you hear a big commotion upstairs, you will know that I've got Mother's attention and it is time for you to go. I will leave the basement door unlocked. Go out the back door off of the kitchen."

"How will I know when to go?" I whispered.

"Don't worry, you'll know," she reassured.

"About when will all of this happen?"

"Shortly after my father leaves for work."

"Is there any chance I could get a cup of coffee to go?"

"Coffee? You mean to take with you?" she asked. I nodded my head and Katherine continued, "We only make coffee for special occasions. How about another cup of tea?"

"Okay, tea it is." It was better than nothing.

"I will leave a cup on the kitchen counter closest to the back door." She once again crept up the stairs and slowly closed the door behind her and this time she didn't lock it.

Shortly after, I heard Katherine's father heading out the front door saying his goodbyes as he left for work. I was ready to make my escape. All I needed was the signal.

About five minutes after Jack Whitney's departure, I heard a loud thud accompanied by the crash of breaking glass. It sounded like it may have come from two floors above me. The thud was followed by a cry that I knew came from Katherine. Katherine's mother screamed, "Oh, dear!" and I heard her run up the stairs. I figured that this must be the signal that Katherine was referring to. Her mother was no longer in the kitchen. This would be the most opportune time to leave, but I questioned if it was really the signal, or was Katherine really hurt? I quickly ran up the basement steps and peered into the kitchen and saw a cup in the exact place that Katherine said it would be and I knew that she was okay. She had created the commotion to avert her mother's attention.

I grabbed the cup of tea before darting out the door into the Whitneys' backyard. I had barely taken a sip before I was frozen with fear by the sound of the deep bark of the Whitneys' dog King. I gathered up my nerve and ran as fast as I could, scaling the six-foot wooden fence that surrounded the Whitneys' backyard. When I landed on the other side of the fence, I was amazed to discover that I hadn't spilled any of the tea. I looked into the cup and thought myself to be pretty nifty to have managed such a feat. I got up and started to proudly walk away, but after a few struts I clumsily tripped over a rock and fell which caused the tea to spill all over me. King stuck his snoot through a crack in the fence and sniffed. It almost sounded as if he was laughing at me.

As I lay there on the ground being laughed at by a dog, I looked up at the sky. It really didn't look any different than the sky in my time. Maybe it was a little bluer, but I hoped I would be able to manage any and all differences here. I got up off the ground and dusted off my second-hand trousers. In the light of day I was able to see how strange the combination of early twentieth-century pants looked with early twenty-first-century sneakers. It didn't help any that the pants were far too short for me. I knew I was going to stick out badly in this time, but believed that Katherine was worth the humiliation I would probably have to face.

After seeing her beauty and grace in the flesh, I was even more captivated by Katherine than I was before I arrived. Of course, seeing and meeting her was one thing. Winning her over was going to be quite another. It was apparent by the Whitneys' breakfast conversation that, despite Katherine's objections, both of her parents wanted her to marry Freddy York. I knew that Katherine and I had created a bond of some sort during our phone conversations, but I also knew that I was going to have to somehow manage to impress her parents to ultimately win her affections. The shabby clothes I was wearing would not help the situation, so step one of the master plan was to be to acquire some decent clothing. Realizing that I had no money and no place to stay, the master plan was immediately revised to step one — acquire money. If I did a good job at step one, step two — acquire decent clothing, and step three — find a decent place to stay, would be much easier.

I decided that I would use returning the tea cup as an excuse to come back to the Whitney house later on and hopefully see Katherine. I hid the cup in tall grass that was growing next to the house and headed toward the road not knowing where I was going or what I was going to do.

Five

The Whitneys' front yard was finely manicured and beautiful spring flowers grew everywhere. The morning was filled with bright sunshine as all of the clouds from the previous day had moved on. The storms had dropped the temperature considerably and it would have been considered cool for a mid-June morning. The front of the property was surrounded by hedges that were not present in my time. I carefully made my way through the yard while trying not to disturb any of the flowers. I found an opening in the hedges, slithered my way through, and found myself on the street.

After barely taking a step on the pavement, I was nearly mowed down by a car that had come to a screeching halt. The car and its driver both looked very familiar to me. The car was a beige Plymouth convertible with dual horns and a rear-mounted spare tire — the same Plymouth convertible that Chuck Manning would drive many years in the future. The driver got out of the car and marched angrily toward me. He was wearing a white collared shirt with a short black tie. His pants were black with thin white pinstripes and his hair appeared to be covered with a combed-in greasy goop. I turned toward the man and said, "You're Freddy. Freddy York, right?"

"Yeah, what's it to you?" the man replied angrily.

"That's quite a car you have there, Freddy." I tried to be friendly even though I knew this man was going to eventually become my nemesis over Katherine's affections.

"Well, you better watch where you're going or you'll find yourself fixed to my front grille like the Johnsons' cat was. You better get back to your gardening or I'll see to it that Mr. Whitney relieve you of your employment."

"Huh?" It took me a few moments to realize that Freddy York had seen me coming out of the hedges wearing shabby clothes and had assumed that I was the Whitneys' landscaper. I felt that I could use this to my advantage. Freddy would never suspect that his rival for Katherine would be someone that he would feel was far beneath him, a lowly laborer. After being berated for some time by the obnoxious young man, I said, "Oh, yes, sir. I'll get right back to it." As the words were coming out of my mouth, I realized that a little girl of about ten years old had been standing nearby listening to my exchange with Freddy. She was wearing a red dress that barely made it to her knees and she wore white knee socks with black Mary Jane shoes. Her dress had a white collar and a tied red bow in the center, and her auburn hair was all in curls and bows. I did a double take, as at first I thought I was looking at Shirley Temple.

"Mother wants to see you," she said snottily as she walked up to Freddy.

Through clenched teeth Freddy replied, "Tell her I'll be right there."

The little girl folded her arms, tilted her head, and said, "She wants to see you right now!" I liked the little girl immediately. She must have been Freddy's little sister which would have also made her Chuck's mother in the future. She had to have a lot of guts to stand up to Freddy like that. Freddy sighed and then got back into his car and drove home which was only a house away. The girl made sure he was gone and then turned to me and said, "You're not the Whitneys' gardener. Who are you?"

"How do you know I'm not their gardener?"

"Because I know their gardener and it's not you!"

"Okay, it's true. I'm not the gardener. My name is Joseph, Joseph Eaton."

"Hello, Joseph. I'm Alice." She extended her hand as if she wanted me to kiss it.

"I know, Alice Manning." I was about to kiss the little girl's hand when she yanked it away.

"Manning? No, I'm Alice York. The Mannings' live across town. I hate that Reginald Manning, I really do!"

"Of course ... you're Alice York. I'm sorry. You may feel differently someday about Reginald Manning, though."

"What were you doing on the Whitneys' property, Joseph?"

"Well, between you and me, I was seeing Katherine. Don't tell anyone though, it's a secret."

"Are you the Joseph she speaks to on the telephone?"

I was surprised that the little girl would know of this. "Well, I guess that would be me. Has she spoken to you about me?"

"Oh, yes. In the past couple of days she has spoken of nothing else. She said you were very charming, but she was afraid you would be homely looking. She was wrong, except for your clothes."

"Yes. I do need to get nicer clothing, don't I? Alice, do you and Katherine speak often?"

"Yes, Joseph, all the time. She sits with me when my parents go out. She usually reads bedtime stories to me, but this week all I have heard about is the charming fellow on the other side of the telephone."

"Really?"

"Really. She said that she has been trying to meet you in person, but so far has been unable to do so. I see that you have finally met face-to-face."

"Yes, we have."

"And?" questioned Alice.

"And what?"

"And, isn't she the most beautiful lady you have ever seen?"

"She is that, Alice. She is that."

"Are you going to marry her?"

"Well … I don't know about that," I said with a laugh. "Besides, I think your big brother would prefer she marry him."

"Oh, he would, but she doesn't like Freddy and I don't blame her 'cause I don't like him either."

"Why don't you like Freddy? He's your brother!"

"All he ever does is tease me and call me a baby. He thinks just because he has a car that all of the girls in town are sweet on him. He has been trying to get Katherine to kiss him for years, but she doesn't want to."

"Why don't you think she likes Freddy?"

"I'm not exactly sure, but she says that she likes to be romanced and that Freddy isn't the romantic type. She thinks that love should be like it is in the movies."

"And you don't think so?"

"Well, I don't know. I'm only ten. Maybe when I'm older I'll know."

"You may be only ten, Alice, but you seem to be smarter than most people two or three times your age when it comes to matters of the heart."

"Thank you, Joseph. I can see why Katherine likes you. You *are* charming!"

Alice York and I both turned to look toward her house where her mother was standing in the front doorway calling her name. "I guess I have to go. It was nice meeting you, Joseph. I hope we can meet again someday."

"I guarantee it!" I replied. "Oh, and don't tell Freddy I'm not the Whitneys' gardener, okay?"

"Okay, I won't."

"And one more thing, Alice. I would like to head toward the main section of town and I don't remember how to get there. Could you point me in the right direction?"

"Just keep walking that way," Alice pointed to her right toward her house, "and go left at Rockaway Avenue. Keep walking down Rockaway Avenue for a few blocks and you'll be right in the main part of town."

I said goodbye to the little girl and started walking. Before I got to the end of the block I stopped for a moment and turned around to look at the Whitney and York houses. I noticed that the houses themselves did not look much different than they did in my own time. Chuck must have had to work very hard over the years to keep the houses in such good condition. I saluted a man who would not be born for nearly a decade and then continued my walk to town.

On my walk I passed by folks that I didn't know, but they greeted me as if I were one of their neighbors. I watched men remove their hats when they greeted women as they passed on the street. It was a more formal yet friendlier time. I wondered why people didn't extend such kind greetings to strangers in the time that I left. I did not have a hat to remove when passing and greeting women, so I decided to bow gracefully instead. Unfortunately, my bow looked like something one might see in an over-the-top version of a William Shakespeare play. After I received just a few too many giggles in return from the ladies in town, I toned down my bow until it appeared more like it belonged in the twentieth century.

After walking for what seemed like an eternity, I finally made it to the main section of Valley View. I was amazed to see that there were a few horse-drawn vehicles that remained in service, but the vast majority of the people in the town used a car or a truck as a means of transportation. The town had recovered nicely from the Great Depression, but when I walked past a bread line that had quite a few takers, I could see there were still some echoes of those bad times remaining. I kept on walking and I eventually came upon Teddy's Ice Cream Parlor, the place where Katherine and I were supposed to have met. It would have a different name in my time, but, from the outside at least, it looked about the same.

Valley View in 1935 really was a small town and everyone, it seemed, knew everyone else. Unfortunately, with the exception of Katherine, not a living soul knew me. Being a total stranger to everyone in town would make finding employment quite difficult. I doubted that they handed out jobs to people who had no one that could vouch for their character. I didn't know for sure that my stay in 1935 would even last long enough to require employment, but I knew I needed money for my plan to woo Katherine to be successful. Money could, at the very least, enable me to buy some decent clothing and look presentable. As I continued to walk, a stranger who drew a striking resemblance to Mr. Monopoly stopped me.

"Sir, might I ask where you were able to procure such extravagant footwear?" the stranger said, all the while checking his pocket watch.

"Huh?" I replied, forgetting that I was still wearing my twenty-first-century sneakers in the first half of the twentieth century.

"Your shoes, sir, they are rather … unique. I was wondering where I might go to purchase a pair of my own?" he said.

My first instinct was to say "Wal-Mart" but I caught the words before they came out of my mouth. I then concocted an elaborate ruse. "I'm sorry, sir, these shoes were made special by the Chinese people as a gift to Prince Nike of Finland. They are one-of-a-kind."

"Prince Nike of Finland, you say? I don't think I have ever heard of him. And they are a one-of-a-kind item?" I shook my head in the affirmative. "Oh, that is a shame. How did you get your hands on such a treasure?"

"Well ..." I tried to think up a good one. "When I was in Finland last year, I saved the prince's young lady, possibly Finland's future queen, from kidnappers. The prince himself presented me with these royal shoes as a thank you for my service." I thought of my phone conversation a few days prior with Katherine when she accused me of being a salesman and tried not to smile.

"That's quite a story, sir. I don't suppose that you would be willing to part with them for, say ... ten dollars?"

This was a man who obviously had not been affected by the Great Depression. "Oh, but if I were to part with these amazing shoes for only ten dollars, that would be quite an insult to Finland's monarchy. It could create an international incident. How about twenty-five?" I connived.

"Would fifteen dollars stop their armies from invading our shores?" the stranger said sarcastically.

"May I remind you, sir, that these shoes are a one-of-a-kind item all the way from China via Finland?"

"I'll give you twenty dollars and that is my final offer."

Inside, I was ready to explode from joy, but tried to keep my calm on the outside. "Yes, I think that would about do it. You will have to throw your shoes into the deal so that I am not walking around barefoot."

"Deal!" the stranger said.

We exchanged shoes and the stranger gave me a twenty-dollar bill. I wasn't exactly sure how far, but I knew that twenty dollars could go a long way in 1935. The stranger's shoes were a little tight on my feet, but with the money he gave me I knew I could buy a reasonable pair of shoes with plenty of change to spare. I laughed hard as I watched the stranger walk down the street in my Nike sneakers and thanked God for small miracles.

Not far from where the stranger was strolling, I spotted a shoe store and I walked there as fast as the stranger's tight shoes would allow.

Shortly after I entered the store, the salesman brought me a pair of penny loafers, which he called "Weejun shoes", and a pair of Oxfords. The penny loafers were less than three dollars and they felt like they would be more comfortable to walk in. Since my feet were my only transportation at the time, I decided on the loafers. As soon as I walked out of the store, my new shoes started to pinch a little and I wondered if I made the right choice.

With more than seventeen dollars still in my pocket, I decided to see what kind of clothing I could buy. Just about anything would be better than what I had on at the time. I asked a passerby where I might be able to purchase a reasonably-priced suit and was directed to Whitten's Department Store at the end of Rockaway Avenue, past the railroad tracks. It was a long walk and my feet really began to throb making me question my choice of shoes even more. When I arrived, I told the clerk at the store what I needed and how much I had to spend. The clerk showed me a sharp four-button Windsor-style double-breasted suit in navy blue with a matching tie, and a plain white collared shirt. Even with socks and underwear, the price came to only fourteen dollars. I picked up a fedora hat for another dollar and hoped that with what little money I had left over I could afford a place to stay for the night and a bite to eat. As I examined myself in the mirror while wearing my new clothes, I thought myself to be quite the charming 1935 man.

I left the store and, sore feet and all, headed back toward the main part of town. There I came upon an eatery called Aunt Shirley's and tried to open the door, but it was locked. I looked in the window to see if there was anyone inside and I saw a rather burly fellow drinking what may have been a cup of coffee. I tapped on the window to get the burly man's attention. After a few rounds of raps and taps, the man finally came to the window and said, "We open at noon, come back in a half-hour."

"May I ask you, sir," I said, pointing to the cup the man held, "is that a cup of coffee, and if so, where did you get it from?"

"Aunt Shirley just made a fresh pot. Come back at noon and you can buy a cup then."

"Tell Aunt Shirley that if I could get a cup right now I will pay her ..." I hesitated as I tried to come up with the proper amount for 1935 that would get action without going too far. "I will pay her fifty cents. Fifty cents if I can get a cup of coffee right now."

"I'll go ask her." The burly man then shook his head and walked toward the rear of the restaurant. I pressed my ear up to the window so that I could hear. He started talking to whom I assumed to be his Aunt Shirley, and then suddenly all I could hear was a woman's shrieking laugh. Soon the man returned to the window. "How would you like your coffee? Cream and sugar?"

"Black will be fine."

"Coming right up, sir." After a few moments, the man returned with a steaming, hot cup of coffee. "Aunt Shirley says that you will have to drink it outside by the door."

"That's fine," I said, thankful to be finally getting my morning coffee.

The man opened the window and handed me the cup. He smiled exposing his nearly toothless mouth and said, "That will be fifty cents, sir. Knock when you're finished so I can bring the cup back in."

I handed the man fifty cents and received the cup of coffee. I stared at the cup for a while as if it were the Holy Grail and then began to drink its contents. Much to my delight, the caffeine began to kick in almost immediately. Aunt Shirley laughed wildly behind the door and she hooted, "Imagine, paying fifty cents for a cup of coffee!" but I didn't care. At last, I had my morning coffee and it was wonderful. "Thank you," I whispered to the sky.

Now that I had my new suit and my morning coffee, I was ready to take on the world. Even the new shoes were starting to break in and become more comfortable. I had a skip to my step that I never quite had before and I walked through town whistling happily.

I never felt so alive before, despite the fact that most of the people I met in this time were certainly dead in mine. There was a level of confidence and self-assuredness I attained that I had never reached before.

1935 seemed to agree with me and I just couldn't stop smiling. I smiled at strangers, at trees, at mailboxes, and even at my own reflection in storefront windows. "I wonder if Aunt Shirley spiked my coffee?" I asked myself aloud with laughter. I didn't care what the answer was because I was in love and it was a beautiful day.

Even though I knew I was going to need more money to continue to survive in this time, the first two steps of the plan were somewhat complete. I had acquired money from the sale of my sneakers and I had bought new clothes and shoes. My next steps to complete would be to find a decent place to live and a job to support this place. During my travels throughout the town, I had been keeping a keen eye out for both but hadn't noticed anything that I thought would suit me. The only lodging that might have had a remote possibility was a partially run-down inn called The Morning Bird which, to me, sounded more like a name for a daily newspaper than a hotel. Hoping to get a different opinion, I asked a heavyset woman who walked by where I might find reasonably-priced accommodations. She quickly responded with, "The Bird on Lincoln." With no other place to go, I decided I would head toward The Bird with the hopes that I would come upon another hotel that was also affordable but less run-down. I walked for blocks and found no such place, and before I knew it I had arrived at Lincoln Boulevard.

The Morning Bird, with its four stories, was the largest building on the street. It was made of brick that may have been red at one time but had faded to an almost orange color. The sign that identified the establishment, as well as its occupancy status, was somewhat crooked as it was hanging by a single nail instead of the two that should have been securing it. The landscaping could have best been described as overgrown chaos with ivy, plants, and trees growing everywhere in and around each other. I opened a screen door that was ripped and loose and entered the hotel. A very young man greeted me with a British accent.

"Good afternoon, sir. What can I do for you?"

"How much for a room for the night?"

"A single costs a dollar a day. Bath privileges are extra and we require payment up front."

"How much extra for the bath?"

"Another twenty-five cents, sir."

"Okay, I'll take the single with bath privileges." I took $1.25 out of my pocket, which left me with only twenty-nine cents left to live on, and handed it to the young clerk.

"Do you have any bags for me to take up, sir?"

"No. Well ..." I thought for a moment and then handed the clerk the paper bag I had been carrying that contained the clothes from Katherine's trunk and the shoes I received in the trade. "Here, you can take this to my room."

The clerk slowly eyed the paper bag he was holding and gently shook his head to signify his distaste for my choice of luggage. "Follow me, sir." I followed him up three flights of stairs and was then led through a very dark hallway. He opened the door to room 402 and light streamed into the hallway from the uncovered window in the room. The unmistakable squeal and patter of rodents scurrying could be heard all around us.

Room 402 was very modestly furnished. The bed consisted of a rickety frame with a lumpy mattress that was covered by a filthy kelly-green-shaded bedspread. The only other furnishing was a beat-up dresser with an oval shaped mirror hanging above it. I mentioned to the clerk that the windows had no covering and he replied, "The maid is laundering the curtains right now, sir. I'll tell her to make haste with them."

"No. It's okay. She doesn't need to *make haste.* Besides, it'll keep the rats away for a while."

"As you wish, sir." The clerk gave me the room key and then put his hand out to be tipped.

I reached into my pocket, took out a penny, and was about to hand it to the clerk, but when I saw it was a 1935 penny I pulled my hand away. Remembering that I still had the task ahead of burying a 1935 penny in a mason jar so that I could dig it back up in the future, I put the penny back in my pocket. I decided that penny would be the very one I would use for the job and fished out another for the clerk. I read the date aloud. "1931. Okay, here you are." As I handed him the 1931 penny, the bell at the front desk rang and he left to answer it leaving him no time to complain about my cheap tip.

***

All that remained was twenty-eight cents. How was I going to live on twenty-eight cents? I sat on the bed of my room and racked my brain until I could come up with some ideas on how I could support myself. Deciding that it might be worth the investment to buy a newspaper that contained "Help Wanted" ads, I left the hotel in search of a newsstand.

I thought that a local newspaper would better serve my job search and the Valley View Mail fit the bill, and for only a penny, the price was right too. As I searched through the paper for the "Help Wanted" section, I came across an article that reminded me of something that my maternal grandfather used to say. The article was about a horse named *Omaha* who would be running in the Belmont Stakes the next day. My grandfather used to say that when he and his platoon stormed the beach at Normandy during World War II, he knew he would live to see another day because it was Omaha Beach and that *Omaha* was lucky for him. He would boast that he bet a large sum of money on *Omaha* to win the Triple Crown of horse racing and that, even though *Omaha* was the favorite, he still won a nice sum of money. My grandfather would always follow that up by saying that the *Omaha* victory had started him on a big winning streak.

I scoured the article for a mention of the words "Triple Crown" but was unable to find them. It mentioned *Omaha's* victories in the Kentucky Derby and the Preakness Stakes, but mentioned nothing about the Belmont Stakes being the third leg of the Triple Crown. I wasn't sure about the year, and even though I was quite a novice about horse racing, I didn't think that any horse could win the Kentucky Derby more than once. I was pretty sure that the Derby was for three-year-old horses only, so this *had* to be the year that *Omaha* won the Triple Crown. Forgetting about my job search, I tucked the newspaper in my back pocket and walked to a nearby phone booth.

"Operator," said a female voice.

"Yes, Operator, I would like to place a call to Harry …" I drew a blank on my maternal grandfather's last name. I thought hard and remembered that my mother's maiden name was Dempsey. "Harry Dempsey."

"There is a Harrison Dempsey in Valley View. Would you like to place that call?"

"Yes, ma'am."

"Please deposit ten cents, sir." I dropped a dime in the pay-phone's ten-cent slot which left me with only seventeen cents. The phone rang for quite a while before a woman with a heavy Irish brogue answered. I asked to speak with Harry.

"Big Harry or Little Harry?" said the woman.

"That depends. How old is Little Harry?" I asked cautiously.

"My boy is nineteen. Who is calling?" the woman insisted.

I then realized I was speaking to my great-grandmother and had to pause to absorb the moment. After gathering myself I said, "This is Joseph Eaton, ma'am, and I would like to speak with *Little* Harry."

"What for? Does he owe you money?"

Her words stunned me. Was my grandfather a no-good bum who owed the whole town money? "No, Mrs. Dempsey, but I think Harry and I could be of mutual benefit to each other. Is he there?"

"No, he's not here, but come to the house tonight at six and he'll be home then." I gratefully took down the address and wrote it on the newspaper with a pencil I borrowed from the newsstand owner.

I had three hours to kill and only seventeen cents to spend. Hunger pains were starting to set in and I wondered what kind of a meal I could get for such a small amount of money. On the advice of the newsstand owner, I found a wiener cart a block away and ordered two frankfurters for five cents each. I'm not sure if it was because of my severe hunger, but even without mustard and relish, they were the best-tasting hot dogs I ever had in my entire life.

With my appetite suppressed, my thirst became the greater issue. I knew that I wasn't going to be able to stop in to the nearest convenience store and buy a bottle of water. It didn't seem that the convenience store had been invented yet anyway. However, Rexall Drugs appeared to be the next best thing. They sold various items including all different kinds of pills, potions, and powders. They also sold pipe tobacco, cigars, cigarettes, candy, and, thankfully for me, bottles of soda. I bought a bottle of Coca-Cola for four cents, and even though it was only room temperature, I drank it all. Remembering how much she would enjoy them in the future, with my remaining two cents I purchased a roll of Five Flavor Life Savers for little Alice York.

I wished I had been smart enough to strap a tool belt filled with valuable items on my body before I time-traveled. I could have arrived in 1935 with assorted valuable items to sell. Instead, I was completely out of money except for my "lucky" 1935 penny. I had hoped to be able to surprise Katherine with flowers and take her out somewhere nice in the evening. My hoped-for date with Katherine would have to be financed some other way. Perhaps, I thought, I could borrow money from my nineteen-year-old grandfather.

***

With time still left to kill before I could meet my grandfather, I walked back to the Whitneys' house to see if Katherine had arrived home from her job. I snuck over to the side of the house where the teacup I had left in the morning was waiting and brought it with me to the front door. I really wished I had some flowers or some sort of gift to present to her, as I figured it would be considered shameful of any suitor of this time to arrive at his sweetheart's door empty-handed.

Mrs. Whitney answered the door and I was presented with a face to match the voice I heard early that morning. I hid the cup behind my back, as I wanted to save it as an icebreaker for a conversation with Katherine. It was clear that Katherine's mother was once a beauty herself, but time and hard work had taken its toll on her appearance. The first of her features to strike me were her eyes. They appeared like a candle that once shone brightly but now was nearly at the end of its wick. Her shoulders were slightly slumped, her hair was turning gray, and her body was soft in the middle, typical of a woman who spent a lifetime taking care of and worrying about her family. Despite the fact that she had no idea who I was, she still greeted me with a beautiful smile, a smile that Katherine apparently inherited. When I asked her if Katherine was at home, her bright smiled dimmed and she began to study me with suspicion. With an inquisitive face she asked, "And just how are you acquainted with my daughter?"

Unable to come up with a better lie on the spot, I replied, "Oh, I'm sorry, ma'am. I'm Joseph Eaton." I removed my brand new hat and bowed slightly. "Your daughter and I met recently at the ice cream parlor." After the words left my mouth, I wished I had said something to make me sound like a better catch for her daughter. I should have said that we met at the library, or even church, but the damage was done. I was now going to be the loser that she met at the ice cream parlor. No match for Freddy York, I supposed.

"Katherine isn't home now." Big surprise, I thought. Of course she's going to say her daughter isn't home. I blew my first impression with her mother and I knew that I might not get a chance for a second. But then she *did* surprise me by saying, "She's running a few errands, but I expect her to be home in about a quarter hour. Would you like to come back then?"

"Yes, ma'am. I'll be back in about fifteen minutes. Thank you." She closed the door. I placed the teacup in a planter nearby and then left the property. As soon as I was at the end of the driveway, I noticed that little Alice York was playing in her front yard with a red ball that was almost as big as she was. I had a present for her, so I paid her a visit. I felt sort of a kinship with Alice since she was the only person I met in 1935 that I had also known in my own time. She was also my best source of information about Katherine and Freddy.

As soon as she saw me she smirked, "Looking for Katherine, I suppose?"

"She's not home so I came to visit you! Here, I have something for you." I reached into my pocket and handed her the pack of Life Savers candy. "I know they're your favorite." Again, I had said something I wished I could have taken back. How would I have known they were her favorite candy? I was hopeful that since she was a child, albeit a smart one, she wouldn't realize my screw-up. Instead, she floored me with, "Mother doesn't allow me to have candy. I can't accept your gift."

"But, they're ... Life Savers." I almost followed up with, "Your favorite."

"I'm sure they are very good, but I don't eat candy, it spoils my appetite."

It then occurred to me that I may have been the one who got her hooked in the first place. Unsure of what the consequences would be if she didn't start loving the candies immediately, I proceeded to entice her. "Oh c'mon," I said. "Look," I opened the roll, put one in my mouth, and took another one out for her to see, "they're small little candies. I'm sure if you had one it wouldn't hurt." I hoped that none of the neighbors were watching. A grown man forcing candy on a little girl probably wouldn't have looked too good from their point of view. She took the candy in her hand and held it up to her nose to smell it. She then shrugged her shoulders and popped it right into her mouth. After swishing it around for a very short time, she bit into it and then chewed it down to nothing.

"May I have another?" Alice asked politely.

"Here," I handed her the rest of the roll, "take them all. I bought them for you."

"What do I tell my mother?" she asked innocently.

"Maybe you should keep this a secret from her." Feeling bad about telling a little girl to be untruthful to her mother, I added, "But don't lie to her about anything else, okay?"

"I won't, cross my heart and hope to die," she said.

A short while later, Freddy's car pulled up in front of the Whitney home and, much to my dismay, Freddy escorted Katherine out of the passenger side. She was smiling at him and thanking him for the ride and at the same time turning my stomach (or was it the hot dogs?). I spied on them as he walked her to her front door. He tried to kiss her goodbye, but she squirmed her way out of his grasp. The rejection of his advances had a settling effect on my stomach, but it didn't seem to affect Freddy at all. He shrugged it off and said that he would be back later. He then zoomed away in his car.

I gave Katherine a few minutes inside before I went back over to her house. The door wasn't answered right away, but I could see someone, possibly Katherine herself, peek through the window to see who it was. Was she making sure that it wasn't Freddy at her door before she would answer it? When she finally answered she appeared relieved that it was me.

"Hi. I've come to return your teacup," I said in a playful tone. She opened the door and I handed her the cup and purposefully grazed her hand with mine.

She carefully put the cup down on a table near the front door and seemed very pleased. "Thank you. I wondered if I was ever going to see you or that cup again." As I was about to ask her why she didn't think she would see me again, she said, "I see your wardrobe has changed dramatically since our last meeting."

"Yes. I decided against the vagabond look. It really wasn't very becoming to me," I joked.

"Well, you would have made an excellent railroad tramp!" she joked back. She then checked behind her, probably to see if either of her parents were nearby, and then joined me at her doorstep closing the front door behind her.

I really wanted to ask her out on a date, but I wasn't sure I would be able to secure the funds necessary to do so. Hopeful that whatever force had sent me here was looking after me and would somehow provide me with the means to take her out, I asked her. "Katherine, would you like to go out with me tonight? The movies or ... anything?"

"Well ... I don't know. I already turned down Freddy York because I'm supposed to help my mother entertain the Wilkersons tonight."

Remembering the conversation between her parents at breakfast I said, "I thought that your parents were just playing cards with the Wilkersons? Surely your mother doesn't need any help with that."

"No. Well, I don't play cards with them, but Mother likes when I serve her guests drinks and hor d'ouerves."

Figuring that she had already rehearsed this excuse with Freddy, I pressed on. "Can't she do it alone for one night?" I asked.

"Well ... I don't know." She was wavering and I was ready to seize upon the opportunity.

"C'mon, Katherine, let's go out tonight. It will be fun, I promise." I flashed my best puppy dog smile in her direction.

"Well, I'll have to ask permission first."

What a different world this was. A young woman in her early twenties having to ask permission to go out on a date was just about unheard of in my time. I pushed her a little more, "Ask permission, then. In fact, I'll ask permission for you if you'd like."

"No, no, that won't be necessary. I can ask all by myself, thank you," she replied. Thank God she didn't call my bluff, as I probably would have wilted away asking her parents' permission to date their daughter. She reached over to me and squeezed my shoulder very hard. "Stay right there, I'll be right back," she implored. I wasn't about to go anywhere, yet, for some reason, she felt the need to physically keep me in my place. She went back inside of her house to ask her mother's permission to go out with me. She was only gone for a few minutes. When she returned, she opened the front door only halfway. She stuck her head out and said, "Okay, pick me up tonight at seven-thirty."

I had no idea with what I would be picking her up in, as I certainly did not own a car in 1935, nor did I have access to one. Would it be appropriate to pick up a woman in 1935 for a date and not have a vehicle of some sort? I played along, but all the while, I was praying in my head for help. "Tonight at seven-thirty it is. I'll see you later, Katherine." I thought about reaching over to kiss her, but I didn't want to give her the impression that I was a guy that was trying to get physical. I didn't want her to think I was at all like

Freddy. Since I knew she really didn't care much for him, being the anti-Freddy seemed to be in order, so I just smiled at her and left. I walked away with the coolest stride I knew to hide the truth that I was ready to burst with anticipation.

Six

If Valley View had a bad part of town in 1935, this was it. I had arrived at the address that my great-grandmother had provided and it quickly became clear that they were not a well-off family. Their house, as well as others on their block, was falling apart at the seams.

It was six o'clock in the evening. I had an hour and a half to convince my grandfather to lend me money and his car (if he had one), clean myself up, and pick up Katherine for our date. I knocked on the door and my great-grandmother, Colleen Dempsey, answered. She wore a plain gray dress and her hair was covered by a kerchief. I asked for Little Harry and explained to her that I was the one she spoke to on the phone earlier.

She stared at my face with suspicion for at least thirty seconds, and then opened the door to step outside. Then she looked me up and down and asked, "You kin?"

At first, the fact that she knew I was related to her was unsettling, but then I realized I could use our kinship to my advantage. I wished I had Margo's knowledge of our family tree so that I could best figure out who to tell her I was. Without that knowledge, the next best thing would be to lie with as much truth as possible. "I am Joseph Eaton from Philadelphia. We're related on my mother's side of the family."

"Oh, you are kin!" Colleen Dempsey threw her arms around me and gave me a very warm hug. "You must be Francine's son." I had no idea who Francine was (she may have been some long-lost relative from Philadelphia), but I acknowledged being her son anyway. "Come inside, child, and I'll get you something to eat." Within seconds of entering the house, a chair was shoved under me and a bowl of steaming hot beef stew was in my face. It had only a small amount of beef, but generous chunks of potatoes, peas, and corn and it smelled absolutely delicious. I was so ravenous that I barely noticed the old man sitting across the table from me. When I was finished, I took a good look at him and realized that he was my great-grandfather Harry Dempsey, Sr. He looked so similar to the way my grandfather looked when I was a child that it was eerie.

A very loud car pulled up to the house making me wonder if the muffler had been invented yet. The front door swung open and a cocky young man entered. His hair was slicked back with the same type of greasy gunk that all the men of this era seemed to embrace. He wore blue work pants and a gray flannel shirt with the sleeves ripped off. "Who's he?" he said to my great-grandmother while pointing in my direction.

"This is your Cousin Joseph from Philadelphia. Joseph, this is Harry Jr." Harry Jr., her son and my grandfather.

I extended my hand for him to shake it, but he walked right by me and stopped at the stove. Looking into the pot of stew he said, "Ma, you didn't give him my portion, did you?"

"There's plenty for everyone," she replied.

"Yeah, but now there is one less bowl for me." I couldn't believe this crass, smart-assed young man was my grandfather. This just couldn't be the same man that would be bouncing me on his knee in forty or so years. He got his bowl, sat down at the table, gave me a wink, and then extended his hand. "Cousin Joseph, pleased to make your acquaintance." It wasn't until he winked that I recognized any of my grandfather in this young punk. His eyes had the same glint of silvery blue that he would have in his later years. I shook his hand and it swallowed mine up like the ocean. He was not a big man, or a tall man, but he had giant working-man hands.

"Joseph has a business proposition for you, Harry. Isn't that right, Joseph?" Mrs. Dempsey said.

"Well, it's not exactly a business proposition. It's more of a business … adventure," I replied. "When you finish eating, we'll go take a walk and talk about it."

"What in the name of Jesus is a business adventure?" I turned toward my great-grandfather Harry Dempsey, Sr. and was surprised to hear him speak, as he hadn't uttered a word since I arrived. "Sounds like a bunch of horse manure to me," he added.

Before I could answer, Harry Jr. came to my defense. "That's no way to talk to a relation."

Harry Sr. barked back, "Hell, he's not my relation! He's yours and your mother's. I can say whatever I damn well please!"

Little Harry went back at his father and then his father returned the volley. This continued for a few minutes and then evolved into a heated argument between father and son. Mrs. Dempsey took me aside and said, "Don't fret about this," meaning the arguing. "They go at each other at least once a day." I then knew why Harry came to my defense. It was simply to be on the other side of an argument with his father. Their spat was almost refreshing, as it reminded me of generational battles that I used to have with my own parents.

Continuing to be the opportunist I had to be to survive in this time, I used their quarrel to my advantage. As I expected, when Little Harry ran out of things to yell at his father, he stormed out of the house. I gave him about a thirty-second head start and then followed after him. "Harry! Wait up!" I yelled down the block. He stopped speed walking and started kicking rocks around instead. When I caught up to him I said, "Man, these geezers, they just don't understand." I hoped the terms *man* and *geezer* had the same, or at least similar, meaning in this time as it had in mine. I also hoped my words would appeal to the young rebel within him.

"He's all wet. I've been saving up my dough to go to college and I've been working real hard. He thinks I'm wasting my time and that I should forget about it 'cause I'm not smart enough." I tried to remember if the grandfather I knew was a college man, but I wasn't sure. He continued, "The old man says he's gonna give me the bum's rush if I don't do what he says," which I took to mean he was going to get thrown out of the house.

"I'm sure he won't throw you out for wanting to go to college. That's ridiculous!" I said.

"Well, to him it's not. He says a man should be able to live on his own by the time he reaches sixteen. He's been trying to kick me out for three years!"

"I guess you wouldn't be able to afford to save for college if you didn't live under his roof."

"I figure I will in about a year. That's all I want is one more year in his house, then I'll leave." He felt in his pockets for something and then said, "Got a ciggy?"

"Sorry, I gave those up a few years ago. Those things will kill ya, you know." He looked at me like I was nuts. Despite our less-than-stellar relationship at that point, I figured it was time to tell him of my plan. "Harry, do you bet on horses?"

I was surprised when he said, "If I were dumb enough to play the horses, I wouldn't have any money at all for college. Why do you ask?"

I had always thought he was a big horseplayer and gambler and worried that it was I who started him on that road. "What if I told you that I know for a fact that *Omaha* is going to win the Triple Crown tomorrow?"

"The triple what?"

"The Triple Crown of horse racing. You know, he won the Kentucky Derby and The Preakness, and tomorrow he's going to win the Belmont Stakes."

He gave me a look of interest. "And just how do you know about this?"

"I could tell you, but you would be better off not knowing," I said without lying, as I gave him a friendly elbow to the ribs.

"Even if it's true, why tell me? We never even met before today," he asked.

The time for outright lying had come. "I was in town and a friend of mine gave me this tip. I was going to share this information with your father, if he were willing to lend me some money to bet with. After talking to you, I thought you might do more with it than he would."

"I don't know. How much do you need?"

"How about twenty dollars?"

"Twenty clams!! What kind of sap do you take me for?"

"How about ten, then?" Harry shook his head. "Five? Five and I'll need to borrow your car tonight."

"Forget it, fella. It's not gonna happen. Nobody drives my baby 'cepts me."

"Okay. Well, I guess I'll fill your father in on the race, then. Is he a betting man?" I started to walk back toward the Dempsey house, but I knew that Harry would stop me. I knew he would like having something going on that his father didn't know about.

"Wait. Wait. Okay, I'll lend you the money and I'll let you borrow my car. After all, you *are* family. But, let me tell you this," he gave me a menacing look, "if your pony doesn't win, you and I are going to have a problem, see."

"Don't worry," I said. "*Omaha* will win. I just wish he wasn't the favorite. We could really clean up." At that moment I started to worry. What if the horse didn't win? What if I had done something to alter history and the horse pulls up lame because of it?

Harry placed five dollars that he had pulled out of his sock into his fist. "You and I are going to the race together tomorrow, so save some money for admission." He hit me pretty hard on the shoulder with the fist and then handed me the money. I never knew that my grandfather was such a tough guy. If the horse didn't win, I was going to be in for a lot of trouble.

***

The moderate temperatures during the day gave way to a warm, but comfortable, early June evening. Harry had given me a crash course in how to start and drive his jalopy, an old Ford Model T that should have been scrapped years before. He showed me how to pull the choke and then cup the crank handle with my palm so that, if the engine kicked back, the handle wouldn't take off my hand. It was beyond strange for me to have to start up a car from the outside. It had also been quite some time since I had driven a car without an automatic transmission, so that was another lesson learned. My driving tutorial concluded when I dropped Harry off at a local pub. I then drove unaccompanied over to my hotel, The Bird, so that I could clean myself up and try to look presentable for my date. As I drove toward Katherine's house, the car's engine backfired so often that I began to envision myself as a cannon loader in a Civil War battle. I got a little too caught up in this vision and almost hit an old lady as she crossed the street.

As I pulled up to Katherine's house, I worried that she would be too embarrassed to be seen in the wreck I was driving. I turned the car off and it fired another cannonball as if to announce my presence. At least with the din I made, there was no need to knock on the door. Katherine had heard the racket and was already outside of her house. She looked beautiful. Her hair was in a pony tail that was held up by a white opaque kerchief. She wore a light-green print dress that fell at about shin level, and, for all I knew, may have been considered risqué for 1935. "Is this your car?" she asked.

"No, it's just a loaner. My car is still sitting in my driveway in Philly." It wasn't a lie. A good start to our date, I thought, but I wondered how long I could go without having to be untruthful to that lovely woman. I really hated having to make up so many stories to get along in that time, but I knew that I didn't really have a choice in the matter. The truth would get me nowhere but the nut house. "Shall we go?" I said as I escorted her toward my grandfather's wreck of an automobile.

"Are you sure it's safe?" she chuckled, but only half-joking, I suspected.

"Yeah. C'mon, get in." We drove into town to the Valley View Movie Theater. At the front window I purchased two tickets to the 8:00 showing of *Bride of Frankenstein*, which apparently was a hold-over hit. As I held the door open for her to enter the lobby, I asked her, "Do you want popcorn and soda? Maybe some Milk Duds too?" Her strange expression prompted me to scope out the theater. I scanned all around and found that there were no concession stands at all. "Oh, I guess they don't sell snacks here like they do where I come from."

"They sell candy and popcorn at the movie houses in Philadelphia?"

"Yes. They also sell hot dogs, hamburgers, chili, tacos, milk shakes, and all kinds of other goodies." After I said this I wasn't sure if I should have. Katherine, or someone else who may have overheard, could use this information and become wealthy with movie concessions before it was time for it to happen.

Katherine smiled at me and said, "Philadelphia sounds like a wonderful place. Maybe someday I could come and visit you there?" She surprised and delighted me by grabbing my hand and squeezing it. She had an expression of joy on her face, but something she saw behind me quickly changed her appearance. "Oh no," she said and she tried to shrink next to me as to not be seen.

"What? What's wrong?" I turned around and saw what was concerning her. It was Freddy York. He was in the lobby of the theater with a pack of his buddies. They were all sipping what I assumed to be whiskey from a flask that was being passed around. I knew I was in for trouble, as there is no man braver than one who is drunk and with a group of his friends.

As soon as Freddy spotted us, he immediately rushed over. "Katherine? I thought you had to help your mother tonight?

Katherine, realizing she had been discovered, un-shrunk herself and said with a quiver in her voice, "Freddy, uh, no, um … she didn't need me after all."

"So why didn't you tell me? If you were hard up for a date you could have told me." He then motioned toward me, "You didn't have to go out with the gardener."

"Huh?" she started to say but was interrupted.

"You can go home now, the lady will be spending the evening with me," Freddy said to me in a loud voice as if I were deaf or couldn't understand English.

I spoke as clearly as I could. "I'm sorry, Freddy, but Katherine and I are on a date."

"Look, I told you to go home now." He took money out of his wallet and threw it at me, "Here, this should cover the cost of the tickets. Go home if you know what's good for you."

I stood there with my arms folded and let the money fall to the ground. I wanted to be civil, but I also wanted to be firm. "Again, I'm sorry, but Katherine and I are together tonight." I looked over at Katherine and she had a pained expression on her face. Unlike me, she had seen what was coming. While my eyes were focused on Katherine, Freddy had reared back and fired a solid punch toward my face. Sensing the danger that was written all over her face, I was able to dodge most of the punch, but a glancing blow struck the left side of my face causing my wound to start bleeding again. A moment of decision had come. Should I knock this doofus to the ground, as I felt confident I could, or should I let him think he got the best of me and take a fall? Katherine didn't seem like the type of woman that was impressed by physical prowess, but I didn't want her to think that I would completely back down from a confrontation. Believing that she would be turned off by the brutality of fighting, but would be equally turned off if I chose not to fight at all, I decided that I would throw a few punches and then take a fall. I threw a quick right cross toward his face that he blocked with his left arm, but I followed up with a straight left that landed squarely on his stomach. He came back at me with the exact same combination, but his straight left merely grazed my mid-section. I pretended that the wind had been knocked out of me and fell to my knees.

"Let's go, Katherine!" Freddy implored as he grabbed her arm, all the while keeping an eye on me on the floor. "You're with me now." He said this as if she had no choice but to go with him because he was the winner of the scrap, or at least he thought he was, and she was his prize.

Katherine was steaming mad and pulled her arm away from him. With constrained anger she said, "Freddy York, I will *not* go with you and I *wouldn't* go with you if you were the last man on earth! I don't care that my parents think you are the bee's knees. You are ill-mannered and incorrigible and I will not go out with you ever again! Do you understand? Do you?"

Freddy stood there dazed, as if some cartoon character had dropped an anvil on his head. His friends laughed at him for being cut down to size by a woman. Katherine's words had hit him harder than my fists ever could. He gathered what was left of his dignity and walked out of the theater alone. Moments later I spotted him driving away in his car at an alarming speed, and, for a second, I was actually worried about what he might do to himself or some innocent person that might get in his way.

Katherine bent down toward me and tenderly put her hand on my shoulder. "Are you all right?" she asked.

My gamble had paid off. If I had beaten Freddy to a bloody pulp, as I had really wanted to do, she may have chastised me instead, and Freddy might have been the one that was gently consoled. I stood up and lightly caressed her arm. "I'm fine. Boy, you really told him off, didn't you?"

"I'm sorry, Joseph. I should have warned you that this could happen."

Her words and their inflection gave me the impression that Freddy York had done this before. He had probably been scaring away her dates for years. "It wasn't your fault," I said. "I probably should have seen it coming too. You know he almost ran me over with his car earlier today?"

"He did? What a dolt!" She reached into her purse and pulled out a lacy handkerchief. With a tenderness that I simply cannot describe, she wiped the blood away from my wound. "Better?" she said. I badly wanted to hold her in my arms and kiss her, but I restrained myself.

We walked hand-in-hand up the stairway that led to the theater's balcony and entered into darkness. I chose seats about fifteen rows from the back that were not quite in the make out section, but close enough to it if that was what she wanted to do. As we entered, a newsreel about Nazi Germany's preparation for the 1936 Olympic Games was being shown. Nobody paid any attention to it at all. Adolph Hitler himself was shown giving one of his usual rousing speeches, but the patrons of the theater cared little; they were too busy talking to each other. These people had no idea how much their world would be changing over the next ten years and that the man on the screen they were ignoring was going to be the major cause of it. For a brief moment, I wondered if I was sent back in time to somehow change the course of history, maybe stop Hitler from all of his evil deeds, but figured that would be too tall of an order for just one man. I made a decision that if I ever met someone of power during this time, I would tell them what I knew about World War II regardless of how they would perceive me.

The Bride of Frankenstein would not hold up well as a horror flick in my time, but for 1935 it was considered downright terrifying. Young girls and women could be heard screaming throughout the theater each time the monster appeared on the screen. Katherine wasn't one of the screamers, but she did grab my arm or my hand with each ghastly appearance. I wondered if she would think *me* to be some kind of monster if she knew the truth. Would a time-traveling man be viewed any differently in 1935 than a man built in a lab from dead bodies? I'm sure I would have been considered just as blasphemous as Karloff's monster to the population in general.

Some of the actors in the movie looked very familiar to me. They may have starred in other films that I had previously seen. It was easy to tell that all of the actors were classically trained. Actors from my time could certainly have taken a lesson from them as they each enunciated every syllable so as to be clearly understood by their audience.

While watching the film, I couldn't help but think of the Mel Brooks spoof *Young Frankenstein* and I laughed at inappropriate times. Each time I did, Katherine playfully elbowed me in the ribs as if she wanted in on the joke. There was simply no way to describe to her what I was laughing about.

Throughout the entire movie, I didn't try to kiss her or even put my arm around her. I just wanted her to get used to being next to me without having to worry about fending me off. However, I did plan on making some kind of move later on in the evening.

The movie ended and we all filed out of the theater. Young men all over the lobby mimicked the Frankenstein monster's groan and walk just to get their girlfriends to scream one more time.

"Did you enjoy the movie?" I asked Katherine.

"Yes, even more so this time," she said.

"You mean you've seen this movie before?" I inquired.

"Oh ... I'm sorry. I must confess that this was the third time for me."

"So why did you want to go again?"

"Because *you* asked me." She smiled and I just about floated on the air.

Not wanting our date to end, I asked, "It's a beautiful night. Would you like to go for a walk before I take you home?"

"A walk sounds lovely," she said, and I hoped she meant it, but I wondered if she really just wanted to avoid getting into Harry's jalopy for as long as possible.

I held the theater door open for her and then held her hand as we walked around Valley View. I was hoping that we could stop for coffee somewhere, but all of the restaurants and eateries had been long closed for the night. We had the town and its streets to ourselves.

"Well, nothing's open. It's your town, Katherine, where can we go?"

She hesitated and then said, "I know a place."

"What kind of place?"

"It's sort of my own secret place."

"Why is it a secret place?" I asked.

"It's a place I go to when I want to be alone or just to get away from my parents. It's really lovely, especially on nights like tonight."

I extended my arm forward, and, with an intentionally bad French accent, said, "Lead the way, madam."

She led me back toward the movie theater, and for a moment I thought we were going to see the movie again. She then led me behind the theater and toward a dirt path that was lined with large pale rocks. The path appeared to lead to a wooded area. She stopped abruptly and then hesitated.

"Is this the place?" I asked. She shook her head no. "Then why have you stopped here?"

"I don't know if we should go any further. I don't want you to get the wrong idea about me."

I joked and said, "I already have the wrong idea about you," but she didn't laugh.

"I just realized that I am leading you into the woods and I wanted to make sure that you didn't get the wrong idea as to why."

"Okay, then, why is the most beautiful girl in the world leading me into the woods?"

"Because in the woods there is this beautiful pond, and I wanted you to see how nice it is. That's all. Okay?" She actually seemed a little nervous.

"Okay, let's go see this pond and that's *all* we will do."

Katherine stared deep into my eyes as if she was checking for any signs of insincerity and then continued to lead me down the path. She then pointed to an extremely large tree stump and turned into the woods. "When you see the big stump, you enter the woods. There isn't really a clearly marked path after that, but you can sort of follow the tree line." She carefully moved through the woods so that neither of us would get clipped by hanging branches as we headed toward her secret place. Then suddenly, there it was.

The pond was as beautiful as she said it would be and the water glistened in the moonlight. It truly was a beautiful night. There were a few low but harmless puffy clouds that would hide clusters of stars as they floated by. Behind these clouds the night sky was so clear that I believed I could see to infinity. Katherine was taken by the night sky as well. She kept pointing out all of the constellations that I had learned in school but had forgotten about. In my time, I almost never looked at the sky. I tended to watch my big screen TV or my computer screen or glance at the occasional book. The closest I would come to star gazing would be when I would sit at my piano, close my eyes, and just play and allow myself the pleasure of letting go of reality. Without the distractions of my time, the world was a larger and more delightful place. I believed that anything could happen here. I had already felt its magic, as I had been here for less than twenty-four hours and had managed to feed, cloth, and shelter myself. I also had completely fallen in love.

Standing near the pond with the stars in her hair, Katherine was so beautiful and desirable that I could no longer contain myself. The time had come to make some kind of move. As she pointed out the Big Dipper and the Little Dipper, I slowly and softly put my right hand on the right side of her face and caressed it. Sensing no disapproval, I moved my left hand into position on the left side of her face. She stopped staring at the sky and started looking into my eyes. I carefully moved my face closer to hers and when I had reached a point of extreme closeness, I closed my eyes. Gently, I kissed her lips. They were as soft as silk and tasted like sweet cherry soda. We both took a deep breath as we opened our eyes and gazed upon each other. I kissed her again, this time with more passion, and tenderly licked her sweet lips with my tongue. She softly moved her tongue over my lips in return. A slight breeze off of the pond blew her hair into her face. I brushed her hair out of her eyes with my fingers and then we embraced. We held each other as if our whole lives had been leading up to that moment.

I was about to kiss her again, but she stopped me and said, "Joseph, I think you should take me home now." I was upset that my romantic mood had been broken, but I realized that I was in the presence of a very respectable girl. We walked back to where my grandfather's car was parked and after starting it, the jalopy's loud engine cooled off my romantic mood even more.

We didn't say much to each other on the drive back. When we arrived at her house, I walked her to the door and, not wanting the night to end, I made another move to kiss her. She pulled away and said, "Not here," and I gathered that she didn't want to be seen kissing me. Was it my embarrassment of a car or was she afraid that Freddy might be watching? I wasn't sure. "My father is most certainly spying on us," she whispered in my ear, and I understood.

"Can I take you to dinner tomorrow?" I asked, not knowing if I would possess the necessary funds to feed either one of us.

She looked deep into my eyes again, as if she was searching for something, and smiled. "Yes. You can come at seven, okay?"

"Okay," I put my hand on her arm and whispered, "Good night, Katherine."

She gently touched my hand and whispered, "Good night," back. I could barely feel the ground beneath me as I walked back to the car. While I turned the car's crank, my mind was deeply indulged into the heavenly world of love, but the deafening boom of the backfire brought me back down to earth.

***

I pulled up in front of the pub where I had dropped Harry off earlier in the evening. The street in front of the place was more hectic than I would have expected for that time of night, and cars were whizzing by at alarming speeds. The bar was dark and smoky, and I didn't see Harry when I first entered. The bartender directed me toward a back area of the pub where a few booths had been set-up. This was where, as the bartender said, "Drunks with no ride home wait until either someone picks them up, or they sober up enough to go home by themselves."

Harry was there with two other guys and they were sprawled out on the booth's benches. I gave Harry a shake, but he didn't respond. I tried again, this time he moaned a little, but was still practically lifeless. I asked for, and received, a cold glass of water and I splashed it in his face. This seemed to help a little as he blew out air and water as if he had been drowned. Still groggy he said, "What the hell are you doing?"

"Harry, it's me, Joseph. I've come to take you home."

"Joseph who?" he asked, while still trying to gain his self-control.

"Cousin Joseph. Remember, you lent me your car?"

The bartender then handed me another glass of cold water and said, "Try it again."

I splashed him in the face again and this time he sluggishly got to his feet. "If you do that again, I'm gonna break your neck!" He was sober enough to stand, so I guided him out of the bar. He couldn't exactly walk in a straight line, but he could walk on his own power.

"C'mon, Harry, C'mon," I said as I led him toward his car. I helped him into the passenger side and then went to the front of the car to start the engine. After a few tries, the old jalopy started, but as soon as I was about to sit down behind the wheel to drive Harry home, I noticed he was no longer in the passenger seat. He had apparently got out of the car on his own and was wandering drunk through the street. A car had to swerve to avoid him as it went by at full speed. Then another car had to come to a screeching halt to keep from hitting him. I didn't even want to imagine what might happen to me if Harry, my grandfather, were to get killed before he even met my grandmother. I had to dodge a few cars myself to get to him, but when I did I safely guided him to the far side of the street. When the coast was clear, we crossed the street together and then I finally got him secured in the car. If there had been a seat belt to put on him, I would have glued it shut to keep him from trying to get out of his seat again.

Fortunately, Harry slept through the entire ride back to his house. When we pulled up in his driveway my great-grandmother, who had been waiting up, helped me get him out of the car and into his bed. I asked her to remind Harry about our appointment in the morning and told her to tell him that I would bring the car back then. She asked me if I wanted to stay the night, but I told her that I was staying at The Bird. She insisted that any future nights I was in town I stay with them. I accepted, as I knew this would save me money, but I was a little leery that Francine, the woman whose son I was supposed to be, might call one evening while I was sitting at the dinner table or in the shower.

With Harry secure in his bed, I enjoyed the short ride to The Bird. It was still a beautiful night and I reveled in its glory. I reviewed the day's events in my mind and was simply amazed. I was in 1935 and I had been out on a date with the woman of my dreams. Thoughts about my old girlfriend Laura saying that I would never go the extra mile in my relationships also entered my head. It seemed to be a lifetime ago when she said that and I laughed out loud thinking about the lengths I had gone to just to be with Katherine.

Seven

It was morning on Saturday, June 8, 1935. Storm clouds had arrived during the night and the sound of the rain coming down gently woke me from my slumber. Still smiling from the previous night's activities, I rolled over into a puddle on the bed which was formed by a leak in the ceiling. This prompted me to sit up on the dry side of the bed. I rubbed my eyes, and when they were nearly in focus I took a good look around me. I was still in my hotel, The Morning Bird, in 1935. Even though I had already successfully slept and awakened in 1935 the previous day, I still had the fear the night before that I would wake up back in my own time. That fear had thankfully been unfounded.

It took me a few moments to realize that for the first time in many nights, I had not dreamed. I guess when you live your dreams by day the night can be completely uneventful. I got dressed, gathered what few belongings I had, checked out of the hotel, and headed for my grandfather's house.

Mrs. Dempsey, my great-grandmother, had let me in and invited me to have breakfast with her family. With the breathtaking aroma of bacon, pancakes, eggs, and coffee, there was no way I was going to refuse. I wondered how the Dempseys, who had a much lower standard of living than the Whitneys, could afford to have coffee with breakfast.

Mrs. Dempsey handed me a cup of her glorious coffee and I sipped it slowly, trying hard to savor it. "You know, we don't drink coffee every day here, Joseph. We're not like some of them high falutin' folks. I made it for Harry, to help him with the hangover I know he's going to have when he gets up."

"I'm sure he'll appreciate it, ma'am. I'll try to leave him some," I kidded.

From my seat at the breakfast table, I observed a small glass curio cabinet that contained the same figurines of well-dressed women that Margo kept in her living room. Mrs. Dempsey noticed the direction of my gaze and said proudly, "Those are my ladies. They come from the old country." She walked toward the cabinet and gently caressed it. "Aren't they wonderful?"

"They certainly are," I replied, and was glad that Margo would later pay homage to our great-grandmother by displaying these statuettes, Colleen Dempsey's pride and joy, in her own home.

"They are my only luxury. I paid a pretty penny for each of them, but they are worth that and more to me." She went back to the stove and put the finishing touches on the scrambled eggs and then placed them on the breakfast table with the bacon and the pancakes. "Wow," I said, "that smells heavenly. I'll try to save Harry some breakfast too!"

"Make yourself a plate, dear," she said.

Harry's father came out of the bedroom, let out some gas, and headed to the table. He still had on his pajamas, which were a one-piece ensemble, and his back flap was not completely secured. Upon seeing me, he let out a heavy sigh and more gas. Mrs.

Dempsey poured him a cup of coffee and he proceeded to drown it in milk. I noticed that there was no sugar for the coffee or syrup for the pancakes on the table. I always drank my coffee black anyway, but I would have liked some syrup for my pancakes. I then watched in horror as Mr. Dempsey spread a large wad of butter on his pancakes. He ate a stack of four in about three bites. The pile of scrambled eggs, upon which he sprinkled a ton of salt and pepper, went down in about two bites. He then stuffed two whole pieces of bacon in his mouth at one time, chewed about three times and swallowed. This was repeated until he had eaten six pieces of bacon. He then proceeded to wipe his mouth off with his sleeve and let out a thunderous belch. Oddly enough, he had enough grace to excuse himself from the table. On his way to the bathroom, he let out more gas and closed the door. He was a man of few words, not unlike my own father.

I accepted the fact that there would be no syrup for my pancakes and spread butter on them, though not nearly as much as my great-grandfather did, and I ate them and the rest of my breakfast very slowly savoring each bite. It was all fantastically delicious, even without the syrup.

The swarm of good smells had finally prompted Little Harry to get out of bed. He was as hung-over from the previous night's antics as Mrs. Dempsey and I expected him to be. His mother tenderly patted his head and poured him a big cup of coffee. She fussed over him until he swatted her loving hands away. At first, he didn't seem to be aware of my presence. He sat somewhat slouched over the table and was scratching his head. After a few big swigs of coffee, he noticed me across the table. "Thank you for driving me home last night, Joseph. Sorry I went on such a toot."

"He also helped get you to bed, you know," his mother chimed in while washing the cookware she used for making breakfast.

"Hey, *thank you* for letting me use your car," I said.

"How was your date with Katherine Whitney?" Harry asked.

"You had a date with the Whitney girl?" Mrs. Dempsey asked, as if that were inconceivable.

"Yes," I answered her, and to Harry I said, "And it went well except for the fight with Freddy York."

"Freddy York?" he laughed his name. "That fella thinks he's a real cake-eater. What a sap! He's always futzin' around."

"Harry!" Mrs. Dempsey admonished her son for what I guess she perceived as foul language. She would be shocked with the way people spoke in my time.

"Did you show him a thing or two?" Harry asked while punching the air. I took that to mean he wanted to know the outcome of the fight. I didn't want to say that I intentionally took a fall, so I just shrugged my shoulders.

Changing the subject, I said, "C'mon, Harry, eat your breakfast and hurry up. We've got to get to the …"

He interrupted and finished my sentence for me, "… the investors. Yes, I know." It was obvious that he didn't want his mother to know he was going out to bet on a horse.

Harry finished his food quickly. While he got himself dressed and ready for the day, I helped his mother with the dishes.

"It's not every day that you'll find a man that'll help with the dishes!" she said. She handed me a dish to dry and then grabbed my hand. "I've never seen such soft hands on a man. These hands ain't seen a lot of hard labor, have they?"

"No, ma'am, I guess not. I have played the piano since I was a child, and my mother thought I was some kind of prodigy so she rarely gave me any chores that could harm my hands. When I did any kind of work at all with my hands my mother always made me wear gloves," I added. "The only real work I ever did with my hands was with small electronics, a hobby of mine."

"Since you were a child? Lad, you still look like a child to me. How old are ya?"

"I'm twenty-nine, ma'am."

"You're twenty-nine? I thought you were about Little Harry's age or even younger. How do you stay so young lookin'?"

After she asked me that question I took a long, hard look at her. Since Harry was only 19, I figured that she was in her mid-forties at the oldest, but she looked much, much older than that. This truly was a hard time to live. The folks that were able to survive the Great Depression would show their battle scars for the rest of their years on earth. Mrs. Dempsey was one of those survivors. Her eyes were proud and fierce, but at the same time they were sad and tired. Her body was already broken down and she would often hold her lower back with her hand to try to alleviate the constant pain she was in. This was not a time for wimps. Even Harry, at age nineteen, could easily pass for someone five to ten years older in my time. I wanted to tell her that my youthful secret was not being born until the late 1970s, but I restrained myself. "Just clean living, I guess," was my answer. Harry finally announced himself ready and we left to go to the race track.

***

Belmont Park in Elmont, New York, was the venue for the annual running of the third leg of the Triple Crown of horse racing, The Belmont Stakes. It was an absolute dismal day and Harry and I got drenched from the heavy rains as we walked from the parking lot to the track. The façade of the building was covered in ivy and the grounds were filled with majestically tall oak trees. I'm sure it would have looked like a nice place if the weather hadn't been so miserable.

I decided to bet all of the money I had left, about four dollars, on *Omaha*. I was extremely surprised to see that there were only four other horses racing that day. The odds wouldn't pay out much for *Omaha* to win, only seventy cents per dollar bet, but I was pretty confident that I hadn't done anything to alter history and that I would win $2.80. Harry removed all the money from his sock, and it was quite a lot. He had brought about one-quarter of his college money with him and was betting all $200 on *Omaha*. I was no longer so confident that I hadn't changed anything and silently prayed for an *Omaha* victory. We got to our seats and sat in what continued to be a driving rain. The overhang of the grandstand helped keep many of the paying customers dry, but the competitors, both human and equine, were completely soaked.

The main event, The Belmont Stakes, was announced and the horses were put into their starting positions. Despite the poor weather, it was a full house. I overheard one patron (who looked like the stereotypical horseplayer) explain to another patron (who may have been his son) that the Belmont Stakes was a real stamina test for the horses. He said that at a mile and a half, it was a longer run than both The Preakness and Kentucky Derby. My program stated that *Omaha's* jockey was named Willie Saunders and his trainer was "Sunny" Jim Fitsimmons. I hoped they both knew what they were doing.

The gun sounded and the horses were released. My heart skipped a beat when I noticed that *Omaha* was not the front runner. I looked over at Harry, and he stabbed me with his eyes. *Omaha* was in third place and covered with mud from the slop the horses in front of him had kicked up. The race continued and with about one-third of it complete, our horse trailed *Cold Shoulder* and *Firethorn*. I was starting to become concerned. "C'mon, Omaha!!" Harry and I yelled in unison. Finally, the horse found a gear that the others in the field apparently did not possess. He motored past *Cold Shoulder*, who had run out of gas, and trailed only *Firethorn*. They ran to the stretch. *Omaha* was still in second place, but trailed by only a neck. Then, as if fueled by a jet-pack, *Omaha* streaked ahead. When he crossed the finish line first, I breathed a sigh of relief.

Officially, *Omaha* won by one and a half lengths at a time of 2:30.60.

Harry jumped up and down with jubilation. "I won! I won! A hundred and forty clams!" Then he did something that he never did even when I was a little boy and he was my grandfather. He hugged me. I realized it was a hug from a man that just won a good deal of money and not a hug of real affection, but it was a hug just the same. It felt good to be able to help my grandfather start to establish himself in life. Having an extra $2.80 in my pocket didn't hurt either. I offered to pay Harry back the five dollars that I borrowed, but he refused to take it. "It was a gift, not a loan," he said. If *Omaha* had lost, I wondered, would the money have been a gift?

The crowd began to clear out of the stadium. With the stands more than half empty, I noticed a familiar looking man who sat in the section to my right with his head in his hands. It was Freddy York and he appeared completely dejected. His fishing outing with Katherine's father must have been shortened or cancelled due to the weather. I guessed he had come with his friends to make some money but apparently picked the wrong horse. I tried to nonchalantly glance away when he caught me staring at him. Harry then noticed him too and, after seeing the expression on Freddy's face, could tell that Freddy's horse was a loser that day.

Harry decided to rub it in a little. "Hey, York! What's a matter, you pick an ass instead of a horse?"

Freddy got up and started to walk closer to our position. He responded with, "Beat it, Dempsey, you Mick!"

Harry, being the hot-head and feeling that he couldn't lose that day, said, "You wanna make somethin' of it?"

"Don't make me come over there, Dempsey!" Freddy remarked. But as he said it, he was doing just that, coming over to where we were standing.

They were now at arm's length from each other and I wasn't sure if I should intervene or not. I didn't know what kind of male fight code would be in order in 1935. Even though Freddy was much taller and probably outweighed Harry by thirty pounds, I felt that Harry could take him on grounds of his sheer toughness, so I decided to keep out of the way. Freddy then surprised both Harry and myself by sticking out his left hand to hold Harry's forehead and then punched him hard in the stomach with his right.

The sight of Harry, my grandfather, being doubled over in pain, and probably with the wind knocked out of him, angered me. When I was a kid, I always thought of him as being some kind of superhero. Now he lay there helpless. This Freddy York character had messed with enough people in my life for the past two days and I needed for him to feel some physical pain. I shoved him and said, "What did you do that for? He was just yapping. There was no reason to hit him."

"Listen, *Gardener*, are you gonna keep giving me static? Do I need to knock you down again like last night?"

I laughed and said, "If you think that you hurt me last night you're way freaking wrong! I took a fall for Katherine's benefit. I didn't want her to see what I am about to do to you now."

My threats didn't seem to bother him any, but I wished they had. It may have stopped the brutal beating he was about to get. As he made a move to shove me back, I hit him with a hard underhanded right to his lower left abdomen. As he reached for that same spot to alleviate his pain, I fired a straight-on right at his lower right jaw. He fell hard to the ground. "That's for my grandfather!" I yelled, and I'm sure I sounded like a lunatic. I then proceeded to pick him up by his shirt and pound his mid-section repeatedly. At this point, even Harry was trying to get me to stop and he tried to pull me off of Freddy, but I wasn't finished yet. I held Freddy up by his shirt collar with my right hand and rabbit-punched his face with my left. Eventually, Harry was able to pull me off. "And that's for Katherine!" were my last words. Luckily, Freddy's friends had kept their distance. It would have made for an ugly brawl. Harry and I left to collect our money while Freddy, who was beaten and bloodied, was attended to by his friends.

We headed back in Harry's car toward his home. The skies had lightened up slightly and the rain was much less fierce. My hands were swollen and bloody, though it was probably with Freddy's blood. I hadn't punched anyone out in quite a while, but I had to admit that it felt good to do it to such an arrogant ass. Still pumped up from the race and the fight, I said, "So, where do you want to go to celebrate our winnings?"

He lit up a cigarette and without answering my question, he asked a new one. "Do you have any other friends with any other tips?"

"I don't think so. Sorry, Harry."

"How about baseball? Know anything 'bout baseball?" he asked.

"Like what? Like, what team is going to win today?" I replied.

"Yeah, like who's gonna win. Know anything about that?" He flicked his ash in my direction.

I thought about the 1935 baseball season and couldn't come up with anything at all that I knew about it. "No, sorry, I don't know anything." Watching him smoke was painful to me. I knew he would die in his early seventies after living through several heart attacks. He would never give up smoking cigarettes, and they eventually killed him when I was only ten years old. "You shouldn't smoke, you know. It's really bad for your health."

He totally ignored me. "How about boxing? Judging by the way you beat up York, you may know something about that. There's a title fight on Thursday, Max Baer versus Jimmy Braddock."

The name Braddock rang a bell with me. "What's the story with Braddock? His name sounds very familiar."

"Oh, the guy was on bread lines not too long ago and now he's fighting for the heavyweight championship."

"Baer is the present champion, right?" Harry gave an affirmative nod. "Does Braddock have a nickname?" I inquired.

"Don't all boxers have one?" he quipped back.

"I mean a new nickname. Maybe something the media is calling him."

"The Media? The papers are calling him Cinderella Man."

That was it. The name sounded familiar because I had recently seen a movie about a Jimmy Braddock who had fought his way out of the Great Depression and eventually won the heavyweight championship. The movie was called *Cinderella Man*. Trusting that Hollywood got the story right, I said, "I think my friend may have whispered something to me about this fight."

"Like what?" Harry asked with his ears perked up.

"Like that Braddock is going to win," I replied.

Without hesitation he said, "I want in. Your horse just won me some big time scratch. This fight will win me even more 'cause Braddock is not favored to win." His eyes were lit up like a Christmas tree. Was I the one that turned him into such a gambler? From what I remember of the stories I was told by family, he was a big gambler until he met my grandmother and she turned his life around. I had just assumed that he had always been a real risk taker and never thought that I would be such a bad influence on him. Well, he was my buddy now and I was going to be staying at his house. I would be getting to know him very well, maybe a little too well.

***

I had made 7:30 reservations at what I hoped would be a decent restaurant for my date with Katherine. By the time I got to her house to pick her up the clouds had almost completely disappeared, but the scent of rain on the roads, grass, and trees still lingered on. I had again borrowed Harry's car and had arrived a little early, it was around a quarter to seven, so I decided to stop and chat with little Alice who was playing with a neighborhood boy. Upon seeing me, the little boy jumped and then ran away.

"Hi, Joseph," she sighed, as if she was a little put off by the interruption of her play. "Was it you who whipped Freddy?"

"Wow, news travels a lot faster than I thought it would in 1935," I said, and then realized how strange it must have sounded to her.

"So it was you. You hurt him real bad you know. You'd better be careful, Joseph. He's real sore at you."

"I'm sorry, Alice. I'm not really a bad guy. He just got me really mad."

"I know. He gets me real mad sometimes too. I'm glad that you beat him up, but did you have to hurt him so bad?"

"Is he really hurt that bad?" I asked, a little surprised that I had inflicted that much damage. I had never been much of a fighter. When I was young I would get into an occasional scrap at school, but my mother kept me busy with the piano at home so there was little time for me to fight with the neighborhood boys. My only escape from the piano at home was when my grandfather would come and take me to the park to play baseball, against my mother's wishes of course. When I was older and had failed to become a concert pianist, there were quite a few bar fights in which I was so drunk I don't remember whether I won or lost.

"Yes, he is. He says he has two broken ribs, a broken arm, and his jaw is very swollen."

I actually felt bad about what I had done. It didn't matter that he had been the aggressor at the movies and had been a thorn in Katherine's side for years. I actually felt compassion for the guy. "Should I apologize?"

"I don't think it would do a bit of good, Joseph. Just be careful because he said he was going to get even with you."

Great, I thought, just what I need. I was going to have to watch my back wherever I went. Then I started to become more concerned about what Katherine would think if she learned that I was the one who had brutally beaten up Freddy. She may have decided that I was no better than he was. "Does Katherine know what happened?"

"I don't know. I haven't seen her today."

Changing the subject, Alice gave me a big smile and said, "Joseph, do you have any more of that candy?"

I *had* been the one who hooked her on the Life Savers after all. "No, sorry, Alice, I don't. I'll bring you more tomorrow, okay?"

"Okay. Thanks, Joseph!"

***

After killing fifteen minutes with Alice, it was time to knock on Katherine's door. Much to my chagrin, Katherine's father was the one who answered. I had heard his voice on the phone, and also while I was hiding in his basement, but this was the first time I actually saw him. Incredibly, he looked almost exactly how I had pictured him to look. He was about 5' 9" tall, stocky but not fat, and he had more grease on his hair than anyone else I had seen in 1935. The grease gave his hair a near jet black appearance. Matching his hair, he had a greased handlebar moustache that was probably considered an old-fashioned thing to have even then. He wore a gray shirt and brown pants that looked as though it had come from an old suit. Over his shirt he wore a striped green and black vest that didn't match his pants. Through his spectacles, he looked at his pocket watch and then gazed upon me as though he were expecting someone else.

"Can I help you, young man?"

"Yes, sir, I'm here to pick up Katherine."

"You're here to pick up Katherine?" When he questioned me, for a moment I thought I was at the wrong house. Then I became worried that she wasn't home and had forgotten our date or, worse yet, she heard that I beat up Freddy and didn't want to ever see me again. "What is your name?" he asked. I told him and he said that he remembered briefly speaking with me on the telephone. "Joseph Eaton? What is your business with my daughter, Mr. Eaton?"

"Your daughter and I have ..." I didn't want to say that we had a date. I wanted to sound more formal and important to her father. "Your daughter and I have a dinner engagement this evening, Mr. Whitney."

"A dinner engagement you say?" The man had the irritating habit of repeating the key words of almost every sentence he heard as a follow-up question. "Are you sure she is expecting you?"

"Yes, Mr. Whitney."

He then shouted out to his wife, "Ellen, does Katie have a dinner engagement this evening?"

"Yes, Jack, with that nice fellow Joseph Eaton," Katherine's mother yelled back from the kitchen.

Looking at me he scowled, "I guess you have met my wife, then." He then yelled so that his wife could hear, "She could have told me!"

"Is Katherine nearly ready?" I inquired.

"Is she ready? I don't know." He then shouted out to his wife again, "Is Katie ready yet?"

Katherine's mother had already left the kitchen and was only a few feet from the door when she replied, "For heaven's sake, Jack, let the young man in. I'll go check to see if she is ready." As she headed toward the stairs she waived, "Hello again, Mr. Eaton."

"Hello, Mrs. Whitney," I waived back.

Mr. Whitney, in accordance with his wife's wishes, said, "Well, come in, won't you?" As I entered the house, I had a better chance to look around than I did when I arrived two nights prior. The layout looked the same as it would in the future when my sister Margo would live here, but, of course, the furnishings were different. The floors were all wood, there was no wall-to-wall carpet, and they shined so bright I could almost see my reflection in them. Mrs. Whitney, and probably Katherine as well, must have toiled for hours to get that shiny effect. The furniture was mostly a mix of traditional American colonial and French provincial. In the living room, there was a wonderful Louis XVI loveseat with a red berry pattern in front of the fireplace. Adjacent to the loveseat was a sofa with a pattern of urns and vines that was the same red as the pattern of the loveseat. Both pieces had walnut-colored wood. Behind the sofa stood a high-backed secretary desk that was also walnut, with neat piles of envelopes and papers on top of it.

"Have a seat, won't you?" Mr. Whitney said trying to be polite, but having difficulty hiding the fact that he didn't want his daughter dating the likes of me. I chose the sofa and hoped I could wait there for Katherine in peace. Mr. Whitney had other ideas.

"So, what's your line, Eaton?"

I wanted to say "degenerate gambler" for the shock value but restrained myself. "Unemployed bum" also came to mind, but I knew that winning over Katherine's parents was important. Her mother seemed to be tolerant of me, but her father would prove to be tougher to impress. Telling him I was unemployed in 1935 would probably have been a mistake, so I decided to tell him about my job in my time. "I work for a company called Reamco and I sell the finest quality paper in a variety of sizes for corporate needs," I said, nearly quoting my company's handbook verbatim.

He wasn't very impressed. "You sell paper, you say? Well, what else do you do?"

"For money?" I replied.

"No. I mean for sport. What do you do in your leisure time?"

I knew that he liked to fish with Freddy York and figured that would be a good way to get him interested in me. "When I have the time, I love to go fishing," I said, despite the fact that I didn't know the first thing about it and I had never gone fishing in my entire life.

His eyes lit up and he began to look at me with much less disdain. "Fishing? Fishing! Fresh water or salt water? What kind of lures do you use? What kind of rod?" he asked in rapid-fire fashion.

It was obvious that the man had a passion for fishing, a passion I did not share. I was in trouble and hoped I could talk my way out of it. "I just use worms, a string, and a stick like they did in the old days."

"Worms and a stick? Oh, you're a real purist, aren't you?"

"Yes, sir, I believe it is unfair to the fish to use all of these modern methods. It makes it much too easy. With the old way, it's more of a fair fight. Don't you agree?"

"Agree? Well I ..."

Katherine had come down the stairs to save me just in time. She was even more beautiful than she was the day before. She wore a fitted black print dress with a white collar. The print was of half moons and stars and her hem came to just above her ankles. Her hair was brushed back away from her face and was fastened by a single clip at the back of her head.

"Ready to go?" I asked, hoping she was so that I could get the hell away from her father.

Smiling, she said, "Yes. I'm finally ready!" Then she said good night to her parents and kissed her mother on the cheek. We walked out the door and were alone at last.

On the way to the car, I asked, "Katherine, has your father ever taken you fishing?"

"Yes. Why do you ask?"

We had arrived at the car, so I opened the door for her and escorted her in. I got in on the driver's side and continued our conversation. "Do you know much about it? Are you any good at it?"

"Yes, I've caught a few. Again, why do you ask?" She started to sound a little annoyed.

"Well, I told your father that I like to fish in my spare time and he jumped all over it. I think if you could teach me to fish, I could fake being a decent fisherman and your father might start to like me."

She laughed and said with a note of pity, "That's what Freddy does."

"What?" I said. "You mean that Freddy doesn't like to go fishing with your father?"

"I don't think so. All Freddy likes to do is get soused with his friends and drive around town in his car honking at pretty girls. He goes fishing with my father to try to get to me."

"What a tool!" I said, as I fired out a cannonball and drove away.

Katherine laughed and said, "A tool? I never heard that one before. That's pretty funny! What does it mean when you call someone a tool?"

"It means they're a jerk, or an idiot, or a …" I wanted to try to sound like I knew the lingo of the 1930s, "a scoundrel."

"Is that something they say in Philadelphia?"

I hesitated a moment and said, "I guess you could say that."

"A tool!" she said, thoughtfully. "The next time Freddy bothers me, I'm going to call him a tool!"

***

I studied the menu at the Valley View Inn and was a little nervous that, after paying for our meals, I wouldn't have enough money left to bet on the boxing match on Thursday. I vowed to spend more time looking for a job in the week to come and hoped for the best.

All of the menu items were a la carte and there were dishes that I never heard of before. Under the heading *Poultry*, there was a dish called *Roast Stuffed Jumbo Squab* for $1.30. I didn't like the sound of "Squab" so I passed on that one. *Relishes* was the word that was used for what would later be called *appetizers* or *starters* in my time. One could start their dining experience with something as horrific sounding as *Sauerkraut Juice* for only 15 cents. For the more sophisticated palette, *Russian Caviar* could be acquired for $1.60. Katherine ordered a cup of clam broth (30 cents), two lamb chops (90 cents), broccoli in a cream sauce (35 cents), and fried sweet potatoes (30 cents). I ordered a ham steak with mushrooms ($1.00), butter beans (25 cents), and, since they did not have a baked potato on the menu, a boiled potato (20 cents). We both had the complimentary water to drink.

As we waited for our meals I glanced around the establishment. There were only a handful of other diners and I hoped that the sparse crowd was due more to the uncertain economic times than bad food or service. The Valley View Inn was decorated to make one feel as though they were dining on board a ship, as it had ropes and anchors and all kinds of boating paraphernalia covering the walls and floors. Large photographs of famous vessels like the *Titanic*, and her sister ship the *Britannic*, also garnished the walls.

When I had finished checking the place out, I noticed that Katherine had been checking *me* out. She had been staring at me for an indeterminate period of time. When I finally met her gaze I asked, "Is there something wrong? Do you not like the restaurant?"

"No, the restaurant is fine," she replied, all the while still staring at me. Though I wished I could say it was, it was not necessarily a stare of love. Her stare could best have been described as being a hybrid of a stare of wonder and a stare of disbelief. It was as if she was trying to look into my soul.

I needed to break the spell and decided that playing the fool would serve me best. "You're staring at me. Is there something on my face?" I contorted my face in all different directions. "Oh my God, there's something on my face!"

She giggled, and to my ears it was like heaven's choir singing in perfect harmony. "No, there's nothing on your face. It's just that ... well ..."

"What?" I said, being serious again. "What is it?"

"Well ... you're just so different than the men I usually meet, Joseph. Why is that? I ask myself, *Is it because you're from a different city?* But my answer is *no, that's not what it is.* That is why I was staring at you, to try to get an answer to that question."

I didn't know what to say, and I'm sure that my mouth must have been open wide in awe of her perception. I wanted to tell her the whole story, but I was afraid that she would think I was kidding her or just plain crazy. Instead, I said, "I just hope that you find my differences engaging and that, in time, we will both fully appreciate all of our disparities."

Taking a page out of her father's book, she said with irritation, "In time? In time! Exactly how much time do we have, Mr. Eaton? At some point you will be heading back to Philadelphia!"

I understood why Katherine was upset. She was angry because she was falling for me and, as far as she knew, I would not be in Valley View for very much longer. What she may not have known was that I had completely fallen for her too and would stay with her forever if it was within my control. Unfortunately, I couldn't promise her anything. Whatever force had brought me there had the power to send me back where I came from whenever it wanted to. "I don't want to go back home. You have to know that I want to stay with you."

"Joseph, I'm sorry. I don't want to put any pressure on you. I realize that we've only known each other for a short time, yet somehow I feel that I know you. But at the same time, I feel that I don't know you at all. I just know that I want to know you … all the time." She said this with such sweetness that I nearly cried.

"I will do anything that I can to stay here with you. I just want you to know that if one day I am not here anymore, it's not because I wanted to leave."

"Then why? If it's not because you wanted to leave, then why would you?" She wanted an answer.

"There are certain things that are beyond my control. I may be here for a very long time or my stay might be very short. I simply don't know."

"Well, none of us knows how long we will be walking this earth, if that's what you're referring to."

"No, I don't mean death. Then again, maybe I do. I can't explain any further."

"You cannot or you will not?" she demanded.

"A little bit of both, I'm afraid."

"Mr. Eaton, do not speak to me in riddles! I am not a child, I am a grown woman. I recognize that life can break people down and make them do things that they ordinarily wouldn't do just so they can survive. I understand that life is not a storybook. Whatever it is that you are keeping from me cannot be all that dreadful."

"I wouldn't say it's dreadful. It's just ... different, but I don't think the time is right to tell you what it is. I just don't know if you're ready for it yet. Heck, I don't even know if I'm ready for it yet!" Our meals had arrived and I wanted the conversation concerning my eccentricities to be over. "I promise that I'll tell you one day soon. I absolutely promise."

"You had better," she said trying hard to keep a firm tone to her voice.

The thought of the absolute possibility of being whisked away from her abruptly, and once again being separated by so many years in time, kept me very quiet during dinner. I could only surmise that Katherine worried about being apart as well and that was what kept her equally as silent. I told myself over and over again to forget about it and try to enjoy the time we had together, but I just couldn't shake the thought of being forced away from her. I had never felt so drawn to anyone before and I was truly and deeply in love. My sensible side advised me to not get too attached to her, as it would make it that much harder on me when I had to leave. I had never been one to follow the recommendations of my sensible side before, and it was not very likely that I would pick then to start. All I knew was that my heart was aching despite the fact that we were still together, un-separated, and in the same room at the same point in time.

The check came to $3.30 and, not being sure what to give for the gratuity or even sure if a gratuity was in order, I handed the waitress four dollars and said, "Keep the change." She seemed to be very pleased with what I had given her and thanked me with vigor. I guess I had over-tipped.

We left the restaurant and neither of us said much to the other. We weren't angry with each other, or at least I wasn't angry with her, but truly realizing my non-secure position in 1935 had put a damper on my evening. In a sour mood, I planned to end our date and drive her home, but after stopping to put a few gallons in Harry's tank I decided to try to force myself out of my funk. "Katherine, where do you and your friends go to have fun?" I had only two dollars remaining so I hoped this fun wouldn't cost me my remaining funds.

She crinkled her face a little as if she really didn't want to tell me. "Sometimes on weekend nights I meet my friends at a place called Milligan's."

"Milligan's?" I said. "Sounds like fun. Wanna go?"

Her mood brightened and she said, "Okay. Let's go! I would really like for you to meet my friends."

She gave me directions to Milligan's and it sounded like it was in the same area where Harry's bar was. As I drove I asked her, "So, tell me about Milligan's? What's so fun about it and why do you and your friends go there?"

"Well, they serve beer and Irish whisky and they have a piano player who plays all of the Irish drinking songs."

"You drink beer?" I asked her. I just couldn't picture her slamming down a beer and singing *Danny Boy*.

She replied very matter-of-factly, "Sometimes I have one or two glasses. I try to leave before the people start to become totally inebriated."

"And you sing the songs?"

"Yes. I like to sing. It's fun. What about you? Don't you like to sing?"

"Of course I like to sing. And I usually need a few glasses of beer to do it! Do your parents know that you go to an Irish bar?"

"No, and please don't ever tell them. Besides, it is one of the few places where I know Freddy won't follow me."

"Why won't Freddy follow you there?"

"Because, he hates everything to do with the Irish."

I parked Harry's car in front of Milligan's. The lack of other automobiles parked nearby indicated to me that there were few patrons inside. I held open the door for Katherine and we entered a dusty, dimly lit, dump. Inside there was a beat-up old bar with beat-up barstools to match, a few rinky-dink tables that appeared as if they were about ready to fall apart, and an old upright piano against the back wall. Two men and a woman at the bar called out to Katherine as soon as they saw us come in. "C'mon," she said, "I'll introduce you." I met a tall and thin man named Walter who was twenty-four and working his way through law school by driving a bus. I met Eddie, twenty-two, the errand boy at Katherine's office but trying to find work as a civil engineer. I also met Betty who did not tell me her age but appeared to be barely eighteen. Betty, like Katherine, was a typist at the law firm of Brown and McCall. They seemed like a nice group, but I wondered if Katherine had ever dated Walter or Eddie.

"Where is everyone tonight?" Katherine asked.

"Ah, the piano player didn't make it so everyone but us regulars went home," replied Eddie, a small man with devilish eyes and a hint of an Irish brogue.

"Joseph plays the piano. Maybe he can entertain us tonight?" Katherine exhorted and then she winked at me as if to say *don't be mad.*

"C'mon, Joseph, play for us. We're bored," Walter implored, while Eddie and Betty agreed.

"I'm sorry. I don't really play all that much anymore. I probably wouldn't know the songs that you want to hear anyway."

Eddie said, "Oh come on, Joe. Play anything. We don't care what, do we?" the group shook their heads *no* all at once.

Since it was unanimous, I decided to give the people what they wanted. I walked over to the piano and went to sit down on the bench but noticed it was very uneven. Walter came over with his handkerchief and stuffed it under one of the legs and that evened it out some. I sat down and said, "Just so you all know, I don't play regularly anymore so I will probably be rusty." None of them seemed to care as they urged me on. "What should I play?"

This time young Betty chimed in, "As we said, we don't care. Just play." She was an attractive young woman with short brownish-black hair and an affinity for talking with her hands.

I slid open the cover and banged out a C-Major chord to try and get my bearings. It sounded horrible. The piano was badly out of tune and if my mother had heard me play such a neglected instrument she would surely have had a fit. At least all of the keys seemed to work.

I started by playing a little Chopin and then switched to Beethoven. The group wasn't getting into it, apparently not fans of the great masters. In jest, I started to play *Mary Had a Little Lamb* with one finger and Eddie started singing along and drank a slug of beer after each line. Walter then joined him as Katherine and Betty danced with each other. I continued the song but added a bass line and full chords. Keeping with the children's song theme, I played *Camptown Races, I've Been Working on the Railroad, My Darling Clementine,* and then ended with *This Old Man* which they didn't seem to know. After each verse, Walter and Eddie continued to take a big slug. After every song, I was expected to drink an entire glass of beer to catch up to the other guys. I told them that I shouldn't drink too much because I would have to drive Katherine home later, but they didn't seem to understand the "too much beer, drunken driving, dangerous situation" connection. I caved to the pressure of my new peers and continued to drink.

By the time I ran out of kiddie songs to play, I was feeling no pain. I couldn't think of anything else, so I started to play, and sing, the Beatles' *Hey Jude* even though I knew the group wouldn't know it. They didn't care for the words of the verses, but I did get them to sing along at the end of the song with each *Na,Na,Na,Na-Na-Na-Na*. We sang the ending for what must have been nearly a half-hour with each person taking a turn singing something nonsensical at the end of each *Na,Na,Na,Na-Na-Na-Na, Hey Jude*. It was all great fun, the kind of fun I hadn't had in years or perhaps never had at all. When Betty asked who wrote such a silly song, I said, "Paul McCartney." When I got the expected blank stare in return, I added, "He's British," and that seamed to explain it all to her.

I never had a regular group of friends when I was young and most of my bar acquaintances of my "lost and always drunk" era were just that, acquaintances. I grew to like this group of people very quickly. I found out that Eddie and Betty had been dating each other for the past six months. I also discovered that Walter had asked Katherine out about a year earlier, but had been scared off by Freddy's antics. Betty later confided in me that Katherine didn't like Walter "in that way" anyway. When I told Walter that I had roughed Freddy up pretty good, he shook my hand and bought me another beer. They were a great group of people who were just starting out in life and had not yet been beaten down by it.

Toward the end of the evening, I pulled Katherine over to sit on the piano bench with me. I definitely had too much to drink at that point, but I lovingly played and, hopefully in key, sang Elton John's *Your Song* to her. She sat up from the bench, stood behind me, and placed her arms softly around my neck as I played, and I couldn't imagine myself having a moment as tender with anyone else.

When I finished playing for her, Katherine started singing a song that sounded a little familiar to me. She sang the words: *Stars shining bright above you. Night breezes seem to whisper, I love you. Birds singing in the sycamore tree. Dream a little dream of me.* I knew this song. My grandmother used to sing it to Margo and I when we were children. Shortly into the song, I started to accompany her on the piano and figured out the chords as we went along. The slightly out-of-tune twang of the piano didn't diminish Katherine's near perfect pitch. She continued: *Say nighty-night and kiss me. Just hold me tight and tell me you'll miss me. While I'm alone and blue as can be, Dream a little dream of me ...* When we finished, the gang at Milligan's gave us a rousing round of applause. Even two men that had only just arrived, and looked like they may have been hobos, were clapping. We performed the song so well together, Eddie and Walter accused us of having rehearsed it.

It was starting to get very late and I worried that if I didn't get Katherine home soon, her father would get very angry with me. Bringing a girl home late from a date when she lives with her parents would not go over very well whether it was the 1930s or the 2000s. There was a problem though; I didn't believe I was in any condition to drive. Despite the fact that I knew I couldn't really afford it, I had the bartender call a taxi to take Katherine and I home. Walter and Eddie both thought I was making too much of a fuss out of driving while I was drunk, but this was one area where people from my generation knew better.

The cab arrived and we settled in the back seat. Katherine had a perpetual smile on her face and I wasn't sure if it was love, alcohol, or both.

"Thank you, Joseph" she said sweetly.

"For what?" I said, as I gently stroked her hair.

"For coming through tonight. The gang loved you and you played so well."

"You're welcome," was all I could muster.

"And that beautiful song that you played for me, what was the name of the composer again?"

"Elton John." It occurred to me that I could have said that I had been the composer, but I had learned by that time that I would always be better off telling the truth when I could. Since she was still a little tipsy, I debated in my head if it was a good time to tell her the *real* truth, all of it. It was something that I knew I would eventually have to do, but this night turned out to be so very special that I didn't want to remove that beautiful smile from her face or that wonderful feeling in my heart. The truth could wait for another day.

Eight

After another dreamless night, I was awakened by my new roommate, an angry Harry who wanted to know where his car was. He gave my buttocks a barrage of kicks and punches until I was awake. Apparently, he would have preferred that I had driven the car home instead of doing the smart thing and ride in a cab.

"I'm gonna ask you this only one more time, see. Where's my wheels?"

"At Milligan's bar," I groused, while fighting sleep.

"What in the name of heaven is it doing there?"

"I took a cab home. I had a little too much to drink last night."

"You were that soused that you couldn't drive?"

"I wouldn't say I was *soused*. I just felt that I was impaired enough that my driving would be affected in a negative way."

"What? You sound like a lawyer," he said with disdain.

"Would you have preferred that I got into an accident and wrecked your car, or maybe got killed?" I clarified.

"Of course not. Hurry up and get dressed so we can walk over to Milligan's and drive the car back. We've only got about an hour and a half till church."

176

"Church?"

"Yeah. What, you didn't know it was Sunday? Did you think you slept clear through to Monday?"

"I haven't gone to church in years," I yawned.

"Well, if you think my mother is going to allow you to miss Sunday mass and still sleep under her roof, you're screwy. Get up and get dressed." He was acting as if he were my grandfather again. In my sleepy haze, he even looked like the Grandpa I used to know. He was ordering me around and I didn't mind because no matter what it was he told me to do, I knew I wouldn't be forced to "practice, practice, practice" on the piano for hours on end. I thought of the times that he would help me with chores or homework just so that we would have more time to play ball at the park, and I remembered my mother screaming at him for taking me there. When I was a child, I thought that my grandfather was the best damn baseball player there was or ever would be.

I did as I was told and got out of bed. While dressing, I asked quite innocently, "Hey, Harry, you want to have a catch after church?"

"You mean with a baseball?"

"Yeah, a baseball, and gloves, and if you have a bat, we could hit a little too."

He was a bit bewildered by my request, but he shrugged his shoulders and said, "I don't see why not. I didn't realize that you enjoyed the grand game."

"Baseball? I love baseball." I winked at him and continued, "My grandfather saw to that." With that statement I finished buttoning my shirt and headed for the kitchen. We each slurped down a cup of tea and grabbed one of his mother's light and fluffy homemade biscuits for the road.

On the walk to Milligan's we talked about baseball, girls, cars, and family. It was strange how the man would come across to me as my grandfather one moment and then some punk kid the next. I had been given a genuine gift by whatever force had sent me here. Not only was I given a chance to be with the girl of my dreams, but I also got to spend quality time with the man who had influenced my life more than any other, including my own father.

My father was a working man who labored at a sheet metal factory for ten hours a day. When he was home he did not want to be disturbed, unless it was to bring him another can of beer. He barely tolerated the sound of piano scales and concertos and I always secretly wished he would make me stop playing. He never did, probably because dealing with my mother would be harder for him than listening to me play. He would only leave the comfort of his chair when it was time for him to go to bed, leave for work, or when my mother had shamed him into taking out the garbage. He and I had a catch once. It lasted about five minutes and he had to stop because his back ached.

Harry Dempsey was the only adult male that spent any real time with me at all in my youth. His arrival usually meant an escape from the piano and a trip to the local park to play ball. He also took me to Veteran's Stadium for my only live major league baseball game, but his visits meant more to me than just baseball and an escape from hours of boring piano practice. It also meant an escape from reality, as he always told such great stories of triumph in both love and war. He was a man's man, but he was also a thinker who could always see an argument from both sides. "Be a pianist and be the best, if that's what you truly want to be. If it isn't, than the lessons and practice won't hurt you and you will make your mother happy for trying so hard to please her. Just leave yourself some time for climbing trees and making snowmen and playing ball. You wouldn't want to miss your childhood," he would often say, and I wished I had listened to his wise words. I guess I became afraid to venture out on my own. Climbing the trees, making the snowmen, and playing ball became meaningless to me when he died, and no one was there to fill the void.

Harry drove us back to his house at what seemed to me to be excessive speeds. I was truly afraid he would kill us both if he didn't slow down. "What are you doing? We have plenty of time before church. Slow down!"

"Ah, don't be such a wet blanket! I'm not going that fast." He *was* going that fast and when he turned a corner he almost hit the same old lady crossing the street that I nearly ran over two days earlier. That barely slowed his pace. He continued at a reckless speed until we arrived back at his house in record time.

As soon as we stepped in the front door, Harry's mother said, "I was afraid you would be late coming back. Go on and get ready for church."

I gave Mrs. Dempsey a sigh and was about to voice my objections when she said, "Go on, boy, you too. We go to church as a family." And that was that. I was going to church after a fifteen-year absence and there was nothing I could do about it.

My relationship with God before my time-traveling experience was akin to "you leave me alone and I'll leave you alone." I didn't question God's existence; I just questioned the relevance of God's existence in my time. The world I left valued status, cars, jewelry, and electronic gadgetry at least as much, and maybe more, than it valued faith. More people turned to the Internet for answers than turned to God. The Internet became this powerful all knowing being that could not only give you the answers that you sought, it could give them to you in an instant. No praying was necessary unless you had a very slow Internet connection or an old beat-up computer.

As I walked toward the front of the large church, I questioned if it was God that had sent me on my journey. I still held open the possibility that it was some freak accident with the telephone and the lightning, or that I actually died holding the old telephone's receiver in my hand and all of what I had experienced since had been the last adventurous thoughts of a dying man.

I entered the Blessed Mother Roman Catholic Church with the Dempsey family and I felt a real sense of belonging that I had never felt before. Everyone was dressed in their best outfits, or as Harry called them, "their Sunday go-to-meeting clothes." Neighbors and friends solemnly nodded to each other. Two men who were arguing about property lines outside of the church joined together to pray inside of it.

The church was filled with the creepy and echoing notes of a pipe organ. Its left and right walls were adorned with beautiful stained glass and there was an enormous cross behind the altar. I looked up and noticed that the ceiling was so high it may have nearly touched heaven. Mrs. Dempsey chose an aisle and we all sat down on the pew. Since I really didn't remember any of the church procedures from my childhood, I followed Harry and did whatever he did. Any crossing, kneeling or praying that I did was in response to Harry doing the same. The entire mass was said in Latin, and since I didn't know the language, the message of the mass, if it had one, did not hit home with me.

I was dozing and nearly asleep when the collection basket was passed to me. I yawned and then dropped in a dime, which left me with less than a dollar, and passed the basket on to Harry.

Bored, I looked around the church for something to amuse me. It was then when I spotted Katherine. She was sitting about five rows in front of me and on the opposite side of the church. She also appeared to be bored and was possibly looking around for something to amuse her. I expected magic when our eyes met, but instead she acted as if she was put off by my presence. She quickly turned away and would not meet my gaze again. At first, I figured that the social mores of the day did not permit a young unmarried woman to acknowledge a young unmarried man while in church. I wanted to believe that, but then I saw the real reason she had turned away from me. Her mother and father were sitting on her left, and Freddy York was sitting on her right.

Freddy was wearing a large bandage across his nose and a few small ones covering various cuts on his face that he received in our fight. His left arm was in a sling to complete his utterly pathetic ensemble. The stare, combined with a subtle smile of satisfaction that he flashed in my direction, said to me that he told Katherine who had inflicted his wounds and that she was not very happy about it. I was sure that he had no fear of me since we were inside a church and in Katherine's presence. I needed some damage control and quick. When the mass ended and all of the worshipers filed out of the church, I made sure that I was near Katherine and Freddy. As Freddy was about to shake hands with Father Quinlan, I quickly jumped in next to them and said, "Freddy, I am so sorry for our fight and any injuries you may have incurred. Please accept my heartfelt apologies." Freddy's jaw hung open and no words came out. Apologizing right in front of the priest left him completely speechless. Although I was pretty sure he could tell that my apology was insincere, it reversed any advantage he may have received in telling Katherine about our fight.

Katherine finally looked at me and gave me a giant smile. It was as if she never really wanted to be mad at me to begin with and was just acting upon some anti-violence moral code she subscribed to. I would bet that if she were forced to reveal her true feelings, she would have wanted to see Freddy beaten to a bloody pulp too. To Freddy she said, "Well, do you accept his apology?"

Being in a house of worship and forgiveness, Freddy had no choice. My apology was very shallow and his acceptance of it was equally so. "I accept your apology," he said in a low monotone voice.

"Wonderful!" Katherine said, "Now you can both be friends!" I'm sure that Freddy didn't want my friendship any more than I wanted his, but at

Katherine's insistence we shook hands. Father Quinlan, a little stunned at what had transpired in front of him, wished us all a good day to get us to move along so that he could greet his other parishioners.

Outside of the church, Freddy and I were left alone for a few moments while Katherine was conversing with her parents. Through clenched teeth he said, "Who are you?"

"I'm Joseph Eaton," I replied smartly.

"No, who are you? I know you're not the Whitneys' gardener. Where did you come from?"

"Philadelphia," I said innocently.

"Eaton, you are not welcome here. Go back to where you came from. Katherine belongs to me and always has. If you know what's good for you, you'll leave here immediately."

His words angered me, but I kept my voice low. "You listen to me and listen good. I am not afraid of you. Your threats mean absolutely nothing to me. Just remember, the last time we tangled I rearranged your face. Katherine does not belong to anyone but herself. And if she chooses to spend her time with me, than I am the better person for it."

Katherine had been walking toward us and could probably see there was still bad blood between Freddy and I. "Everyone getting along?" she said with a smile, trying to diffuse the situation. Neither one of us answered. "Joseph, would you like to come over for dinner tonight?"

I really wanted to ask if Freddy was invited as well, but asked instead, "Are you sure that your parents would want me to come?"

"Of course! They just told me to invite you. They like you a lot. Well, Mother does anyway. We eat early on Sunday. Come around three, okay?"

"Okay." What else could I say? When the girl of your dreams invites you over to dinner with her parents, you say yes. I just hoped that Freddy wasn't going to be there to get in the way.

***

"So, you really like that skirt you're chasing, don't you?" Harry said as he soft-tossed the ball to me.

I caught it in what may have been the same glove that Harry would use many years later to have a catch with his grandson. It was, I think, an infielder's glove, but it had less flexibility than even a catcher's mitt from my time. It was basically five padded fingers tied together with leather straps. There wasn't much of a pocket, and catching the ball with one hand was nearly impossible. At least it was for me. Harry was holding his cigarette with his right hand and had his glove on his left and had no problem corralling the ball without the use of his right hand. He was good. Maybe not as good as I remember, but he was good. I wasn't crazy about him referring to Katherine as a "skirt" but answered, "Yeah, I really like her. She's very different than other women I've dated. She's beautiful, smart, she seems to get me, and she's definitely not a bimbo." I tossed the ball back to him.

Harry looked at me strangely as he caught the ball. Apparently the word *bimbo* had a different meaning in 1935. He explained that a bimbo was some kind of big tough guy, like a bouncer in a bar. I guess with the way I handled Freddy at the race track, Harry may have thought me to be a bimbo! He threw a curveball and said, "You're lucky, Joseph."

I struggled to catch it. "Why's that?" I attempted to throw a knuckleball and it barely reached him.

"You really seem to know what you want and you go after it." He ran toward me and fielded my failed knuckler. He then threw the ball sky high to me.

I covered my eyes from the sun and did a basket catch. "You know what you want, don't you?" I asked. I tried a split-finger fastball this time and threw it wildly past him.

He chased it down while shouting, "Sometimes I think I do, sometimes I don't. One day, I really want to go to college and become some kind of intellectual. The next, I think about going into business." He tossed the ball softly to me.

"You'll figure it out," I assured him and lightly tossed the ball back.

"I also think about finding a good woman and starting a family, but I'm afraid that no good woman would have me," he pined with all sincerity.

"One will. I guarantee it," I promised.

"I suppose you're gonna need the car later?" He threw some kind of weird sidearm pitch that started to rise and would have hit me right on the nose if my reaction time were a little slower. I caught it, but at the same time grazed the wound on my face with the glove and started to bleed again. I wiped off the blood with my finger.

"Yeah, if it's okay with you? I would put more gas in it, but I don't have much money left." I threw him a hard grounder.

He fielded it with ease and then fired a hard overhand fastball at me. I missed it and had to chase it down. I picked the ball up and as I got ready to throw it back, I noticed Harry take out a wad of money from his sock and start to walk toward me. With his right arm extended he said, "Here. Take five dollars."

"I can't take more money from you. I just can't."

"Sure you can. If it wasn't for you telling me to bet that pony, I'd be much poorer now. And you're gonna make me some more dough on the prize fight too, right?" I didn't answer right away and he started to look a little nervous. He repeated his last word, "Right?"

"I guess so. I mean, there is no such thing as a sure thing, but I'm pretty sure about this."

"Good. So take it." He again put out the hand with the five dollars in it. He was my grandfather again and he was giving me money like he used to when I was a small child. And just like when I was a small child, I took it.

***

I could smell the chicken cooking before I even got to the Whitneys' front door. Katherine's father let me inside where even more olfactory delights awaited me. I could smell homemade biscuits, baked potatoes, corn on the cob, and fresh string beans. It smelled just like the Sunday meals my grandmother used to make for my family when we would visit her house. The pleasant, down-home feeling I had didn't last very long.

I heard a familiar voice coming from the Whitneys' study and it belonged to Freddy York. He left the study and entered the living room holding a leather bound copy of Charles Dickens' *A Tale of Two Cities*. With an unlit pipe hanging from his mouth he asked Mr. Whitney if he could borrow the book. Before his answer arrived, he saw me. Freddy removed the pipe and snickered, "Oh, I see that you finally turned up." I was at most five minutes late, if I was late at all. With a heavy note of sarcasm he added, "It's just so wonderful to be graced by the presence of Philadelphia's top paper salesman." Apparently, he had been asking questions about me and had received some answers. The bandages he wore on his face earlier in the day were no longer present and his arm was no longer in a sling. Either he received a miracle cure at church or he had been playing up his injuries to acquire sympathy from Katherine.

"I see the Lord works in mysterious ways. You seem to have been relieved of your injuries, Mr. York," I replied with equal sarcasm.

"The bandages and sling were precautionary on the advice of my doctor. I removed them upon his say so as well."

"Ah, I see. Yes, never underestimate the power of a good doctor."

"Are there any good doctors in Philadelphia, Mr. Eaton? I guess you can find out when you go home. Will that be soon?"

I was about to answer when I spotted Katherine at the top of the stairs. She was wearing the same white linen dress that she wore to church, but she had let her hair down. The sunlight through the front window adorned her hair in such a way that she looked like an angel coming down from heaven as she descended the stairs. With my eyes on Katherine, I said, "The length of my stay here has not yet been determined, Mr. York. I may decide to stay here permanently."

Freddy appeared ready to fire a sarcastic shot back at me when Jack Whitney declared, "Okay, we're all here. Let's go to the dining room and eat!" I greeted Katherine's mother who was busy putting the finishing touches on her marvelously aromatic meal. Katherine then helped her bring all of the food out to the table.

Freddy and I were seated next to each other and Mr. Whitney sat at the head of the table to my right. Once all of the food and drink were out, Ellen Whitney took her seat at the opposite end of the table from her husband and Katherine sat across from Freddy and I. Katherine's plate and chair appeared to be purposely situated so that she was right in between the two of us, only on the opposite side of the table. Katherine's father said grace and the taking and passing of food commenced.

Mr. Whitney cleared his throat and said, "So, Freddy, what kind of plans do you have for the future?"

"Well, Jack," Freddy called Mr. Whitney by his first name and Katherine rolled her eyes, "I plan to make my first million in the real estate market by the time I'm thirty. I would love to buy a nice big house on the ocean and raise a large family."

With a stern look that could have burned a hole right through me, Jack Whitney said, "How about you, Joseph, what does your future look like?"

I don't know why I was taken by surprise, but I was. I had become an unwilling contestant in a twisted version of *The Dating Game*. It was twisted because Freddy and Katherine's father had apparently worked out all of the questions and the right answers before my arrival. "Well, I don't know, sir. I'll be looking for a job in town this week. I'll see where that will lead me."

"Aren't they looking for help in the mail room at your company, Jack?" Freddy quipped.

Katherine's mother, not realizing that Freddy was taking a shot at me, said, "Oh Jack, do you think you can help the boy out?" I looked at Katherine and playfully kicked her under the table. She kicked me back and gave me an innocent look that told me she didn't know that I was going to be pitted against Freddy for a valuable prize, her. The Whitneys' humongous St. Bernard then entered the room. Perhaps he was going to be my parting gift. The dog started to growl and bark, first at me and then at Freddy. Maybe he was upset that he wasn't asked to be a contestant.

"Actually, Mr. Whitney, if there is anything you can do to help me find local employment, I would truly appreciate it. I would really like to stay here in town." He was some kind of bigwig at an insurance company, so I thought he might have some pull.

Jack Whitney was perplexed. "Local employment? Well ... I guess I could ask around. You're some kind of salesman, right?" I nodded. "I'll see if I can get you a sales position in my company."

"That would be great, sir. Thank you."

I glanced over at Freddy and he was steaming. His game plan had backfired and he started reaching. "Did I mention that I was valedictorian of my graduating class at Brooklyn Business College? How about you, Eaton? I suppose you went to Yale or some other Ivy League school."

"Actually, I received a music scholarship to Juilliard."

"Joseph is quite a musician," Katherine interjected.

"So you graduated from music school?" Mr. Whitney inquired.

"Well, I didn't exactly graduate. I left after my first year."

"You left, or they asked you to leave?" Freddy said snottily.

"I left. I couldn't keep up with the other students and I started to question my love of music." I didn't tell them that I started to look for answers at the bottom of a bottle.

Mr. Whitney responded, "Your parents must have been very disappointed."

"Well, it didn't matter much to my father. Nothing I did mattered to my father, but leaving school devastated my mother. She wouldn't see me after that."

"Do you have contact with your mother now?" Mrs. Whitney asked with care.

"No, ma'am. She passed away a few years ago."

Mr. Whitney chimed in, "How about your father? Do you see him at all?"

"No, sir. He died a few months after I left
Juilliard. According to my sister Margo, my mother
grieved heavily over the loss of my career and my
father just couldn't bear to see my mother in pain
anymore. He suffered heart failure and died on the
way to the hospital. At least that's the story Margo told
me. I tried to comfort my mother, but even upon my
father's death she still wouldn't see me."

My story caused Katherine's mother to tear up.
She blew her nose and said to her husband, "Jack, find
this boy a position in your company." She was not
making a request. It was a demand.

Jack Whitney got up from the table and rushed
toward his wife. He gently put his hand on her
shoulder and said, "I'll see what I can do, dear. I'll see
what I can do." With that, I declared myself to be the
winner of *The Dating Game*. Not only had I won over
Katherine's parents' sympathies, her father was going
to try to set me up with a job. I looked over at Freddy
and could see he was piping mad. He had been
working on Katherine's parents for many years. I
doubt if I had completely undone all of his work (he
was still Jack Whitney's fishing buddy), but I had made
inroads in the life of the Whitney family. This small
victory would come at a price as Freddy would not
underestimate me ever again.

When dinner was over, I helped Katherine and
her mother with the dishes. "Nice job!" Katherine
chuckled as she dried a plate with a dish towel. "I've
never seen Freddy at such a loss for words." With the
absence of her father and Freddy she must have felt
free to speak to me as she normally would. I was,
however, surprised to hear her talk about that subject

in front of her mother. "And Father's going to find you a job!" she roared.

Ellen Whitney rinsed off a glass, handed it to Katherine to dry, and added, "Then you can stay here in town, right, Joseph?" She turned away from the sink and faced me directly, almost staring me down. Something had happened between mother and daughter that I was not aware of. The last I had known, Katherine's mother wanted her daughter to marry a man like Freddy York, but something had changed. Had Katherine told her mother of her feelings and won her over for me? Apparently, *The Dating Game* was not as stacked up against me as I had originally thought. Katherine and her mother must have known what Freddy and Jack were up to and had leveled the playing field. It slowly became clear to me that Ellen Whitney was an ally of mine.

"Yes, Mrs. Whitney, if I find a job, I could stay here in Valley View." I smiled at Katherine, then at her mother, and said, "I want that more than anything else in the whole world."

Freddy York ruined the moment by poking his head into the kitchen. He frowned at me and then said to Katherine, "Your father wants to take some photographs of us. Go to the backyard."

"Only if Joseph can be in some of the photographs too," she replied.

Freddy started to get angry and said, "Why must he ..." He stopped himself and begrudgingly said, "Okay, just go out back."

"Can we, Mother?" Katherine asked.

"You kids go ahead. I'll finish up in here."

We went out the back door off of the kitchen and found Jack Whitney setting up the best location for his photo shoot. He had an expression of delight when his daughter came into his camera's eye view and a look of disdain when he saw me. The camera was an odd looking accordion-shaped thing that was much smaller than I would have expected a camera from that time to be. I would find out later that it was made by Kodak.

Jack continued to set-up his shot and Freddy was his subject. "Katherine, get in the picture with Freddy."

"Only if Joseph can be in it too," she replied to her father.

Trying to win a few brownie points with the old man, I said, "Go ahead, Katherine, get in the picture. I'll get in the next one." I moved out of the camera's range and stood next to Jack.

Jack had his shot all ready and said, "Okay, Katherine, now get a little closer to Freddy." She moved a few inches closer but was still almost at arm's length.

"Come closer, Katherine, I won't bite you," Freddy said. She unhappily moved a little closer.

"Now smile ... Katherine, you're not smiling!" her father said. I moved my position so that I was almost behind Jack Whitney and made a funny face at Katherine which prompted her to smile. "Good, now hold it." Jack snapped the picture. "Great!"

"Now take one of me with Joseph," Katherine demanded.

Jack raised an eyebrow at me and nodded in Katherine's direction, "Go ahead and stand next to my daughter." I walked over to Freddy and playfully pushed him out of the way. "Okay, ready? Smile." As Mr. Whitney was about to snap the picture, Katherine moved extremely close to me and put her hand on my back. I smiled wide as it became even more obvious that she preferred me over Freddy. Her father then took the picture. There were a few other pictures taken that day. Ellen Whitney had finished the dishes and joined the rest of us for photos. I took a crack at 1935 photography and took photos of Katherine, a few of her parents, and even one of Freddy (he insisted that his picture be taken in front of his car). All of these snapshots would end up in Katherine's photo album and be found many years later inside a trunk in what used to be her family's attic.

***

I awoke from a restless night after a disturbing dream. Chuck and Margo, both wearing clothing that would be more suited to 1935, had come to take me back to my own time. Margo repeatedly pointed to a suitcase that was supposed to belong to me and insisted, "Pick it up! Let's go!" each time she pointed. Chuck had an evil expression on his face, as if he planned to do me harm, and snapped, "You did ruin my Uncle Freddy after all, didn't you? Well, it's time to go back and pay the consequences!" I had difficulty shaking off that dream for the rest of the day.

The penny that I had been putting off burying had been weighing heavily on my mind the night before, and was a likely contributor to that terrible nightmare. I had become afraid that if I buried the penny as I originally planned, that some kind of circle would be completed and I would return to my own time. I was also afraid that if I didn't bury the penny, and made a definite decision not to, that I would return back to my own time as well, but with no recollection at all of ever having been in 1935. Neither scenario was acceptable, so I figured the longer I put off making a move, one way or the other, the longer I would stay.

Being in a relationship with a man displaced in time was not very fair to Katherine, but I wasn't strong enough to end it. I also wasn't strong enough to allow myself to just vanish without a trace. I knew I had to tell her the truth, and soon, even though I doubted she would believe any of it.

Monday morning was beautiful. The birds were singing sweetly and there was very little humidity in the soft breeze that whispered through the trees. Mrs. Dempsey had asked me to earn my keep some by painting the wooden fence that framed the front of their property. I regretted having to ask her if she wouldn't mind if I put that chore off for another day. I knew I had been nothing short of a freeloader to the Dempseys, but Katherine had the day off and we had a date to go fishing. She was going to teach me the finer points of catching fish so that I could at least pretend to know what I was talking about with her father.

Harry had the car, so I had to walk to the Whitney house, and it took me nearly an hour. Before I had even stepped on their property, Katherine came running out of the house to meet me. I greeted her with a big hug and a peck on the cheek (her mother was watching). She had important news for me.

As we entered the house, she said, "Joseph, my father called and there is a sales job at his office for you if you can get there before ten o'clock." It was a few minutes past nine so I could make it on time, even on foot, but I wasn't appropriately dressed for an office job. The jacket and tie that came with my suit were hanging in Harry's closet. I was wearing the pants and dress shirt, but they were in desperate need of laundering. Unaware that I had already gone through them, Katherine's mother offered the old clothes from the trunk in the basement.

After I declined the old clothes, Mrs. Whitney asked, "How much money would you need to buy a new suit?"

"I don't know, about fifteen dollars, I guess, but even if I had fifteen dollars there isn't time to shop for one," I moaned.

"Yes, there is." Ellen Whitney then opened a small white purse and removed money from it. "Here's twenty dollars. Take Katherine's bicycle to Whitten's Department Store and pick out a suit off the rack. Then pedal to Jack's office and start your new job. You can bring the bicycle back later." She ordered Katherine to get her bicycle and bring it out to the front of the house.

"Mrs. Whitney, I can't take money from you. It just wouldn't be right."

"Don't worry about it. I know that you'll pay me back when you can."

"I don't know. It just doesn't feel right," I sighed.

She looked me square in the eye and with conviction she said, "You staying in Valley View would make my daughter very happy. Having employment can make that possible, so take the money, get a suit, and start the job." She was not going to take no for an answer. I often wonder how someone from another time would survive in the era that I left. It certainly wouldn't be on the kindness of strangers, yet without the help of people who barely knew me I wouldn't have been able to survive in 1935.

"Thank you, ma'am, I promise to pay you back as soon as possible." I took the money, walked out the front door, grabbed Katherine in my arms, dipped her and gave her a giant goodbye smooch. I didn't care who may have been watching.

It had been a very long time since I was on a bicycle, but it's true what they say: you never forget how to ride one. The sight of a man riding a girl's bike must have been considered high comedy in 1935. The basket with fake flowers in the weave that was attached between the handlebars didn't help any. Every person I passed either laughed, had something derogatory to say, or just rolled their eyes with a smirk. I didn't have the time to be bothered by it.

I made it to Whitten's in record time and explained my situation to the same clerk that had waited on me a few days prior. He remembered me, and even my size, and picked out a black pinstriped suit that was of similar style to the one I already owned. The whole suit, with matching shirt and tie, was on sale for only eleven dollars. I hurriedly tried it on and decided it would have to do since I didn't have time to try on anything else. For another dollar more, the clerk offered to have cleaned the pants and shirt that I had been wearing. He said I could pick them up after my new job had finished for the day. I took him up on his offer, paid him, and got back on the bicycle.

Smith and Cooper Casualty and Life Insurance Company was situated in the main section of town, at the center of Franklin Avenue. It seemed out of place, as the majority of the businesses in that area were mom-and-pop shops.

I walked the bike through the main door, parked it, and greeted the lovely receptionist. I identified myself and mentioned that Mr. Whitney had set-up a sales position for me at the company. The receptionist got up off of her seat to fetch him and after only a few minutes Jack Whitney emerged from the corridors. Surprisingly, he was very happy to see me. He was walking with a colleague who, for some reason, didn't appear to be pleased to see me at all.

"Joseph!" Jack Whitney extended his hand for me to shake it and I did. "I was afraid that you weren't going to make it and that Gordon's nephew would get the job." That was why I had to get there before ten o'clock. Apparently, I was up against the nephew of someone named Gordon for the job and whoever arrived first would get the prize. It turned out that Gordon was the man that Jack was walking with and he wasn't happy to see me because my arrival meant no job for his nephew. "Come with me and I'll introduce you to your new boss." As we walked away, Gordon handed Jack what appeared to be a five-dollar bill. "Better luck next time, Gordon!" Jack said. I then understood why Jack was so happy to see me. He had a bet with Gordon on who would arrive first and he bet on me. I probably should have been upset about being wagered upon as if I were a racehorse, but I wasn't. I was glad to be on Jack Whitney's good side.

Jack led me up a flight of stairs and then to a room on the second floor that resembled a classroom. Inside, three young and eager-looking men paid close attention to a balding, stout man with a dark moustache, big protruding ears, and large thick glasses. "Now go out there and sell these people some policies. Remember, money can't replace a loved one, but it can come damn close," the odd-looking man said, followed by a Santa-like laugh. He then noticed Jack and I standing in the doorway and motioned for us to come in. "Ah, is this the new recruit?"

Jack responded before I could, "Yes, this is Joseph Keaton."

I walked up to the pudgy man and tried to ignore the terrible cheap cigar odor he exuded, "Actually it's Joseph *Eaton*, sir. It's a pleasure to meet you." I extended my hand for him to shake it, but since he was focused on Jack, he didn't notice.

"So, Jack, your son-in-law got here before Gordon's nephew, did he." I wondered if I had heard him correctly. Did he say *son-in-law*?

Jack Whitney looked at me with a wry smile and then said to my new boss, "Yes, I guess Gordon's nephew couldn't get out of bed this morning!" The two men shared a chuckle. "Joseph, this is Mr. Pottershed, your supervisor."

I didn't know if it was because I was nervous or because I was stunned by being referred to as Jack Whitney's son-in-law, but I said, "Very nice to meet you, Mr. Potato Head." I doubted if the Mr. Potato Head toy had been invented yet, the resemblance was uncanny, but I guess what I said was still considered pretty funny to the young guys in the room, as they all looked at each other and tried to hide their laughter. Luckily, neither Jack nor my new boss noticed the faux pas. Jack left the room and I would have to wait until another time to find out why I was referred to as his son-in-law.

Mr. Potato Head instructed me to take a seat. He was wrapping up what I gathered to be his daily pep rally for the young salesmen. When he finished, each young man grabbed a briefcase and left the room. On his way out, one of these men gave me a friendly elbow and said in a whisper, "Mr. Potato Head! You slay me!"

I spent the rest of the day being taught the finer points of being a door-to-door insurance salesman. I discovered that Mr. Potato Head was once the best door-to-door salesman in the history of the company. Back problems had limited his mobility and he was forced to take a job teaching the next generation of salesmen. He taught me more about sales in one day than I had learned my entire time selling paper in Philadelphia. He actually had me believing I could do it. Starting the next day, I was going to sell insurance to anyone who would answer their front door.

I got so wrapped up in learning the job that I had no idea how I was going to be compensated. I was almost afraid to, but I did eventually ask Mr. Potato Head about my pay. I was shocked when he said I would earn only a dollar per day. If I wanted more than that I would have to sell some policies. I guess it was better than earning strictly commission, which I was told was how most companies compensated their sales force, but I wasn't sure if I could live on such a small amount of money. After giving the matter a little thought, I decided that it was a start and five dollars per week was better than nothing at all.

When my first day of work in 1935 was over, I hopped on Katherine's bike and headed back to Whitten's Department Store to pick up my shirt and pants. As soon as I entered the store, a strange feeling came over me. I started to get extremely cold, as cold as I was when I first arrived in 1935. The sudden cold made me feel extremely numb and I lost control of my body. As if I were a marionette whose strings had been released, I slumped to the floor near a rack of suit jackets. After watching me fall to the floor, the clerk left the customer he was waiting on and rushed over to see if he could be of assistance. I was nearly passed out and I had lost my ability to speak. It was as if my entire body was paralyzed.

For a brief moment I felt as if I were somewhere else. People walked past me wearing clothing that would have been more consistent with the time I left. Not one paid any attention to me with the exception of a little girl who stopped to stare before her mother abruptly whisked her away.

I blinked and was relieved to see the clerk's familiar face. He touched my shoulder and asked if I was all right. I replied, "Yes, I'm okay," but I couldn't really *feel* the words come out of my mouth. Unsure if he had heard me, I tried again. "Yes, I am all right," and suddenly I was. The other people that had walked past me were no longer visible and the numbness and overall cold feeling had left me. I felt almost as though it had never happened at all. I picked myself up off of the floor, with the assistance of the clerk, and brushed off my clothes with my hands. "Thanks for your help. I think I'm okay now."

"You gave me quite a scare. By the look on your face I thought you were a goner," the clerk said.

Once my recovery was near complete, I became very curious as to what had just happened to me. "I'm going to ask you a strange question, okay?"

"Okay, sir," the clerk replied with a puzzled look on his face.

"Did I ... disappear?"

"What? Disappear?"

"Yes, did I disappear? Was I, for a short moment, not here?"

"You were here the whole time as far as I could tell, sir." He tried to hold back his amusement, but couldn't. Once he got the laughter out of his system, he paused as if he were in deep thought for a second and said, "Well, for a moment I thought you might be dead, if that's what you mean. You certainly had a look on your face that said you weren't here anymore."

"But my body ... my body was here, right?" This was important for me to know. If I really did travel back to my own time in that instance, as I had already hypothesized, and my body was also present in 1935, then my body might have stayed in Margo's apartment when I first time-traveled. The thought of my sister finding me in her living room in some kind of coma was unsettling. I needed to know if my body could be present in two different time periods simultaneously.

Again, the clerk could not hold back his laughter. "Yes, your body was here the whole time," he said with merriment.

The customer that the clerk had been helping stepped forward and answered me in a more serious manner. "Yes, as far as I could tell, your body has been here since you entered the store." I glanced at the man and had to do a double-take. He looked a lot like Chuck Manning, only he appeared to be about fifteen years younger, had muttonchops and a poorly groomed moustache. He was dressed in a heavy brown suit that appeared to be more appropriate for winter wear. I was astonished and stared at him with awe. He offered his hand to break the spell and said, "My name is Professor Manning. How do you do?"

Still aghast, I shook his hand with caution and said, "Joseph Eaton. Glad to make your acquaintance."

"Mr. ... *Eaton,* was it?" I nodded in the affirmative. "What would make you think you would disappear?"

I didn't know what to make of this Professor Manning. He couldn't have been Chuck's father unless he had completely robbed Chuck's mother Alice from the cradle. He could have been Chuck's grandfather, the father of Reginald Manning – Alice's future husband. I lied to cover myself. "I'm sorry, Professor. I didn't really mean *disappear.* Of course I wouldn't *disappear.* I meant what the clerk said. Did I look dead?"

"Mr. Eaton, other than thinking you can perform parlor tricks, you seem to be a reasonable and bright man. Again I ask, why would you think you would disappear?"

He saw right through my lie. I desperately tried to think of a better one, but came up empty. I don't know if it was because he looked so much like Chuck, or if it was because of the scholarly way he carried himself, but I felt I could tell him the truth without ridicule. I smiled and said, "Professor, take a walk with me."

The clerk at Whitten's shook his head at both of us and handed me my cleaned pants and shirt. Professor Manning told him that he would be back the next day to complete his purchase and we left the store together.

I pushed Katherine's bike up Rockaway Avenue while I walked and talked with Professor Manning. I tried some small talk first. "Which institute of higher learning are you associated with, Professor?"

"Right now, I am setting up the science department in a local branch of New York University. We start classes in the fall."

"So, you're a scientist?"

"Yes. That's why I was so interested in you. You said that you thought you might have disappeared. A few years ago I worked with the government on a project to make a man seemingly disappear using small mirrors attached to various locations on his clothing."

"Did it work?"

"Well ... only if the lighting was just so and the viewing angle was a certain way. When I saw you and you asked if you disappeared, I was almost hoping that they had continued this work after I left and that you were doing a test of a special disappearing suit or something of that nature."

"No, sorry, I'm not with the government," I said.

"Then why did you think that you may have disappeared?" he insisted.

I came right out with it. "Professor, do you believe that man has the ability to travel in time?"

He cleared his throat and said, "Of course. Each man travels forward in time from the moment of birth until the time of his death."

"How about backward? Do you think that it is possible to travel backward in time?"

"Backward? Well, according to a Nobel Prize winning physicist, it can be done if you can move fast enough in space. But no, I don't think that it can be done, or at least not with the tools available to us today."

"What if I were to tell you that I am personally acquainted with your grandson and that the last time I saw him he was fifteen to twenty years older than you are right now?"

"How can I have a grandson that is older than me? Besides, my own son is only a boy."

I decided to try and test my theory that he was Chuck's grandfather, and I hoped that if I were right he would be in awe of me. "You mean Reginald?"

"Yes." It worked. He stared at me with wonder. "How did you know my son's name? I didn't tell you ..."

"Not only do I know his name, I also know the girl he will marry and I will become very good friends with their son on the days that precede my time-traveling here."

The awe factor had worn off and the scientist in him took over again. He started to ask valid questions. "What method did you use to get to this time, Mr. Eaton?"

"I'm not completely sure. You see, I found this old telephone — well, it was old when I found it — and I ..." I went on and told him the whole story about the phone, the lightning, and Katherine.

"Okay, young man, what specifically can you tell me about future events?"

"Do you mean in your near future or further away?" I asked.

"Well, what about tonight? What will be the top news item in tomorrow's paper?"

"I'm sorry. I don't know anything specific about today. The closest event that I have foreknowledge of is the big boxing match on Thursday."

"I think everyone knows that Max Baer is going to win the fight on Thursday," the professor said smugly.

"No, he's not. James J. Braddock is going to win."

"Really? That's a bold prediction." He was a little more intrigued, and from the glint in his eye I gathered that he really hoped that what I told him was true so that he could win some money. He changed the subject and said, "So, where is your proof that you are from the future?"

I thought about it and realized that I probably had no evidence to support my time-traveling claim. I dejectedly said, "I have none."

"You mean to tell me that you came from the future, but brought no objects from the future with you?"

"The only objects that came with me were the clothes and shoes I was wearing."

"Okay," the scientist said, "Go fetch them so that we can study them. Perhaps there is something unique about them that would support your claim."

"I sold my sneakers to a stranger on the street, but I still have my sweatpants and t-shirt. I can get them, but I have to return my girlfriend's bicycle first."

"How about you bring your, whatever it was you called them, to my lab around eight o'clock this evening? We can study them then." He wrote the address of his lab on a piece of paper and gave me general directions on how to get there. I hoped Harry would be able to lend me his car because I would never make it on foot or even by bicycle. As he walked away from me he shouted, "You certainly are an interesting man, Mr. Eaton! I'll see you tonight." I watched Professor Manning walk away and was still amazed at his resemblance to Chuck. Even his voice and mannerisms were similar. Once he was out of view, I got on the bike and headed to Katherine's house.

I was on the bike for only a short period of time when it happened again. An icy cold feeling crept into my body and I could no longer feel my feet, which made it especially hard to pedal. I somehow managed to launch myself off of the bike and I landed at the front of an empty lot in a residential area. The cold became deeper and deeper and I felt myself begin to lose my temporal hold. One instant I was lying on an empty lot, and the next I was on a lawn of freshly cut grass. Judging by his path, the operator of the lawn mower had gone over the spot where I landed only a moment before and was approximately ten feet away from me. Had I arrived any sooner I may have ended up in pieces inside the clipping bag attached to his mower.

He was mowing away from my position and, since his back was to me, didn't notice me lying there. The man's dog, a little midget mutt that was tied to a tree, *did* notice me and began to bark, but the sound of the mower drowned it out. I may have been back in my own time again, but I wasn't sure. The mower was definitely not from 1935 but could have been from the 1970s on up. The house looked like it may have been built in the 1950s so I was definitely not in 1935 anymore. Other than being able to move my eyes, I was completely paralyzed. I tried to blink my way back to 1935, as I thought I might have done earlier, but was unsuccessful. The man on the lawn mower had started to change direction and would have been able to see me lying on his property in mere seconds, but in less time than that, I was gone.

The blood had just started to rush back into my body when I saw two young and startled boys about to make off with Katherine's bicycle. "Hey, bring that back!" I tried to yell, but to my own ears it sounded more like "Ey, ring a rack!"

"Mister, where did you come from?" the older of the two boys asked.

Able to speak more clearly, I said, "I've been here next to the bike." Then I questioned myself aloud, "Haven't I?"

"We didn't see you there, mister. We wouldn't have taken the bike if we saw you there," the younger boy said while pulling on his suspenders.

"Boys, are you saying that you really didn't see me here at all?"

"Yes, mister, we didn't see you," the older one said. This confounded me as my body seemed to have disappeared when I left 1935 on this occasion but not earlier when I was in Whitten's Department Store. The only real difference between the two incidents was that I was away from 1935 longer on this occasion. Perhaps, I wondered, there was some sort of time lag where my body would be present in both times simultaneously, but after it was in the new time for a while it would disappear in the old one. This would make interesting conversation with Professor Manning, I thought.

"We're real sorry, mister. Please don't tell our dad. We thought someone left the bike here and didn't want it no more. We weren't gonna keep it anyway; it's a girl's bike."

They gave me the impression that they were truly honest boys who thought they had found an abandoned bicycle. "Don't worry about it. It was an honest mistake." I groaned as I tried to move, "Can you do me a favor and help me get up?"

"What happened? Did you fall off the bike?" the youngest asked.

"Sort of," I replied.

"I know. It happens to me all the time," the youngest one confessed.

The older boy then teased his brother, "That's why you have training wheels, baby!"

The boys were not quite strong enough to get me back on my feet by themselves, but they sure did give it a try. Eventually, I regained enough strength to be able to get up without their help. I was about to get back on the bicycle when the older boy said with concern, "Are you sure you want to get back on that bike, mister. You might fall again."

The younger one added sweetly, "You can borrow my training wheels."

I laughed and said, "I'll be all right now, boys. Don't worry about me." The feeling had completely come back to my legs, though my arms were still a little cold and numb. I thanked them for their help and was back on my way.

Nine

Concerned about falling off the bicycle again and getting hit by a car, I decided to walk the bike the rest of the way to Katherine's house. I stayed as far away from traffic as possible and made it there without any more time-slip incidents.

With the hopes of obtaining another free meal, I knocked on the Whitneys' front door. I would have preferred to take Katherine out for a nice dinner, but I didn't have enough time. Saving as much money as possible to bet on the fight with was also a concern. While there, I also hoped to have a private talk with Katherine's father and ask him why he referred to me as his son-in-law at the office.

Katherine's mother answered the front door. I thanked her once again for loaning me money for the suit and promised to pay her back on Friday. She pursed her lips and put her forefinger in front of them to tell me to keep my voice down. Apparently her husband was not to know that I borrowed money from her. That was okay with me. I left the bicycle outside the front door and entered the house. "Your suit is nice," she whispered. "But why are your pants all dirty already?"

"I fell off the bike. I guess I didn't do a good job of brushing myself off," I said.

Katherine had overheard my words and came running from the kitchen. "Are you hurt?" she asked with concern, while she smacked more of the dirt off my backside.

"I'm fine," I said, but I wasn't. The thought of time-slipping again and disappearing in front of the Whitney family's eyes scared me to death. Even more mortifying was the thought of never again returning to 1935 and being without Katherine for the rest of my life. I tried desperately to get those thoughts out of my head, but couldn't. The very real possibility that it could happen tortured me.

Mrs. Whitney asked, "Would you like me to set another place for dinner?" and it was music to my ears. I used to be such a picky eater in my own time, but after traveling to 1935 I ate whatever was offered to me. Food, in general, was not in large supply and it wasn't taken for granted as it was in my own time where every street corner possessed a convenience store, a supermarket, or a Red Lobster. There was an incident, while in a drunken stupor, when I wasted a whole plate of spaghetti by throwing it at a waiter in an Olive Garden because it was overcooked. The waiter cursed me out and I proceeded to pound the hell out of him in front of the entire restaurant. My girlfriend at the time tried to pull me off and I accidentally knocked her unconscious. Eventually, the police came and hauled me away. When my mother came to bail me out of jail, her expression of total disappointment told me all that I needed to know about her feelings. I was nothing that she could be proud of and she wouldn't pretend that I was. My father had only been gone for a month and putting up with my antics was more than she could take. It was the last time I saw her alive. The judge gave me a choice of jail time or the ten-step program. For the record, I became a reformed alcoholic, but off the record I still drank like a fish for a few more years. I was never able to completely stop drinking, but I was able to keep it under control.

Responding to Mrs. Whitney's dinner invitation, I said, "That would be great. Thank you."

"What took you so long to get here?" Katherine asked.

Referring to Professor Manning, I replied, "I ran into an old friend. In fact, I'll be seeing him again in a few hours." I then remembered that I had to call Harry so he could pick me up and drive me to the professor's lab. "Mrs. Whitney, would it be a terrible imposition if I used your telephone?"

"No imposition at all. It's over there," she replied, while pointing to the phone's location.

"What old friend are you going to meet?" Katherine asked, trying not to sound too inquisitive.

"His name is Professor Manning. He's going to be teaching at the university in the fall." Katherine seemed relieved that my "old friend" was a man.

The phone sat on an oak table, the same table that Margo used to display our great-grandmother's figurines, and was the only piece of furniture that Margo used that was originally from the Whitney house. I walked over and picked up the receiver and it felt eerie to have it in my hand again. I was able to reach Harry and, after a little prodding, he agreed to pick me up and drive me to the professor's lab.

I managed to make it through dinner without time-slipping. There was a moment when I began to feel very cold, but it passed quickly. While Katherine helped her mother with the dinner dishes, I had an opportunity to talk with her father alone. He was in his study smoking a fat Cuban cigar. I ducked my head in through the doorway and said, "Thank you very much, Mr. Whitney, for getting me a job. I truly appreciate it."

He was reading his newspaper and didn't seem to want to be bothered. "Huh? The job? Oh, yes. You're welcome," he grunted.

"I have just one question, sir, if I may?"

He reluctantly took his eyes off of the paper and looked up. With unhidden annoyance he said, "A question? What is it?"

His tone shook me, but I kept on. "Why did my new boss refer to me as your son-in-law?"

"Son-in-law? Oh, yes ... well, the only way I could get you the job was to tell them that you were related to me." He continued with a laugh, "I had an opportunity to win money from Gordon and I couldn't pass it up!" My ego was deflated. I had hoped that the man had started to feel some affection for me, that I had managed to get on his good side without having to pretend that I knew everything about fishing. He noticed my disappointment and inquired, "Did you think that I wanted you to marry my daughter?" My lack of a response was response enough for him. "You did, didn't you?" He laughed hard and it sounded like a wolf howling at the moon. Abruptly, his laughter stopped. He put down his newspaper, stood up and snarled with certainty, "Understand this. The only reasons that I got you the job was to win a bet and because my wife asked me to help you. You are not good enough for my daughter, but if I forbid her to see you, she will pine for you, never forgive me, and want you more than ever. I am sure that the longer you stay around, the more my daughter will see what you are and that there can be no future with you. Enjoy your time with her now, son, because your time is running out."

It was like all of the air went out of my body at the same time. I felt crushed. I knew that Katherine's feelings for me were real, but I also knew that plans for a life together were not always made based on love in that time. If I couldn't provide for her, and provide for her well, I would never get her father's blessing.

When Katherine had finished helping her mother clean up, we went outside and I pushed her on the tire swing that hung from a branch of an oak tree, the same oak tree that was my marker for burying the penny. The tree was, of course, smaller than when I had first seen it, but not by as much as I would have thought. It was still a very large tree.

I had little to say; I was still reeling from the conversation I had with Katherine's father. King, the Whitneys' behemoth St. Bernard, didn't help matters by barking and growling at me. Yet another male Whitney family member that did not appreciate my presence, I thought. Katherine's mother called off the pooch and brought him inside of the house.

My mood did not reflect how lovely an evening it was. The sun had not quite begun to set, but the big orange ball was getting ready and a few far off puffy clouds framed it as if it were a pretty picture.

"What's wrong?" Katherine asked. "Did something happen between you and Father?"

"Yes," I said dejectedly. I decided to break the news to her. "Katherine, he ... he doesn't want us to be together."

I expected her to ball up into tears, but instead she said flatly, "So, what's the big surprise?"

"It doesn't bother you that we would never get your father's blessing?"

She skimmed her feet on the ground to stop the swinging motion and turned toward me. "His blessing for what? Marriage? You can't even commit to staying here in Valley View! Why would I think you would commit to something as serious as marriage?" she railed.

"I am committed to staying here! I started a job today, and if that works out I will try to find a permanent place to live. I am as committed as I can possibly be under the circumstances."

"The circumstances? What are the circumstances? Oh, that's right, you can't tell me. And I'm supposed to just accept that?"

"No, I don't expect you to just accept it. I will tell you. I just ..."

"You just what?" She swallowed her anger and said in a calm but firm manner, "What is it, Joseph? Why can't you just say that you will stay here forever?" She turned away from me and started swinging again.

The time had come. I was about to risk it all and tell her everything when I suddenly went cold. My legs could no longer support my body and I collapsed to the ground. Katherine didn't notice me fall and said with her back to me, "Joseph, do you have any answers for me at all?" She was truly annoyed at me, but I couldn't speak. I wanted to tell her that everything would be okay, but I was nearly gone. Then, in an instant, she and the swing disappeared and I was all alone.

I noticed that the Whitneys' backyard had changed and knew that I was no longer in 1935. My neck was still paralyzed, but I was able to observe my new surroundings by moving my eyes. I saw holes in the yard that appeared to have been recently dug and knew for sure that I was back in my own time. I blinked my eyes to send myself back, as if I had the power of a genie, but to no avail. My paralysis began to subside enabling me to move my neck and I caught sight of Margo in her kitchen window. She didn't notice me at first, but when she did she dropped the pot she had been drying and ran outside.

"Little Joey, Is that you?"

I wasn't quite ready to speak, so I nodded my head.

She bombarded me with questions. "Are you okay? Where have you been? Do you know that everyone has been looking for you? I even called the cops." I tried to answer her, but my frozen throat and mouth couldn't manufacture the words.

Even though I was grateful to see Margo again, I wanted to get back to Katherine as soon as possible. I felt extreme frustration from time-slipping again and I started to cry. The warm tears began to defrost my cold face. Margo gave me a hug that warmed me up even more. As much as I missed her, I pushed her away for fear that if I warmed up completely I would never get back to Katherine.

I was finally able to get out a few words and said, "I did it!" but I wasn't sure if Margo was able to understand me. I repeated, "I did it! Tell Chuck I did it."

"Did what?"

"Traveled to 1935! I time-traveled to 1935!"

"Oh, you can't be serious, Little Joey. You ..."

I interrupted and was able to speak much more clearly. "Look at my suit. Would I walk around town in a suit like this?"

"No, I suppose a sane individual wouldn't do that," she wisecracked.

"Margo ..." I gained even more control of myself and said calmly, "Margo, I made it. I'm glad to see you again, but I have to get back."

I could see that she had started to believe me. She gave me a wry smile as if she understood everything completely and said, "Then go back, Little Joey, go back now." It was almost as if she made it happen. The extreme cold set back in again and I was glad that I had never got up off of the ground because I would have fallen right down again. My body became numb and I was gone.

When I was able to open my eyes, I was still in the Whitneys' backyard, but Katherine was not. I didn't think much time had passed since I left and began to worry that I traveled back to a time other than 1935. When my ears defrosted I was relieved to hear her calling for me from the front of the house. Unfortunately, I was not quite ready to reply to her. I wondered if she had seen me disappear or reappear. She walked back toward the swing, saw me lying there all twisted like a pretzel, and began to run the rest of the way. "Joseph!" she screamed while running. Upon reaching me, she knelt down in front of me and said,

"Are you okay?" I was just beginning to get the feeling back in my body and was unsure if I could speak, so I nodded instead. She asked, "What happened to you? You were next to me by the swing and then all of a sudden you weren't." She started to sob while she kissed my face, "I thought that you left me. I'm so sorry, Joseph. I don't mean to put so much pressure on you, but ..." She pulled away from me so that she could look me straight in the eyes. She held my head in her hands and said, "I love you and I don't care if you won't say it back. I don't care if you leave for Philadelphia, I will still love you."

I didn't hesitate. "I love you too." I started to sob as well and said, "I love you and if I do have to go back, I'm going to find a way to take you with me." I hugged her and didn't want to let go, but the sound of a car backfiring signaled me that Harry had come to take me to see Professor Manning. I wiped my tears, got myself up off of the ground, and then helped Katherine up as well. Harry sounded his horn, as if announcing his arrival was necessary. Katherine looked at me as if to say that she couldn't believe I was going to go with Harry after the words we had just said to each other. I tried to assure her. "I will tell you everything." I hesitated, but then continued, "Tomorrow. I promise to tell you everything tomorrow. I'm sorry, but I gotta go." She buried her face into my chest and I kissed the top of her head. I released her and headed to the front of the house where Harry was waiting. I turned my head for another goodbye and said, "Tomorrow." She nodded in acceptance of the fact that she was in deep with a crazy man.

***

Harry tossed me the bag of clothes that I asked him to bring and we drove away. "So who is this Professor Manning and why do you need to see him at his lab?" he asked, as he turned onto the main road.

Even though we had become very close, I was still afraid to tell him the truth. "Oh, he may have a job for me," I lied.

"I thought you just started a job today?"

"I did, but ... I've got to keep my options open, right?" I said with a nervous laugh.

Harry surely realized that I hadn't been completely truthful with him and he protested with silence the rest of the way to the professor's lab. When we arrived, he finally spoke. "Do you want me to wait for you or should I just come back later on to get you?"

I hopped out of the car. "I'll probably be a while. Why don't you pick me up in about an hour?"

"All right, one hour." Harry then attempted to speed away, but the car backfired a few times and eventually stalled. I asked him if he wanted me to wait, but he got out of the car, got it started again, and waved for me to go.

***

I knocked on the slightly open door of Professor Manning's lab, but no one was there to answer. I slowly pushed the door open and saw a room in complete disarray. Half unpacked crates of books, vials, beakers, and test tubes were everywhere. Also inside the room were unmarked chemical containers, jars containing unknown parts of unknown animals, and a human skeleton. Peeking out from underneath a cloth cover was what may have been an electrical generator. I lifted the cover and saw different color wires of assorted gauges and they were completely entangled with each other. The only part of the lab that was neatly kept was a corner that contained a bench with a microscope on top and empty slides next to it ready for use. As I walked toward the bench to get a closer look, Professor Manning entered the room.

"Ah, Mr. Eaton, I see you have arrived," he glanced at his pocket watch, "and almost on time. Have you brought the garments that you mentioned?"

"Yes, Professor." I handed him the bag with my clothes from the future which included my sweatpants, my plain white t-shirt, and, unfortunately, my dirty socks and boxers. "I hope this can somehow give you the proof that you wanted." I stared at him as he handled the articles of clothing and he caught me.

"Why do you watch me with such intensity, Mr. Eaton?"

"I'm sorry. It's just that you look so much like my friend Chuck. You know ... your grandson."

He looked cynically at me and said, "Oh yes, the grandson that I don't yet have." He changed the subject and, while holding my sweatpants, said, "These garments are very different. They are lighter than I would have expected. What material are they?"

"I think they are all 100% cotton, but they may be blended with some other kind of fabric. I don't know."

"I see there is a tear at the knee. May I cut off a small portion of the fabric to examine under the microscope?" the professor asked.

"Of course, do what you need to do with them. I would probably only wear them to bed in this time anyway. If I wore this outside I would probably get arrested."

"This is not an undergarment in your time?" he asked, and he wasn't joking. It was comforting in a way that he was taking it very seriously, as if he might believe my story a minute amount.

"No. The way people dress in my time would probably be considered indecent here. Heck, it's considered indecent in my time too!"

"Oh really?" He cut off a small portion of my sweatpants and affixed the clipping to a slide. "And why is that?"

"Well, some of the young women in my time wear clothes that barely even cover their underwear. I think it's considered fashionable to show their bra straps or show parts of their panties."

He looked up from the microscope and said with shock, "Their brassieres and underthings are visible in public? Is there a shortage of fabric in the future?"

"No, it's just the way some women dress," I said with amusement. "There is plenty of fabric in the future." I thought for a moment and said, "Perhaps all of the extra fabric they save from the women's clothes they use for the men."

"What do you mean?"

"Well, the men sometimes wear pants that are so big on them that they fall down while they walk."

"They have no belts or suspenders?"

"Well, those things still exist in my time, but it's just considered fashionable for the younger men to wear their clothes oversized."

Professor Manning shook his head in disbelief of my story of the future and then concentrated his gaze on the fabric sample in the microscope. After a few moments he said, "What's this?" He took his eye off of the microscope and then back on again. "I can see the cotton, but there is another material that I do not recognize. Come here and take a look. Maybe you can identify it."

I looked at the slide, but it just appeared to be a random pattern of lines to me, some slightly broken up and others not. "I'm not a scientist. I don't know what I'm looking at."

The professor nearly pushed me out of the way to take another look. As he did, I grabbed my sweatpants off of the bench and turned them inside out. "What is that? I've never seen anything like it. It's like some other fabric has been woven with the cotton," he remarked.

I noticed the tag on the sweatpants and read it aloud, "Fifty percent cotton and fifty percent polyester."

"What did you say?" he said, while keeping his eye on the sample.

"Fifty percent cotton and fifty percent polyester. Here, look at the tag."

He took the sweatpants from me and looked at the tag with a magnifying glass. "A marker that identifies the material the garment is made from? Ingenious!" He turned the tag over and was even more astonished. "And it even gives you proper washing instructions!" He looked at my t-shirt and boxers and noticed that each had a similar marker. He asked why my tube socks didn't have the tags, but I had no answer for him. He then switched the subject back to the material of the sweatpants. "P-o-l-y-e-s-t-e-r?" he said trying to decipher the word. "Do you have any idea when it was developed?"

His question, and the manner in which he asked it, made me realize that he had become a believer in my story. "I don't know. There is no polyester in this time?"

"I never heard of such a thing. When I worked in the government, I handled all different kinds of metals, fabrics, and adhesives. I even worked with plastics, but nothing that was called polyester and nothing that looks like this does under the microscope."

I was happy that polyester was my ticket to believability, but I didn't know what else to say. "I don't know when it was developed, but I know it's definitely a man-made material."

"Oh my boy, you and I are going to go public and talk about your time travels! We can show off your clothes from the future on the lecture circuit! I've got to get started on our presentation right away."

The professor was extremely excited, but I had to rein him in. "Whoa, hold on, Professor. Slow down. I'm not going public with this."

"Why would you want to show me proof, then? Why go to the trouble of providing proof only to keep it to ourselves?"

"I just wanted to talk to someone who is much smarter than I am about it. It's important for me to

have someone to confide in. I'm way too afraid to talk
to my girlfriend Katherine about it. I'm terrified she's
going to think I'm a lunatic, but I know I have to start
telling her the truth and *only* the truth."

"Why did you choose me to confide in?"

"Like I told you, you're smart — you're a
scientist. But, I also think it's because you look so
much like your grandson that I feel I can trust you. I
trusted him and he helped send me on this journey in
the first place."

"You can't really expect me to keep mum on
this, can you? A time traveler, well that's just too
extraordinary! A scientist works his whole life to make
a discovery that will give his name a mark of
distinction in the scientific community, and here you
just fall from the sky to make that happen."

"Please, Professor Manning, don't say anything
to anyone. I have to be able to get along here, and if
everyone were to know my story, well, it would make
things extremely difficult for me. It's already tough
enough as it is with all of the time-slipping I did
today."

"Time-slipping? What do you mean by *time-
slipping*?" he asked.

"When I met you earlier today, I had just
returned from being back in my own time for a brief
moment. When I time-slip I get really cold and numb,
and I become nearly paralyzed. Then I find myself
back in my own time, stay for a little while, and then
return here again. That's why I asked you if I had
disappeared."

"Why do you think this comes about?" the
scientist asked.

"I was hoping you could tell me."

"How many times has this happened to you?"

"So far, as far as I know, three times — all today. The first time was at Whitten's when I met you, then on my way to Katherine's house while I was riding her bicycle, and then later on while I pushed her on a swing. I'm worried that it means my time here is coming to an end. What do you think I can do to stay here permanently? I really want to stay."

"I don't know, Joseph. You may need a doctor more than you need a scientist. You may even need a priest for all I know. Tell me more about how you came to be here. You said that my grandson helped you. What did he do for you?" I told him about digging up the penny in the jar. "Well, did you bury the penny like he told you to do?"

"No. I'm a little afraid to."

"Why?"

"I'm afraid that if I bury the penny my life here will end and I will be sent back to my own time."

"Logically, if logic even applies here," he laughed at his own words, "you need to bury the penny, because if you don't, or should I say if you didn't, you wouldn't have come here to begin with. That may be why you keep getting sent back. You have not performed the necessary task that helped bring you here in the first place!"

"Oh, I don't know. I'm so confused, Professor."

"Trust me. You must bury the penny. It may not guarantee that you stay in this time, but, if I may theorize, the longer you wait, the more often you will slip back to your own time, and then, eventually, you will slip back permanently. This is all most fascinating!"

"Well, I guess it would be fascinating to you, but it's not a whole hell of a lot of fun for me."

Professor Manning looked me square in the eyes and said with controlled passion, "Life is never easy for the special ones, Joseph."

"Special ones? Professor, you sound more like a clergyman than a scientist."

"Well, sometimes someone special like you comes along and blurs the lines between science and theology. I never believed that either of them were mutually exclusive from the other anyway."

"Careful, Professor, you sound like a real radical," I laughed. "You better keep those kinds of comments to yourself or you might find yourself blacklisted."

"Yes, I'm quite the rebel," he chuckled, and then flashed a toothy grin.

Over an hour had passed and I figured that Harry must have been waiting for a while, so I departed company from Professor Manning. He had agreed to keep quiet about my story, but said he was going to try an experiment of his own. He was going to attempt to duplicate my time-travel experience with the use of another telephone and electrical current. I wished him well, but worried that he might accidentally kill himself.

Harry had been waiting for me for more than a few minutes and apparently that was too long for him. He smelled like he may have killed the hour in a bar and it brought out a nasty side of him. He did not hide his displeasure about being my chauffeur and barked,

"You've got to get your own wheels," and said nothing else the rest of the way home.

Mrs. Dempsey got on me as soon as I walked in her front door about painting the fence. I promised her I would take care of it shortly and truly hoped that I would before she called Francine, my supposed mother, to complain about me. One thing was becoming clear: I was wearing out my welcome in the Dempsey home.

Ten

Weather-wise, Tuesday morning was not as pleasant as Monday morning was. There were dark clouds in the sky, but the rain was reluctant to fall. During the night, I had either a very odd dream or another time-slip. It was very dark and difficult to see, but I believed I was in some kind of factory. In this factory there were machines with sharp-looking blades that may have been used for cutting wood or metal. I was unable to move any part of my body except for my eyes. That was all I remembered.

I was becoming increasingly concerned about slipping back to my own time permanently and decided I would take Professor Manning's advice and finally bury the penny. Unfortunately, since I had to go to work, that undertaking was going to have to wait until later in the day, but I hoped that merely making a definitive decision to act would be enough to keep me from time-slipping.

Harry had already left by the time I was ready, so I had no ride to work. In order to make it on time, I had to run, not jog, but run, all the way there. While running, I decided that, until I had enough money to buy my own automobile, I was going to try and purchase a gently-used bicycle. By the time I darted in the door and greeted the pretty receptionist, I was out of breath, my clothes were completely disheveled, and I was a sweaty mess. Despite my unkempt condition, I was happy that I made it on time and extremely relieved there were no time-slip incidents on the way.

As soon as Mr. Potato Head, my boss, laid eyes on me he squawked, "Joseph! We can't have you greeting people looking like that! Go to the washroom and clean yourself up!" he commanded.

I did as he said. I went into the bathroom and attempted to straighten out my suit. To try and cool myself down, I put water on my face and hair. While looking at myself in the mirror, I began to get extremely cold and I knew what would happen next. In an effort to keep myself from time-slipping, I tried to envision myself burying the penny and said out loud, "I will bury the penny tonight." I repeated this phrase a number of times and it seemed to help, since I never went completely numb and I did not slip back to my own time. For the first time in a long while, I felt that I had some control over my life. With renewed confidence and conviction in my belief that I belonged in 1935, I left the bathroom.

I was told that I would be teamed with one of the other salesmen for the remainder of the week to further my training. Fortunately for me, this partner was to be Sam Lerner. He was the salesman that found my Mr. Potato Head remark completely hilarious the previous day. Sam was a young man in his early twenties, smallish, and prematurely losing his thin blond hair. "Joseph, I'm going to show you my foolproof sales method. Soon you will be so good you'll be able to sell an icebox to an Eskimo," he joked and then lightly elbowed me in the ribs.

"Or how about eyeglasses to a blind man," I quickly jested back.

My quip should have been considered slightly amusing at best, but Sam was nearly bent over with laughter. "Oh, that's a good one!" he said. He would laugh in that same manner for all of my jokes that day, both good and bad, and he probably thought I was the funniest man in the world.

After Mr. Potato Head's daily pep rally, we headed out for our first sales call. We were assigned Carpenter and Argyle Streets for the morning and Cornwall Avenue and Beverly Parkway for the afternoon. The first door that we knocked on was answered by a tiny boy. As soon as he had reached up to open the screen door to let us in, a huge German shepherd came out of nowhere and knocked me to the ground. Why dogs had been so hard on me since my arrival in 1935, I wasn't sure. It was as though they knew that I had come from another time and, to them at least, I didn't belong in theirs. Expecting to be utterly mauled, I covered myself up as best as I could. When the anticipated attack didn't take place, I opened my eyes and looked up to see the dog licking Sam's right hand while being pet by his left. Sam looked down at me while I was prone on the ground and said, "Bologna."

"What?" I gasped, still stunned that I wasn't being gnawed on.

He repeated, "Bologna," and showed me a bag which contained sliced meat and gave me my first pointer. "Always carry bologna with you. It helps you make friends with the watchdogs."

I got up off the ground, shook my head and acknowledged, "I have a lot to learn." I had wondered why he smelled like a delicatessen.

The woman of the house, the small boy's mother, was shown the benefits of taking out a life insurance policy on her husband who had a dangerous job loading and unloading large ships with a crane. Sam was masterful. He *could* sell an icebox to an Eskimo. She signed on for a one-thousand-dollar policy and gave us the first payment of five dollars without even consulting her husband. I would come to realize that Sam had a way of making it seem like the offer he gave had to be acted upon immediately, that there was no time to think about it, as death could occur at any moment.

We were not as successful at the next three houses, but at least they didn't have any attack dogs. As we walked toward the fifth house, I began to feel as though I was going to time-slip again. The last thing I wanted was to disappear in sight of my co-worker, so I told Sam that I had to pee and ducked behind a pack of tall bushes. As usual, I began to feel numb and I fell to the ground. I told myself repeatedly, "I will bury the penny tonight. I will bury the penny tonight. I will bury the penny tonight," and envisioned myself doing just that. This ritual apparently kept me from slipping all of the way back, just as it did earlier in the day in the company washroom. My legs quickly regained feeling and I was able to stand again. I noticed Sam peeking over in my direction to see what was taking me so long, so I pretended as if I was finishing up my business. "Ahh," I said to Sam as I came out of the bushes, "that's better!"

In a deadly serious manner, Sam intoned, "I have to report this to the boss, you know. He's fired people for much smaller offenses than public urination." He held his serious expression for a few moments, but he couldn't hold it long. He blew air out of his mouth as if he had been holding his breath and he began to laugh hysterically. "You should have seen your face!" He continued to hoot, "You looked so worried!" He didn't know that it wasn't my job status that worried me. Staying put in 1935 was. I had a few more near time-slip incidents during that workday, but each time I was able to keep from leaving 1935 by telling myself that I would bury the penny that night.

When my workday was over, I started to walk to Katherine's house. I had hoped to have a serious talk with her that night about my time-traveling experience and I also hoped to leech another meal from her parents. In my mind, I practiced telling her my story. I tried out many different approaches, but, unfortunately, none of those approaches made me sound anywhere near sane.

Half of the way to Katherine's house, I decided to take a shortcut down a dirt road that was lined with woods. A car passed me and then, seemingly on purpose, spun out of control before abruptly stopping. Even through the cloud of sand, dirt and dust it kicked up, I could tell it was Freddy York's car and I feared what would happen next. I tried to appear cool and kept walking as if nothing was wrong. When I got within a few feet of the car, Freddy and two of his friends got out.

"Going to Katherine's house?" he asked, but I was sure he knew the answer.

I took a hard and firm tone. "What is your business with me, Mr. York?" His friends laughed at my formal tongue.

Freddy got very angry and spit out, "I asked you a question!"

I spouted back, "Yes, a question you damn well know the answer to! Of course I'm heading to Katherine's, you jackass!"

Freddy's friends reacted to my insult with "ooohs" and "aaahs" and one of them followed up with, "Freddy, you're gonna take that from this sap?"

Freddy slowly moved closer and closer to me, and as soon as he believed he was in the right position he sneered, "Hold him, fellas!" On that command, his friends came from behind me and tried to hold my arms. I fought them off for a while, but eventually they held me in such a way that I could not break free. Freddy then began an assault on my midsection. He threw punch after punch at my stomach until I wished that my stomach wasn't empty so that I could have at least vomited on him for defense. Pain started to sear through my entire body and I worried that he had inflicted major internal damage.

"I told you! I warned you!" he screamed as he threw more punches. "Katherine is mine! I know it! Her father knows it!" He then changed it up and hit me with a dizzying uppercut that knocked me and my handlers to the ground. As soon as I hit the dirt, he continued, "Now *you* know it!" He started to walk away, but changed his mind and came back to spit on me. As if on cue, the skies opened up and it began to pour. I wanted to shout back to him that *Katherine didn't know it,* but there was no point in fighting further.

It was a battle I could not win. I lay on the ground beaten, bloody, and bruised, and was content to stay there in a puddle of rainwater and my own blood. Freddy looked up at the raining sky and said to his friends, "Let's go, fellas." Both of his friends gave me a parting kick in the ribs and then obediently followed Freddy back to his car. They drove off and left me there alone to lick my wounds.

As I lay there, I thought to myself that it would have been great if I could have time-slipped while I was getting my beating. When the numbness set in, I wouldn't have felt any pain and I could have shocked them by disappearing right before their eyes. Maybe I would have reappeared behind Freddy's back and taken him by surprise.

I got back to the reality of my situation and thought about shouting for help, but realized the street was completely desolate and it was unlikely that anyone would hear my cries. I started to take a self-inventory and realized that walking would be a possibility. It wouldn't be without severe pain, but it was possible. I was certainly bruised and beaten, but I didn't think I had any broken bones. A few teeth had come loose and I was bleeding from the mouth courtesy of Freddy's uppercut, but I believed I could plod along and make it to Katherine's house. Eventually, I picked myself up off of the ground and headed in that direction.

It took a very long time, but I made it. Mrs. Whitney answered the door and was appalled at what she saw. "Joseph! Oh my! What happened to you?" I didn't want to tell her that Freddy and his friends had beaten me up, so I lied and said that I had fallen on the way. She didn't believe my fib, but let it go. "Please come in. Can I get you anything? Something to eat?"

I was starving but afraid I wouldn't be able to chew a normal dinner, so I asked, "Do you have anything soft to eat? Maybe a banana?"

She could tell that my mouth was hurting. I'm sure the blood was a dead giveaway. "First, let's get you cleaned up, and then we'll see what you can eat."

Mrs. Whitney then shouted for Katherine, and when Katherine caught a glimpse of me she did not react with pity or with horror as I had expected. Instead she got very angry. Through gritted teeth she said, "Mother, can you get me a wet washcloth, and see if there is any ice in the icebox." Mrs. Whitney did as she was asked and when she was out of hearing range Katherine whispered angrily to me, "Freddy did this to you, didn't he?"

"No. I just fell down," I insisted.

"Just once, Joseph Eaton … just once, tell me the truth! Did Freddy do this to you?"

Her eyes were on fire and I knew that I had to tell her the truth. I had planned to tell her the whole truth that night anyway so *this* truth, I thought, would be a good place to start. "Yes … yes, Freddy and his friends beat me up."

"You see!" She no longer whispered and she could not contain her anger any longer. "This is what happens! He pushes you! You push back! Then he pushes you more! Can you see why I hate fighting?" She paused for a moment, but I was sure that she didn't really expect an answer to her question. "Now look at you!"

I didn't know what to say to her, but I knew I had to say something. "Katherine, you're right of course. Fighting is ... well, it's wrong. It doesn't help anything. I know that now."

"Do you? So it takes Freddy beating you up for you to learn that lesson? You couldn't have learned it before, when you beat him up?" She was still furious. Her mother came back with the ice and the washcloth and Katherine proceeded to clean me up. Despite her anger, she was gentle with me while wiping the blood off my face and holding the ice pack to my jaw. She stroked my hair as if to tell me that, despite the brawling animal in me, she still loved me.

Mrs. Whitney had prepared some broth with soft noodles that I was able to eat, and I started to feel a little better. My suit was being hung to dry, so I was given more clothes from the trunk in the basement to change into. The new ensemble was worse than the clothes I had acquired from the trunk a few days before. I was given a pair of heavy green knickers that fell barely below my knee and were far too large around my waist. For a top, I received a yellow-stained white linen collared shirt that would have been too big for an offensive lineman in football. I was hardly GQ material with my ridiculous outfit and my beat-up face.

When I asked Katherine what she would like to do that night, she said that she was going to be sitting for little Alice York next door. She asked if I would like to join her, but I was reluctant to go into the house where the man who had just beaten me up lived. "Don't worry. Freddy won't be there," she said. "He and his friends drive around town every night getting soused and being a nuisance to every girl they come across."

After giving it some thought, I said, "Okay, I'll baby-sit with you. But first, let me borrow your bicycle. I want to get Alice a present."

***

Pedaling a bicycle shortly after receiving the beating of my life was not all that easy. Finding an open store after seven o'clock p.m. that sold Life Savers candy proved to be equally as difficult. All of the drug stores had been closed for at least an hour. There were no 24-hour convenience stores or mini-marts. It was hard to adjust to a world where everything you desired was not easily at hand. Fortunately, I passed by a newsstand that also sold candy and it had not yet closed for the night. I bought Alice's Life Savers and headed back to Katherine.

On the way back I started to sway a little on the bicycle. Parts of my body had begun to throb from all of the punches and kicks I received, and controlling the bike became even more difficult. The rain had completely stopped, but it left an obstacle course of puddles for me to circumvent. I misjudged the speed of an oncoming car and nearly got hit going around one of the large puddles. I was a bit shaken up by the near miss and said a prayer hoping it would facilitate a safer return back.

When I arrived back at the Whitney house, Mrs. Whitney informed me that Katherine had already started baby-sitting, so I walked to the house next door.

Alice was glad to see me and let me in. "What happened to you?" she asked, while studying my bruised face.

"Well, I got into a fight with your brother and a couple of his friends."

"I told you he was sore at you! Are you okay?"

"Yeah, I'll be all right. Nice of you to ask." I patted her on the head.

"Do you have anything for me?" she asked, barely able to control her anticipation.

I played dumb and said, "What would I have for you?"

Alice looked disappointed and with a pathetic tone said, "I was hoping that you had some candy for me." She put her hands behind her back and shuffled her feet around.

I couldn't tease her anymore. "You mean like this!" I took the Life Savers out of my pocket and handed them to her. She jumped up and down and was ecstatic with the expectation of a sugary high. I had created a candy monster.

Katherine saw Alice with the candy and scolded her. "Where did you get that from?"

Alice pointed at me and said sheepishly, "Joseph gave it to me."

Katherine looked at me with scorn, but calmly said, "Mrs. York does not want Alice to have candy, especially just before bedtime!"

"Oh come on, Katherine! She's a kid and kids should have candy. What fun is it to be a kid without candy?" I campaigned.

"Yeah, kids should have candy!" Alice chimed in.

"She won't have any after she brushes her teeth, okay?" I added.

"Yeah, I won't have any after I brush my teeth." Alice repeated.

"Well, okay, I guess. Just don't ever tell your mother about it. She'd skin me alive."

"Hooray!" Alice said, as she paraded around the house thankful that she was going to be allowed to have some of her candy. I just hoped that she wouldn't be bouncing off the walls all night.

Later on that night while Katherine cleaned up in the kitchen, Alice and I played a game of hide-and-go-seek. She left the kitchen to hide while I closed my eyes and counted to fifty aloud. Since she had the home advantage and knew all the good hiding spots, it took quite a while to find her, but I eventually discovered her in a small closet under the stairs.

It was then her turn to find me, so I left the kitchen on a quest to find a good hiding place of my own. I settled on a spot behind a big oversized chair in the living room. I crouched down behind the chair and hugged my knees to better conceal myself. When Alice reached forty-five in her count, I started to become cold and numb. I told myself that I was going to bury the penny that night and envisioned myself doing it, but this time it didn't work. Alice finished her counting and started to seek. While she searched the closet under the stairs, her favorite hiding spot and the best place to hide in the house, I began to lose all feeling in my body. The sound of the thud from my body slumping to the floor gave away my hiding place. She may have caught a glimpse of me laid out behind the chair before I disappeared.

When I was able to open my eyes again, it was as if Alice had been the one who disappeared. The room, at least what I could see of it, looked exactly the same as the room I had left. The lights in the living room were off, but I could see a light shining in the kitchen and was able to hear the sound of a man humming. The man continued to hum as he walked past the living room and I was able to identify him as Chuck Manning. He hadn't seen me lying on his living room floor partially hidden behind the big chair. I started to get the feeling back in my body, but as soon as I was able to yell out to him, I had gone cold again and was back in 1935.

When I reappeared, Alice trembled terribly and stared at me in disbelief. Apparently, she *had* seen me disappear. And to make matters worse, she was also a witness to my reappearance. I wanted to comfort her, but I had not sufficiently thawed enough to do so. To her credit, she didn't scream, but she may have been in such a state of shock she was unable to voice her fear. I hoped that she wouldn't tell anyone what she saw. I didn't want to have to say that my disappearing act was simply a product of a little girl's vivid imagination and give her the reputation of being a real storyteller. As soon as I was able to speak, I said to her, "Alice, don't be afraid. What you saw was real, but you must not tell anyone."

She lunged toward me with her arms open and hugged me while softly crying. "I thought you were dead. Mommy said when Grandma died that she disappeared to heaven. I thought that's what happened to you."

"No, sweetie, I didn't die." I laughed, as if what she said was preposterous. Then, when I realized what I was about to say was even more preposterous, I laughed harder. "I just left this time for a little while. I don't know if heaven would want me yet anyway."

"Oh," was all she said, so I offered no further explanation.

"Please promise me that you won't tell anyone that you saw me disappear, okay?"

"Okay. I promise."

"Cross your heart and hope to ..." Die didn't seem appropriate after what she had just said about her grandmother, so I shortened the expression. "Cross your heart?"

She crossed her heart and said, "Okay?"

"Okay," I replied, satisfied that the little girl wouldn't tell.

Katherine had come into the living room and, unbeknownst to me at the time, had seen Alice crossing her heart. "What's going on here?" she asked.

At the same time that Alice cutely replied, "Nothing," I said, "I'll tell you later."

Katherine focused on me and said with a slightly raised voice, "You'll tell me *what* later?"

I calmly replied, "Everything."

***

Alice had been put to bed and her parents had returned, so our sitting services were no longer needed. The skies were clearing and the night turned out to be a fairly pleasant one, so I asked Katherine to take a walk with me. We had walked only about twenty feet from the edge of the Yorks' property when she stopped and blurted out, "Well?"

"Well, what?" I replied.

"You said you would tell me everything. So, let's have it," she insisted.

"I'm not really sure where to begin."

"Start from the beginning and end with what it was that you made Alice promise not to tell." I tried to think about what words to use, but she didn't allow me time to think. "You told me that you would tell me, so tell me. We're alone. No one else can hear, so tell me!"

I didn't think. I just spoke. "I traveled in time from over seventy years in the future so that I could be with you."

"What?"

"I've been having difficulty staying in this time the past couple of days and, unfortunately, I traveled back to my own time right in front of Alice. To her, it looked like I disappeared. The night that you found me lying on the ground in your backyard, I had slipped back to my own time. That's why you couldn't find me right away. I have to bury a 1935 penny inside a mason jar in your backyard around ten feet from the base of the big oak tree. I ..."

"What in the world are you talking about? You disappear? Is this what you offer as your reason for not being able to stay in Valley View? Do you think I am that gullible, Mr. Eaton?"

I was in trouble. I knew my story would be hard for her to swallow, but I never really expected her to just dismiss it as a total fabrication. I continued, "Over seventy years from now, I find the photograph that your father took of us in a trunk in the attic of what was *your* house. I looked so happy that I couldn't really believe it was me in the picture. When I found out that it was me, I had to come to 1935 to be with you. I know this all sounds very strange. Well, that's because it is strange! But, it's also very true!"

"True! You don't know the meaning of the word!" she scoffed.

"Katherine, I came here, or I was sent here, to be with you. I love you and I have never said that to anyone else in my entire life. You have to believe me!"

"Why can't you just be honest? Why not just tell me that you're already married to a girl in Philadelphia, or that you're on the run from the police, or whatever the real truth is?"

"I know it's hard to believe! I probably wouldn't believe me either. Can't you see that I didn't want to tell you because I was afraid that you wouldn't believe me?"

In a very businesslike manner she said, "You're right. I don't believe you. Your story is nonsense, Mr. Eaton. Please leave now."

"Katherine, please ... please believe me. You have to help me. If I don't bury the penny tonight I may slip back to my own time and never return. It has to be done! Please!"

She began walking toward her house and I followed her. Without turning her head to look at me she reiterated, "Please leave now, Joseph! Go away!"

"Katherine?" I begged. "Talk to Alice. She'll tell you that she saw me disappear and then reappear again." She started to run toward her front door, so I raised the volume of my voice to be heard. "Talk with

Professor Manning at NYU. He will tell you that everything I said to you is true!"

She stopped and then turned to look at me. With an expressionless face, she said, "Our association is over, Mr. Eaton." She pointed in the direction opposite of her house. "Go, now."

I stared at her hoping to see the look of love return to her face, but it didn't. I just couldn't believe that she was ending our relationship. I had no choice but to leave, though I held out hope that time would change her mind. As I walked away, I heard her fighting tears and knew that there were still feelings for me within her.

Without Katherine's help, I would not be able to bury the penny that night as planned. I thought about waiting until the Whitneys' were all sound asleep, but I didn't even have a shovel to do the job with. I began to devise a plan that I would carry out the next night.

Eleven

Even though Katherine had told me that it was over, I didn't believe her. I knew that I didn't come to 1935 just to win money on horse races and boxing matches. *She* was my reason for being in 1935, of that I was certain.

My confidence in the future of our relationship was made more secure by a dream I had that night. I dreamed that some kind of spirit guide, who appeared to me as merely a thin outline of light, gave me a sneak preview of what my life with Katherine would be like. We were both about twenty-five years older and we lived in an old house by a lake. As if I were a fly on the wall, I watched an older Katherine work on a painting of a sailboat while my older self joyfully played nautical-themed music on the piano to inspire her. It was difficult to say what year it may have been. It may have been the 1960s or the 2030s or some time in between. The lake and the house each had a timeless quality about them that could lie anywhere between never and eternity. At the end of the dream, my older self and Katherine's older self held hands as we walked down to the lake shore to watch the sunset. It was a beautiful dream and it gave me plenty of hope that our love was not as over as she said it was.

When I awoke from the dream, I appeared to be in the same factory that I had either dreamt about, or had physically been in, the night before. I was pretty sure that it was not just another dream. I had time-slipped while sleeping and landed in this damp, cold, and dark place. Harry's neighborhood must have changed into some kind of industrial area at some point after 1935. It was a little unsettling, but it could have been worse. If Harry's family had lived somewhere else, I could have time-slipped into a landfill or a sewage plant. Surprisingly, I had feeling in my body (I must have been there sleeping for a while) and was able to walk around the place. It was very dark, but it appeared as though I was inside a factory that built wooden furniture. There were piles of wood near a lathe with each individual piece marked where cuts would be made. A few nearly finished products were nearby that may have just needed painting or sanding. While investigating the factory further, I tripped the alarm sensors and the resulting flashing lights and sirens made the place look like a discothèque. I was very thankful when the numbness set in and I slipped back to 1935 before the police arrived.

Unfortunately, since I had roamed around the building in the future, I did not reappear in my bed when I got back to 1935. Instead, I found myself in Harry's parents' bedroom. I shivered on the floor as I regained my senses. When I stood up, Harry's father saw me and sat up in his bed. He was still half asleep when he asked, "What do you want, boy?"

"Nothing," I replied while gasping for air, "it's just a dream. Go back to sleep." With that, he passed gas and then slipped back under the covers. I crept back to my bed in Harry's room and did not have any other time-slip incidents during the night.

TIME CALL

***

It was a sunny and warm Wednesday morning. I woke up extremely sore from the beating I took the day before and also from spending an unknown amount of time on a hard factory floor. I had secured Harry's car for later that evening and I packed it with a shovel that I borrowed from his father's toolshed and a mason jar that I stole from his mother's cupboard. I really wanted to skip work that day and find a safe place to do my time-slipping, but I still needed to make as much money as possible. Even the small amount they were paying me was better than the nothing I would have received for not showing up for work at all. I decided to go to my job and do my best to deal with any time-slip incidents as they came.

I had allowed myself enough time to not only walk to work at a leisurely pace, but I also had enough time to enjoy a quick breakfast from the Dempsey kitchen. Mrs. Dempsey asked when I would be painting her fence, and she held my breakfast bowl hostage until I had an answer for her. While she held the bowl away from me at arm's length, I told her that I would try to get to the fence on the weekend, and if I didn't, I would pay someone else to paint it the following week. This answer satisfied her and she handed me my breakfast. She even patted me on the head, though it may have been more like a light smack. The old-fashioned oatmeal with a little cream and butter really hit the spot and was easy chewing for my sore mouth.

It was a pleasant walk to work and I was in a good mood despite the fact that I was in emotional pain from being dumped the night before by the love of my life, and I was in physical pain from getting beat up by my rival. The temperature was above normal and I felt warm, but it was an energizing kind of warmth. I felt like a flower that had been out of the sun for far too long. I didn't know why, but, despite the disasters of the previous day, I felt more determined than ever to make a life for myself in 1935. I just knew that somehow everything would work out and Katherine and I would end up together. While I walked, I came up with an idea to acquire more money to bet on the boxing match with. I would ask my boss for an advance.

As soon as Mr. Potato Head wrapped up his daily pep talk, I asked for an advance in pay. As expected, it didn't go over well.

"An advance? I don't know, Joseph. Even the most seasoned employees would likely be turned down for an advance in pay," he said with candor while picking debris out of his ear.

"Mr. Potters Head," I broke his name up into two words so that I wouldn't mispronounce it, "I realize that an advance in pay is likely against company policy, but I was hoping the company would make an exception." I made full eye contact and with my best expression of innocence I continued, "You see, sir, I must find a new place to live. Right now I'm living with relatives in town, but they can no longer afford to feed me and keep a roof over my head. I'm afraid that without an advance in pay I will end up on the street. It is extremely difficult to find a decent and permanent place to live on only a dollar a day. I will sell some policies next week when I am on my own, I'm sure of it. Ask Sam Lerner and he'll tell you that I am good for it and that I show a lot of promise." I was sure that my sob story had pulled on his heartstrings.

Mr. Potato Head sighed and I expected him to say that he would do what he could do for me. Instead, he said, "Toughen up, Eaton! This is a harsh world and it will eat you for breakfast if you let it. You have to fight for what you want. Look at that guy ... what's his name ... the boxer that's fighting for the heavyweight title."

"You mean Braddock?"

"Yes, James J. Braddock. Now there's a man! He had to literally fight his way from the bottom to the top and now he's fighting for the title. Of course he has no chance to win, but you have to admire the man for how far he's come."

A light switch turned on in my head and I said, "I'm going to the match tomorrow, can I place a wager for you?"

"Well, I'm not really a betting man and the wife would have my head if I were to lose," he said sheepishly.

I playfully elbowed him in the ribs and noted, "You said yourself that Braddock has no chance to win. Why not make a little money for his pain?" Wow, I really was a salesman!

He replied with uncertainty, "You think so?" I had him hooked. Now all I had to do was reel him in.

"Of course! Hey, those guys make a bundle whether they win *or* lose. Why not make some money for yourself?"

I had him! He reached into his pocket and pulled out his wallet. I expected him to remove a five or at best a ten. Instead, he handed me five twenty-dollar bills! "Here's a hundred. Put it on Baer for me." Then he put his hand firmly on my shoulder, peered around to make sure no one was within earshot, and said, "Do me a favor and don't tell anyone about this, okay?"

I was in shock. The guy had trusted me to place a one-hundred-dollar bet for him. Despite his trust, I had no intention of placing the bet on Max Baer. I would be placing every bit of money in my possession on James J. Braddock to win the heavyweight title. Mr. Potato Head would simply think that he lost the bet. With that kind of money to bet with I didn't need an advance in pay. I just hoped that I had my facts correct and that Braddock would really be the winner of the fight. "Y-y-yes, sir. I will place the bet tomorrow and nobody will know anything about it."

"Good boy! Now go out there and sell some policies!" he barked, with a pump of his fist.

When I exited the room, Jack Whitney and I caught sight of each other in the hallway. I knew for sure that he didn't like me and I was reasonably sure that he would never like me no matter what I did or said. I was surprised when he smiled at me and uttered, "Joseph, come see me in my office," as he passed by.

Jack Whitney's office was not very fancy. It was smaller than would have been expected, especially for someone in his position, and it was completely undecorated. There was a desk in the middle of the room with papers scattered all over it and a filing cabinet just behind the desk situated so that the cabinet's drawers would not interfere with the desk's drawers. A small wheeled table with a typewriter stationed on it leaned against the wall. Besides Jack's far from luxurious desk chair, the only other place to sit was a three-legged stool that was shoved under the table. I pulled out the stool, sat on it, and was ready for a man-to-man talk.

"What are you doing?" Jack questioned.

"I'm sitting. Didn't you want to talk with me?"

"No. I just wanted to give you this." He reached behind his filing cabinet and produced a paper bag that contained my stained and formerly soaking wet suit that I had left at his house the night before. He took the suit out of the bag, rolled it into a ball, and tossed it to me. "Katherine doesn't want to see you anymore, so don't come by the house tonight. I told you! I knew she would eventually come to her senses!"

I said nothing. I just got up from the stool and walked out of his office. As I was leaving he added, "Oh, and one more thing." I stopped to listen. "If you screw up anything at all around here, even the minutest detail, I will see to it that your employment will come to an abrupt end."

I was angry, but I had nothing to say to the man except for, "Is that all?"

"No ..." he paused and then put on a giant fake smile and snickered, "Enjoy your day!" I knew the man was glad that I was, at least temporarily, out of his daughter's life, but did he have to be such a jackass about it?

**

I was, once again, teamed up with Sam Lerner and it was another adventurous day of selling life insurance. After taking mental notes on Sam's smooth approach, I deemed myself ready to try and sell a policy on my own. As we walked toward the next house on the block, I asked Sam if I could give it a try alone.

"You really think you're ready, Joseph?"

"Yeah, as long as they don't have a big dog I'll be able to keep my composure. What do you think?"

"Go ahead. I'll just watch from the street. Good luck."

The door was answered by a woman with gray-streaked hair who was wearing a very tight and low cut dress. She looked as though she might have been quite beautiful in her youth, but at that point in her life she was just trying to hide her age in a sexy dress. With a sultry voice she said, "Yes, what can I do for you?"

"Yes, ma'am." I went into my spiel about the benefits of a policy with Smith and Cooper Casualty and Life and I ended with, "Can I sign you up?"

"Well, I don't know … Why don't you come in, Mister? …"

I walked into her house and noticed that it was very sparsely furnished and that there was an overall look of incompleteness to it. "Eaton. My name is Joseph Eaton," I said.

She extended her hand in a very graceful manner and I shook it. "Hello, Mr. Eaton, I am Mrs. Harrison." She batted her overdone-with-mascara eyes at me. "I'm new in town, Mr. Eaton. As you can see, I've just recently moved in." She waved her hand toward the empty spaces in her home as if she were presenting them as a showcase on *The Price is Right*. "I truthfully don't think that life insurance interests me at this time."

I continued my spiel, "Well, ma'am, might I say that you cannot afford to NOT be interested in life insurance in this day and age with the rising costs of a proper funeral and all. Perhaps your husband would be more interested. When might he be at home?"

"My husband passed away last year. I guess I am an unmarried woman, Mr. Eaton." She sounded as though she was about to cry, but she restrained herself. "How about you, are you married?" She batted her eyes at me again and I believed that she was attempting to flirt with me, but she seemed uncomfortable about it.

I was uncomfortable about it too. I didn't want to deal with a still-grieving widow, who appeared to be looking for a new husband, on my first solo attempt at a sale. "Yes, I've been married for five fantastic years," I lied. At that point I was no longer interested in making a sale. I just wanted to get out of there. "I'm sorry to have bothered you, ma'am. I'll just be on my way."

I headed for the door, but she continued talking to me. "You know, we bought this house just before Roger died. I could have moved in a long time ago, but … I just wasn't ready."

The poor woman clearly needed someone to talk to. For some reason I felt obliged to be that someone. "Did you have any kids?"

"No. We were never blessed with children. Roger really wanted a family, though. We talked about adopting children, and we were going to look into it after we moved into this house, but of course that never happened. Why don't you sit, Mr. Eaton?"

I sat on what looked like a dining room chair, and she sat on the only other piece of furniture in the room, a loveseat. "If you don't mind me asking, how did your husband die?"

"He worked in construction, and one day while working on a new building in the city, the scaffolding he was standing on collapsed. I was told that he died instantly."

"Did he have insurance? Please know that I'm not trying to sell you anything right now. I'm just curious."

"Yes, he had a small policy, and I will be able to live on it for a while longer, but eventually I will have to go back to work." She cried and continued, "I really miss him! I just know that our lives would have been wonderful here in this house. We would have adopted a child or two and this house would have been filled with laughter instead of these tears."

While she spoke, I studied her more closely and decided that she was not as old as I originally thought. In fact, she may not have been much older than I was. Apparently, her grief had turned her hair prematurely gray. "You can still adopt a child, can't you?" I asked.

"I don't think they would give a child to an unmarried woman," she scoffed.

"Why not?" I barked back.

"A single woman who will eventually have to go back to work? I don't think so."

"Well, you'll never know unless you try."

"That's a nice thought, Mr. Eaton, but who would care for the children while I was at work?"

"Your parents can help if they are still with you. Also, if you have brothers or sisters they could help too. Maybe you will meet some nice neighbors that would pitch in as well."

"That's a lot to ask of my family and friends. I don't think I could do that. They have had to put up with so much from me in the past year as it is."

"Well, ask them first. If they say they can help, then do it. Someone once said that "it takes a village to raise a child" anyway. Why don't you try and raise one in your village? No one ever has to raise a child alone." She got up off of the loveseat and hugged me. As she did, I noticed that Sam was peering through the window at us and he was laughing.

Through tears, Mrs. Harrison said, "Maybe I will try, Mr. Eaton. Thank you for listening. And if I ever do decide to buy life insurance, I will surely call you first." I left her my calling card and wished her luck as I exited.

"What happened in there?" Sam hooted as we walked toward the next house.

"Nothing happened. She's just a lonely widow who misses her husband, that's all," I explained.

"She was all dolled up and she had a nice chassis, but from what I could see, she was a real face stretcher. I'll bet in her day she was a choice piece of calico, though. It looked like she thought *you* were the bee's knees!" He laughed hysterically. "I guess you were even better than you thought you would be on your first attempt at a sale!" He continued laughing uncontrollably, as if he were being tickled.

"She was new in town and she just needed someone to talk to. She was a nice woman," I continued to explain.

"Hey, well you're new in town too. Maybe the two of you could get together?"

"No thanks," I said with confidence. "There's only one girl for me."

***

I made it through the entire workday without anyone seeing me time-slip. There were two incidents that day. In the first, I time-slipped into an empty dumpster while Sam was in the bathroom of a potential customer's house. The customer was in her kitchen fixing us lemonade and didn't see me disappear or reappear. When she re-entered her living-room with a tray of drinks, the woman yelled at me for getting dirt and grime all over her couch, but was perplexed as to how I had managed to keep her carpet clean.

In the second incident, I could have been seriously injured. While walking through a vacant lot during the tail end of my lunch break, I time-slipped into a road project that had closed what would have been a busy street. The crew was on a break after finishing paving the street and they didn't see me slip in or out. When I met back up with Sam after lunch, it was difficult to explain why I had dark and wet asphalt on my suit. Time-slipping was becoming more and more of a problem, but I had to accept the fact that it could happen again at any moment.

After work I stopped at the cleaners to drop off the filthy and wrinkled suit that Jack Whitney had returned to me earlier in the day. I wished I could have given them the suit I was wearing as well, but I didn't have any other clothes with me to change into.

Since I had over one hundred bucks on me, I decided I would treat myself to a nice dinner. Once again, I happened upon Aunt Shirley's diner and I just couldn't resist the temptation to walk in. Aunt Shirley recognized me as the man who overpaid for a cup of coffee and she had difficulty holding back her laughter.

"Good evenin', sir. Tonight's special is pot roast with gravy, red cabbage, and yams," she couldn't contain her cackle anymore and spit out, "All for only fifteen dollars!"

"Yeah, yeah, very funny," I acquiesced. "Actually, the special sounds good. Bring me a fresh glass of water too. Oh, and also, bring me some slices of bologna."

"Just slices? No bread?" she questioned.

"Yes, that's right, no bread," I confirmed.

Aunt Shirley looked at me as if I belonged in the loony bin. She then shrugged her shoulders and grinned, "Comin' right up, sir."

I heard a familiar voice a few tables away and saw a man that, from behind, looked like Professor Manning. I got up from my table and walked over to the man and saw that he was dining with a woman and a young boy.

"Excuse me." I tapped the man on the shoulder and when he turned around I could see that it was indeed the professor. He looked as though he had been through a fire as one of his ears was puffy red and his hair and eyebrows were singed.

"Joseph! Fancy meeting you here. I'd like you to meet my wife Martha and my son Reginald."

"How do you do, ma'am," I bowed slightly to the professor's wife then extended my hand to his son. "Nice to meet you too, Reginald."

Professor Manning winked at me and then smiled at his wife and gushed, "Honey, this is the man from the future I told you about!"

I was lucky that I wasn't eating anything because I would have choked on it. "Umm, Professor, can I talk to you in private for a moment?"

He got up off of his chair, finished chewing and swallowing his food, and then followed me to the back of the restaurant chuckling all the way.

"I thought I told you that I didn't want anyone else to know about me, Professor," I whispered in as angry of a tone as I could.

"I share everything with my family, Joseph," he said in his normal speaking voice. "Don't worry," he assured, "my wife doesn't believe it anyway."

"And what about your son?"

"Oh, he's just a small boy. He believes in Santa Claus too. You needn't worry about him."

I shook my head and said, "Well, I don't know." I got another glimpse at the burns on his face and asked, "By the way, what happened? Something blow up in the lab?"

"Yes, as a matter of fact. I tried to recreate your time-travel method and I nearly set the whole school ablaze."

"How did you manage that?"

"Well, I used the electrical generator in the lab to generate as much electricity as I possibly could. I connected the generator to a telephone and held the receiver up to my ear and then ..."

"It blew up?" I said.

"It blew up," he grimly repeated. With an optimistic tone he continued, "But that was only my first attempt. I am borrowing a much more powerful generator from another school for my second trial. I need you to find out exactly which model telephone you used."

"Hold on, Professor. Maybe you should use an inanimate object for your next attempt. Better yet, don't make another attempt at all. I'd really hate to see you get seriously hurt."

"Don't you want to know how you got here? Maybe if we can figure out how you got here, we can devise a way to keep you from slipping back to your own time. Don't you want that? Don't you want to stay with your sweetheart forever?"

"Of course I do, Professor. Unfortunately, at the moment she doesn't even want to see me. Forget about forever and ever."

"You two have a quarrel?"

"Yeah, I guess you could say that. I told her the truth about me and she didn't believe a word of it."

"Did you tell her about the clothing and what we found in the lab?"

"I tried to, but she told me to leave and never come back."

"What are you going to do?"

"Well, maybe you could talk to her and explain everything. If a genuine scientist were to tell her the validity of my story, then maybe she would believe it."

"I'll do it if you think it will help, Joseph," he offered.

"I certainly don't think it would hurt. When can you talk to her? Can you do it tonight?" I begged.

"Give me the address and I'll go and have a talk with her tomorrow."

I wrote down Katherine's address on a napkin and handed it to the professor. "Please talk to her and try to explain ..." As soon as the words left my mouth, I began to go into the deep freeze. I had started to time-slip right in front of Professor Manning. I noticed a look of concern in his face as I slumped to the carpet. I'm sure that my disappearance changed his expression from concern to amazement, but I wasn't there to witness that facial transformation.

In the blink of an eye, I found myself on a tiled floor and the professor had been replaced by a tall shelf. On the bottom of this shelf were stacks of bar soap of a brand that I had never heard of. I began to get some feeling back in my neck and was able to roll my head in the opposite direction. There I saw another tall shelf that contained cans of baked beans of a brand that I was also unfamiliar with. As I continued to defrost, I became more and more able to observe my surroundings and I noticed I was in an aisle of shelves that contained all different kinds of items ranging from toothpaste to candles to kite string. I had time-slipped into some kind of dollar store. It appeared that the store was closed for the night, as I heard and saw no one. I hoped that no one had heard or saw me either. Just as I was about ready to push myself up off the floor, I started to slip back.

Professor Manning's face was practically white when I reappeared and his mouth was wide open in awe. He spoke to me, or at least I saw his lips move, but I was not yet able to hear him. After a few moments, my hearing began to return and I heard him say, "… n't completely believe it until I saw it! Joseph, this is absolutely incredible! Are you okay? Can you get up?"

With a frozen tongue I said, "Give me a moment."

"Yes, of course. Do you need help?" he offered.

My circulatory system had restarted and I was able to move my arms and legs again. "You can help me up." He pulled my arms and with his help I was able to stand again, albeit unsteadily. With a mouth that felt more like my own, I asked, "What did it look like when I left?"

"You just slowly faded into a light frozen mist."

"Did anyone else see?"

"No. No one saw you but me. You were only gone for about ten seconds. Where did you go?"

"I guess I was in my own time. Aunt Shirley's restaurant becomes a dollar store in the future."

"A dollar store? What's that?"

"It's a store where all different kinds of junk cost only a dollar."

"Why would you spend a whole dollar on something if it is junk to begin with?"

Unwilling to attempt an explanation about the inflation of the dollar, I said, "I don't know. People will buy anything, I guess." I was more interested in the professor's opinion about my time-travel experience. "So, now that you have seen it for yourself, do you have any new theories as to why I keep slipping back to my own time?"

"Well, have you buried the penny by the tree like you said you would?"

"No. I couldn't go back to Katherine's house last night after being told to leave. Besides, I didn't even have a shovel or a jar. Tonight I will be more prepared. I have everything I need packed in my grandfather's car."

"Joseph, I truly believe you will continue to be untethered in time until you bury that coin. You must do it tonight or risk never making it back here!"

"I will, Professor. Tonight is definitely the night." Aunt Shirley brought out a dinner plate and placed it on my table, but I wanted to make sure that the professor would do as I had asked before I left him. "You have Katherine's address, right?"

"Yes."

"And you will visit her tomorrow, right?"

"Yes, Joseph."

"Okay. Thanks for everything, Professor." Once again, I observed the burns on his face and his ear and added, "And don't do any more experiments! I've really started to believe that science had very little to do with why I'm here anyway." I acknowledged the professor's wife and child on my way back to my table and then sat down and ate a delicious home-cooked-style meal that cost less than a dollar.

When I had finished eating, I realized that I had no place to go until much later that night. Fearing that his mother would put me to work, I decided that I wouldn't go back to Harry's house until I knew he would be home and ready to lend me his car. I chose to kill the time walking around the streets of Valley View, hoping to enjoy some pre-WWII Americana.

As usual in this time, the people I passed on the streets were friendly and graciously acknowledged my presence. I had learned the proper way to acknowledge women (tipping my cap with a slight bow) and other men (a firm nod while making good eye contact). In my own time, I always felt like an outsider or an outcast and I never really fit in anywhere, but I didn't feel that way here.

There was no need to drink away the pain of Katherine telling me to leave, which I would surely have done had I met and lost her in my own time. It had been less than a month since I had done precisely that.

When Laura left me, I was truly alone for the first time in my life and I really didn't know how to handle my self-imposed isolation. I had been sober for a long time before she left and, even though I never loved her, I felt that she was the glue that kept me from breaking apart. For some reason, I believed that her presence was an absolute necessity if I wanted to hold on to my sobriety and my sanity. It was not the best base for a relationship, but it was less dysfunctional than some other relationships I had been exposed to. Fortunately, I knew it was not a good enough foundation for a marriage. Laura, however, didn't agree and I was sure that she left more because I had no intention of marrying her than because I didn't love her. When she left, I needed to find a way to keep my own sanity. After a week off of the wagon, I realized that excessive drinking was not helping me any. That was when I decided that a little dose of family was what I needed and I gave Margo a call.

The warm day led to a hazy night that created a picturesque sunset. On my walk, I stopped in front of a barbershop that had not yet closed for the night. The men inside were talking about the events of the day and the prize fight that would take place the following day. I thought seriously about getting a haircut that would give my hair a style more appropriate for the times, but changed my mind and decided to put that off for another day.

I passed a butcher shop, a five-and-dime store, and a shoe repair shop. They were all closed for the night. The drug store was still open for business so I stopped in for some supplies and I made sure to get more Life Savers for Alice. Every other shop nearby was closed as the time approached seven o'clock p.m. There were small signs of life at the end of the street and, after walking in that direction, I realized I was in front of the bar that Harry frequented. Noticing his car parked in front, I went in to spend some quality time with my grandfather.

The pub was empty with the exception of Harry and a few rummies that were likely regulars. I hopped up on the barstool and requested two beers, one for me and one for Harry. Harry turned and greeted me with the same smile that he used to greet me with when I was a little boy. He held up his mug of beer and said, "Cheers!"

"Cheers," I replied as we clinked our mugs together.

"So, when are you going to tell me where you're going tonight?" I didn't answer. "I see you put the old man's shovel and one of my mother's jars under a sack in the back of my car. What do you plan on doing with them?"

"Harry, I really want to tell you, but I can't."

"Is your scientist friend having you do some kind of experiment for him?"

He gave me an out that I couldn't ignore. "Yeah … yeah, that's it. It's kind of a secret, though, so I can't tell you any more about it."

He accepted the fact that I wasn't going to tell him, but added, "If you ask me, that guy's batty. He'll get you into all kinds of trouble if you let him."

I grinned and looked him straight in the eye. "What about you? Don't you think I'll eventually get myself into trouble simply by associating with you?"

Harry laughed hard and quipped, "You got me there!" He then downed the rest of his beer, lit up a cigarette, and yelled to the bartender, "Barkeep, two more beers." We drank another round after that and talked about life, work, and women. It was different than the time we spent playing catch a few days before when I was still in awe at being in the presence of my grandfather as a young man. The night at the bar we were more like two men on the same level talking and figuring out our way through life. I treasured the hours I spent with him that night at least as much as the time we spent having our catch.

***

I parked Harry's loud car in a non-residential area a few blocks away from the Whitney house and traveled the rest of the way on foot. It was about two o'clock a.m. and I was worried that I would wake the entire neighborhood with each accidental clank of the shovel against the jar or each banging of the jar against the Eveready flashlight that I used to light my way. Fortunately, I didn't make enough noise to disturb the tranquility of the street. There were no lights on in the Whitney house, so I deemed the coast to be clear. I walked to the east side of the house and carefully dropped the shovel over the fence. I then gently dropped the jar in a different spot so that it would land on soft grass and not hit the shovel. Once I had hooked the flashlight on the opposite side of the fence using its convenient ring, all that was left was for me to go over. I climbed about halfway up, positioned my right foot on top of the fence, and then hoisted myself up and over.

Before time-traveling to 1935, it had been quite a while since I had last hopped a fence, but backed by my recent experience, I landed like a pro. I pressed the *ON* button on the flashlight and navigated my way to a spot about ten feet from the big oak tree's trunk with shovel, jar, and penny in tow. I drew an imaginary line between the tree and the kitchen window and tried to remember approximately where I had unearthed the penny in my own time. Bowing in reverence to the big tree, I thanked it for its part in bringing me to Katherine and then put shovel to ground and attempted to dig.

I had barely made a dent in the grass when I heard the faint sound of a dog growling. At first, I thought it may have come from another yard in the neighborhood, but as the volume of the growls grew, I realized they came from King, the Whitneys' colossal St. Bernard, and he was only ten feet away. He continued to growl and it got louder and louder with each slow step he took toward me. When he was about arm's length away, he leaped at me. I calmly thanked Sam Lerner for preparing me for the moment and pulled out of my pocket the slices of bologna that I had ordered with dinner. I shoved the slices of meat in King's face to divert his attention and then held them in my open hand for him to accept as a token of our newfound friendship. He sniffed my hand and the bologna for quite a long while. Finally, he came to a decision. He sat like a good dog should and just when I thought he was going to be my pal, he leaped toward me like a frog with a vengeance. A head fake to my right made him change his jump in mid-air toward that direction. I ran as fast as I could while he chased me around the backyard and he barked louder with each stride he took. I was amazed that the entire Whitney family had not been jarred awake by the commotion.

While being chased, I continued to fake out the big bear of a dog. I made a move and headed for the fence on the west end of the property and prayed that I would be able to leap over it as swiftly as I had done days before. After one last head fake to my right, I jumped on the fence. This time King did not fall for my false move. Apparently, the animal was smarter than I had given him credit for and after being fooled a number of times had learned to ignore the head fakes. He knocked me off the fence with his tremendous snout and pinned me to the ground. I felt relieved when I saw a man from the other side of the fence shining a flashlight in my direction.

"Good boy, King, good boy," the man said in a familiar voice. To my dismay, I discovered my savior was Freddy York. He jumped over the fence and saw that King had captured his arch enemy. He flashed the light in my face and croaked, "Eaton? What the hell are you doing here?"

"Nothing, just call off the dog, will ya?" My face was covered in dog drool and I was afraid to move the muscles necessary to wipe the slobber away.

"I called the police, you know. They will be here any minute." He laughed and shook his head, "I warned you to stay away from Katherine. Even King here knows that she belongs to me, don't you, boy." He patted the giant creature on the head which caused even more drool to drop on me. "Oh, and just in case you weren't informed, I asked Mr. Whitney's permission to marry his daughter and he gave it. We are having an engagement party this Friday. It's quite a pity that you won't be able to attend. I guess you'll be too busy breaking up rocks or making license plates."

"She'll never marry you, Freddy! She'd rather marry King here than you." The dog then gritted his teeth and shot another menacing growl at me.

"We'll just see about that. Maybe I should have King rip you to pieces. What would you say to that?"

"Call the dog off, Freddy!" I demanded. King barked at me with each spoken word.

"I'll call him off when the police arrive." We could hear the cry of the police car siren as it entered the neighborhood. "… And here they are."

Jack Whitney stormed out of the front door of his house still wearing his long nightshirt. "What in the hell is going on here? Who called the police?" he bellowed.

Freddy called his attention to our position. "Over here, Jack. King has caught an intruder!"

Mr. Whitney opened up the lock on the gate and entered his backyard. "Who is that?"

I tried to speak, but the dog's bark drowned me out. Freddy replied smartly, "It's Eaton. He was prowling around your property. I heard King barking so I called the police."

Jack Whitney looked at me cowering under his mountain of a dog. "What in hell are you doing here? It's the middle of the night, boy!" Again, I tried to speak only to be drowned out by the dog. "Let him up!" he commanded, but King did not do as he was told. Jack Whitney pointed to the other side of his yard and hollered, "King, go!" The dog obediently did as his master commanded and I was then able to get to my feet.

"Thank you," I said.

Jack Whitney's sleep had been interrupted and he was in no mood for any nonsense. "Boy, you've got some real explaining to do and you better do it fast. What in the world are you doing here in the middle of the night?"

I had no explanation that anyone, with the exception of Professor Manning, would believe. I opened my mouth to speak in my defense, but nothing came out. Freddy shouted from thirty feet away, "He brought a shovel. It looks like he was digging for something!"

"Digging for something? What were you digging for? There's nothing of value buried in this yard. Explain yourself!" I wanted to tell Jack the whole story, but I knew that the truth would only make matters worse so I said nothing.

Two police officers arrived at the scene. After consulting with Freddy, the taller of the two cops asked Jack Whitney, "What do you want us to do with him?"

He didn't hesitate to answer. "Send him to jail!"

The other officer asked, "What do you want us to charge him with?"

"Charge him with trespassing and criminal mischief." The shorter cop then handcuffed me and led me out the gate toward the front of the house.

Katherine, who was standing at the front door with her mother, cried, "Father, no!" when she saw that it was me the police were taking away.

Mr. Whitney screamed at his wife and pointed, "Take her inside!"

Katherine continued to scream from inside the house as I was led to the police car. A crowd of curious onlookers in their pajamas were present to watch as I was put into the car and driven away. Apparently, I ended up waking the entire neighborhood after all.

Twelve

The Valley View Police Station looked pretty much like how one would expect a police station in a small town to look. There was an old wooden desk that was covered with police files that appeared to be in different stages of disarray. The corner of the room contained two dusty filing cabinets and a locker that may have been used for storing weapons. On the wall hung a huge photo of President Franklin D. Roosevelt, a banner which contained the official New York State seal, and, for some reason, a painting of Charlie Chaplin.

After being booked, I was led to a stale and smelly holding cell, which was the only one in the station. My cuffs were removed and then the steel cell door was slammed shut and locked behind me. It was certainly not my first time in jail, but it was the first time I had been sent to jail while sober.

The cell contained nothing except for a small sink, a rickety chair, and two bunks that were attached to the wall — one atop the other. If I needed to use the toilet, I would have to either utilize the sink for that task or ask the guard to be let out. At least I was alone, but I wished I had been drunk, as it would have made falling asleep easier. "When do I get my phone call?" I asked Officer Schmitt.

"In the morning," he replied. "We don't want you waking up any more people tonight," he snickered. "Why don't you just lay back on your bunk and sleep? Pretend you're a guest at a nice hotel."

I did as he said and tried to sleep. I laid on my back and wondered how I could possibly have screwed up something as simple as burying a jar so badly. I managed a smile thinking that if this arrest had been in my own time, it would have been my third strike and I would have been in for some real trouble. After some serious Zen and self-hypnosis, I managed to drift off to sleep.

I was only asleep for a short time when I was jarred awake by the sound of the cell door opening. I was getting a roommate for the night and I wasn't happy about it. Officer Schmitt bellowed, "Eaton, you're gonna hafta move to the top bunk. This rummy is too plastered to hop up there." I recognized my new bunkmate as one of the regulars from Harry's favorite pub. As a result of his public drunkenness, he was a frequent guest of the Valley View Police Department. I could relate, so I climbed up to the top bunk without being asked twice. The intoxicated man sat down on the lower bunk and hung his head. He was asleep even before the police guard could place him in a horizontal position. The cell door slammed shut signaling the end of the hullabaloo.

I settled in and attempted self-hypnosis again, but this time it didn't work. Next, I tried taking deep and relaxing breaths, but that didn't work either. I was no longer able to sleep, and to make matters worse, my bunkmate snored so loudly that it made the cell bars vibrate resulting in a humming sensation that sounded like a tuning fork. I tossed and turned and tried counting backward from one hundred, but I just couldn't fall back asleep. I was beginning to realize how grave my situation could become. What if they never let me out of here? Would Katherine really marry Freddy?

My head was spinning so I hopped down to the floor and walked over to the sink. The cold water that I splashed myself with made me even more awake and alert. Not wanting to climb back up to my bunk, I sat on the old rickety chair and watched the town drunk sleep. He snored with each breath he took, but he looked so very peaceful. I was alarmed when he opened his eyes and caught me gazing at him.

"What do you want?" he growled. "Ain't you ever seen a man sleep before?"

"I'm sorry, I couldn't sleep. I didn't mean to disturb you. I had nothing else better to do so I figured I would watch you sleep." Immediately after I finished speaking, I began to get cold and I started to time-slip. If I wasn't so worried about never coming back to 1935, I would have been delighted to time-slip right out of jail. It was then my cellmate's turn to stare at me as I fell off the chair and faded out right in front of his eyes.

When I was able to open my eyes again, I was alarmed to see what appeared to be an Asian man ready to attack me with some kind of martial arts kick. I tried to move, but my body was still frozen from the time-slip. While I was still in fear for my life, my eyes began to focus better and I was relieved to see that my attacker was actually a life-sized poster of a martial arts master in a kicking pose with a menacing look on his face. As my body thawed, I could feel that I was lying on some kind of cushioned mat. I slowly began to realize that I had time-slipped into a martial arts school. Luckily for me it was the middle of the night and the school was empty of punching and kicking youngsters. I was extremely thankful that their instructor was not present either.

When I was sufficiently thawed and able to walk again, I got up off the mat and explored. I noticed that I was in the rear of the building. No bells or whistles sounded from my movements, so I was reasonably sure that the place did not have a motion sensor alarm. Hoping to find an unlocked door, I walked to the front of the building. The reverse of the white silk-screened sign on the front window told me that I was in Sagong's Tae Kwon Do Academy. I looked outside and noticed a few parked cars that were definitely not from 1935 and knew that I was back in my own time again. I pondered breaking the lock or the window to be set free, but, while thinking about it, I began to time-slip back.

When I was able to see again, I found that I was back in the police station but no longer in the holding cell that I had occupied just a short while before. Officer Schmitt spotted me just as I had regained the full use of my body. He was not very happy to see me out of my cell. "Eaton, what in blazes are you doing out here? How did you get out?" Before I could answer, he ran in my direction, grabbed me by the collar, and started to drag me back toward the cell. "Don't give me any trouble or I'll smash you with this." He held out his nightstick to show me what he would hit me with if I put up any resistance. He opened the cell door, shoved me in, and then locked it again. The inspection he gave the locked door and bars of the cell yielded no clues as to my escape. "I don't know how you did it, but if I find you out of here again tonight you'll get what's coming to you." I was glad that he didn't press me for an answer, as the truth may have netted me padded walls instead of bars.

Worried that I might time-slip out of my cell again and feel the wrath of Officer Schmitt, I decided that I had better sleep on the floor in the middle of the cell. I measured the distance in feet (my own feet) from the center of the cell to the bars. That way, if I time-slipped again, I would know how far I could move and still be within the confines of the cell when I time-slipped back. My cellmate, a little less drunk at this point, looked at me like I was crazy. With the safe zone measurements in my mind, I curled up in a ball on the floor in the middle of the cell and went to sleep. I was pretty sure that I time-slipped to the tae kwon do academy at least one more time during that night because the pain in my pelvis from lying on the hard floor was relieved for a short while, as if I had been lying on a cushioned mat.

***

"Wake up, you lousy thievin' bastard! It's time for your phone call!"

I awoke and looked up at the police guard. He was a different officer from the last one I had seen (the other one's shift must have ended). His name tag identified him as Officer Walsh and he wore the standard navy blue uniform with copper buttons. He had sandy-colored hair and a bushy moustache that contained a small piece of his breakfast. I was still lying on the floor in the middle of the cell and my body was in pain from spending the night there. "What time is it?" I asked.

"It's nearly eight a.m." Officer Walsh replied in a slight brogue, and it made me wonder why so many policemen were Irish during this era. "Get up now! Let's go!"

I stood up and dusted my clothes off. "Can you take me to the toilet first? I've got to pee."

"All right," he said with contempt. "Get yer lazy behind moving, you slothful bastard." He led me to the bathroom, and while I relieved myself I thought about whom I should call. My first instinct was to call Mr. Potato Head and tell him that I'd be late for work. Then I thought about calling Harry or his mother, they must have been wondering where I was. No, I knew Professor Manning was the one I should call, but I wondered if it was too early to call him at his lab. I didn't have a home telephone number for him and I wasn't even sure where he lived. I was barely finished when the guard dragged me out. "That's enough," he said as he grabbed me and then yanked my arm half out of its socket.

"I can't wash my hands?" I objected.

The officer laughed and spouted back with sarcasm, "You can wash your hands later when the Queen arrives." He pushed me toward the telephone and picked up the receiver. "What number do you want me to dial?" he asked.

"That depends," I replied.

"On what?"

"Do I get another shot at it if the person I'm trying to reach isn't there?"

"Just who do you want to call, Eaton?" he asked in anger.

"I want to call Professor Manning. He is a teacher at the university. I have the phone number to his lab, but I don't know if he's there yet."

"Just give me the number and I'll call," he said impatiently.

"If he doesn't answer, can we try to call him at home — maybe look up his number?" I asked with desperation.

"We'll see. Give me the number!" He dialed the number I gave him and then shoved the phone's receiver in my hand.

"Pick up, pick up," I grumbled aloud.

"*Hello?*" The relief I felt at hearing the professor's voice was immeasurable.

"Professor, this is Joseph Eaton. I need a favor, a really big favor ..." I explained that I was in jail and that I might need him to come and bail me out, though, to my knowledge, no bail had been set. He said he would be down to help me as soon as he could.

I was placed back in my cell and discovered that my cellmate had been released. How the town drunk was let loose on Valley View before I was, I'll never know. With nothing to do, I played solitaire with a deck of cards that I borrowed from one of the officers. After an hour or so of not winning any hands, I was told there was someone there to see me.

I assumed my visitor was going to be the professor, but I was pleasantly surprised to see it was Katherine. Her eyes were somewhat swollen, perhaps she had been crying over me. She was dressed in a gray linen suit with a long fitted skirt that flared at the hem and her hair was wrapped in a tight bun. She dressed like she meant business and she did. I offered her a seat on the lower bunk and she accepted.

"Katherine, I can't believe you're here. You have no idea how glad I am to see you. Can you get me out of here?"

In a very professional tone she replied, "Father will drop the charges against you if you agree to a few things."

"What things? I'll agree to anything that will keep us together."

She swallowed hard and said, "You must agree to leave town and never see me again." She tried to keep her serious tone, but the words *never see me again* made her shed a light tear that slowly rolled down her cheek. She regained her composure and refused to wipe the tear, letting it roll unimpeded down her beautiful face. "You must also agree to never set foot on our property again for as long as you live."

"Katherine, you can't possibly expect me to agree to that. Don't let Freddy win. He thinks that the two of you are getting engaged. You're not really going to marry him, are you?"

"Mr. York and I are to be engaged this Friday," she replied with painful dignity.

"No way, Katherine! I know you. You don't want to marry Freddy, I know you don't! I know you want us to be together, but your father and my erratic behavior has kept that from happening. Please stay for a little while. My friend, Professor Manning, will be here soon and he and I together will explain my situation. What I told you was true. I have traveled here from the future to be with you."

She softened her business-like tone slightly. "Joseph, it doesn't matter anymore."

"It has to matter!" I yelled, which caused Officer Walsh to pay us a visit.

"Everything all right here, ma'am?" he asked.

Katherine looked at me crossly, then peered up at the officer and said, "Yes. Everything is fine." When he was gone, she whispered to me, "You had better keep your head. My father has threatened to keep you here for a very long time if you don't cooperate."

She seemed genuinely concerned for my welfare. I wondered if her father and Freddy had colluded to force her to come down to the station to tell me to leave town. If so, it was smart of them to do so, because if either of them had come instead I would have told them to jump in a lake. Sending Katherine at least forced me to listen. I was sure they told her to keep as composed as she possibly could while speaking to me. "Katherine," I said, trying hard to keep my own composure, "you don't have to listen to them. I'm sure your father and Freddy put you up to this." I looked into her beautiful but sad eyes and then looked away for fear of falling so deeply in love with her that I would not be able to function. "I know your heart doesn't want to be with Freddy." I lowered my head and continued, "I know it wants to be with me."

I raised my head and she peered into my eyes as if she was looking there for an answer as to how to get us out of our predicament. With a dry mouth she commented, "If I don't promise to marry Freddy, they will never let you out of here."

"Then let them try to keep me here. How long of a jail sentence could I get for attempting to dig a hole in someone's yard anyway?"

"Father says a long time."

"I don't think so," I rebutted.

"He knows very important and powerful people. He could keep you here a long time, or, at the very least, make life very difficult for you in Valley View."

"Does your father love you?" I asked bluntly.

"Of course he does ... I think," she replied.

"Would he want to make *your* life difficult?"

"No, I don't think he would."

"If we were together and your father tried to make my life miserable, wouldn't that make your life miserable as well?"

"I suppose so. What are you driving at, Joseph?"

"Just that if we were together, your father would not make good on his threats toward me because he loves *you*."

At that moment I heard a throat clear and I turned my head expecting to see Officer Walsh coming to end our time together. It was indeed the officer, but Professor Manning had arrived and was at his side. The officer opened the cell door to let the professor in and then asked Katherine if she was ready to leave.

"Katherine, please stay," I pleaded before she could answer him. Pointing to Professor Manning I continued, "Here is a man that I'm sure you would consider an upstanding citizen and he can tell you that I'm not lying. Please stay and listen to what he has to say."

"Ma'am." Professor Manning removed his hat and bowed slightly to acknowledge Katherine.

"Are you staying, Miss?" Officer Walsh asked again.

She hesitated for a moment and then looked over at me and saw the desperation in my face. She allowed herself a wry smile before she replied, "Yes, I'll stay for a while longer."

I was truly relieved. Finally I could explain my situation to Katherine and had a truly respectable man present who could vouch for my character and my story. "Professor, please explain my situation to Katherine. Maybe if she hears it from someone other than me it won't sound quite so crazy."

Professor Manning was put on the spot, and was obviously uncomfortable about it, but did his best. He turned to Katherine and, after clearing his throat a few times, started his speech. "Well, Joseph told me that he is from the future. I believe his story because he brought me the clothes that he was wearing when he arrived and they are made of a material that does not exist in our time." Katherine didn't seem impressed, but the professor pressed on. "As a scientist, I needed proof as to the validity of his story to believe him and he provided it. I can show you this proof if you'd like to visit me in my lab." She still appeared skeptical. "I understand your apprehension," he said to her. "Even with the provided proof, I didn't completely believe the young man until I saw him disappear."

Her eyes opened wide. "Disappear? He really disappeared?"

"Yes," the professor continued, "right in front of my eyes! It was remarkable!"

Katherine turned to me and asked, "Where did you go?"

"I went back to my own time, to the exact same spot where I left this one. It was the same when I disappeared in your backyard and also when I disappeared in front of Alice and made her promise not to tell. This is what I tried to tell you." I made a move to put my arm around her and hold her, but she stiffened so I pulled my arm back.

"It's impossible. People don't dart around from time and place to time and place." She put her head in her hands, "It's just impossible. Isn't it?"

Professor Manning offered, "I thought so too, my dear. It doesn't make logical sense to me either, but I believe whole heartedly that he is telling the truth."

She raised her head and asked me with tear-filled eyes, "Why on earth were you digging in my yard in the middle of the night?"

"I tried to tell you, when I was still in my own time I needed to convince myself that I really had traveled to yours to be with you. At a séance, you told me that if I truly believed that it could happen, it would happen, but I wasn't a true believer until I found the penny."

"I told you in a séance?" she questioned and then looked at me like I was a lunatic.

I continued, "Yes, in a séance. The professor's grandson, who will also be Alice's son, suggested that when I get to this time I bury a 1935 penny in a mason jar. Assuming it to have been done, we dug until we found it about ten feet from the trunk of the big oak tree in what was your family's backyard. Once I saw the penny that was buried for over seventy years, I was convinced that it was all true and I time-traveled here later that afternoon. Of course that left me the task of burying the penny, which, for one reason or another, I have not yet been able to do since I arrived in 1935."

Professor Manning chimed in, "I think, and I believe Joseph agrees with me, that the reason he has shifted back and forth in time since his arrival here is because he has not yet buried that 1935 penny. Until it is put where he will find it in the future, he will continue to be in a sort of time limbo — not firmly grounded in either time."

Katherine appeared confused, and although she was not completely receptive to the idea of me actually being a time traveler, she seemed to be more open to the idea than she was previously. With two sets of eyes looking to her for some kind of acceptance, she said slowly, as if she were still in deep thought, "I don't know what to think. I really don't know." She lightly tapped on the cell bars to get Officer Walsh's attention, and when she wasn't successful she banged on the bars with her purse. When the officer finally came, she asked to be let out of the cell.

"Katherine, please don't go!" I begged. "You can't leave until I'm sure that you believe what I have told you — until you believe in me!"

She reapplied her business-like face and said calmly, "Joseph, I need time to think. I need to figure this all out."

"Will you at least try to get your father to drop the charges against me?"

"I will try," was all she would give me. She then nodded to the professor and said politely, "A pleasure to meet you, Professor." The officer then opened the cell door and she was gone. I suddenly felt completely helpless and hopeless.

Professor Manning tried to lift my spirits, but I was inconsolable at that moment. "Joseph, if Katherine's father doesn't drop the charges, I will get you out of here myself, I promise. And don't give up on that pretty girl. Nothing worthwhile is ever easy." He left and I was all alone again with only a deck of cards to keep me company.

The rest of that morning was rather quiet. There were no other cellmates for me to deal with and the phone in the station rang only once. Officer Walsh took a power nap and I tried to do the same but couldn't. While I was busy plotting an escape on my next time-slip, the phone rang for just the second time that day. The officer woke from his nap to answer it. He stared in my direction during his entire conversation and when it was over he walked over to my cell with key in hand. "It's time to let you loose on society again," he said with sarcasm. "Jack Whitney has dropped all of the charges against you." He opened the cell door and continued, "You're a free man after you sign some papers." I was suddenly ecstatic. I didn't know if Katherine had worked some kind of magic with her father or if I was being set free for some other reason. At that particular moment, I didn't care. I was just happy to be out of my cell and was thankful that I didn't have to time-slip to do it.

After leaving the police station, I stopped at the first pay-phone I could find to inform Mr. Potato Head that I didn't make it to work that day due to a "family emergency." I apologized for not calling him earlier and assured him that I'd be placing his bet on Max Baer later in the evening. My next order of business was to get Harry's car back to him and explain what happened. I walked for many blocks and was relieved to see that his car was exactly where I had left it the night before.

There was more cars than usual heading south on Rockaway Avenue that day and to compound the problem, lunch hour was about to begin. The unusually heavy traffic forced me to stop Harry's car dead on the road which, in turn, caused the jalopy to stall. I got out of the car and was cranking the engine to try and get it started again, when Freddy York drove by in the opposite direction with his usual companions. He spotted me struggling with the car and pulled into the next available parking spot. He then got out of his vehicle and headed toward me with his gang of thugs. I was in no mood for a fight and had hoped to get the car going and drive away before they reached me, but the engine wouldn't start.

"Hey!" Freddy yelled from twenty yards away, "I thought you were told to go back where you came from."

I knew that arguing with him would only make matters worse so I replied, "I'll be leaving tomorrow." Freddy continued to walk toward me at an accelerated pace and was practically right on top of me when I added, "I have a few loose ends to tie up before I go."

He grabbed me by the shirt and with loose saliva said, "You'd better tie up your loose ends fast, Eaton! And if you ever show your face around here again, you'll be sorry!" He released me with a shove, kicked the passenger side door of Harry's car, and marched back to his car with his small army following closely behind. I wasn't proud of cowering to him, but I did what I had to do. Fighting him again was a no-win situation and it could have landed me back in jail.

Eventually, I got the jalopy started again and I drove it back to the Dempsey house without further incident. Harry had received a ride to work in the morning from a neighbor and the same neighbor had driven him back home for lunch. He was glad to see his car, but he wasn't exactly thrilled to see me. I tried to explain to him what had happened, but he didn't want to hear it.

Even though I was unable to make amends to Harry, I was able to show my gratitude for Mrs. Dempsey's hospitality by, at long last, painting her fence. Doing a little manual labor was good for my soul. Something about the simplicity of repetitive work would always free my mind so that it could concentrate on other more important issues. Practicing piano scales had a similar effect on me. Most aspiring pianists hated doing scales, but sometimes I liked the fact that I could remove my mind from the equation and let my fingers do the thinking.

How I was going to try and further convince Katherine that we were meant for each other became first and foremost on my thought agenda. The whole time-travel problem was also a major issue. If I finally bury that penny, would I really stop time-slipping? And what if I didn't? Would I be time-slipping for the rest of my life? Would that kind of life be fair to put upon Katherine? My mind started to race. What was it that Katherine said to her father that made him drop all of the charges against me? Was she actually going to get engaged to Freddy York? After pondering those questions in my head all afternoon, I knew that the only way I would learn any answers at all would be to ask Katherine directly.

I finished painting the fence and even got a "good job" from Mrs. Dempsey. It was around four o'clock in the afternoon and I expected that Katherine had already made it home from her job and was helping her mother prepare dinner. I decided to do something I hadn't done since arriving in 1935, call Katherine on the telephone. She answered my call and didn't seem surprised that it was me on the other end of the line.

"Katherine? It's me, Joseph."

"Yes, I know."

"I just wanted to thank you. How did you do it?" I asked.

"Do what?" she replied with false naivety.

"You know, get me out of jail."

With a steady voice she said, "I told my father that you agreed to leave town and never see me again." I laughed briefly but stopped when I realized that she wasn't joking. With a note of acceptance of her situation she said, "Joseph, you have to go back to Philadelphia. There is no other way."

"You still don't believe me? What can I do to prove to you that I am telling the truth? Do you know how much I love you? I know that you have feelings for me too. I know you do. I can't believe that you're willing to throw it all away to be with Freddy. Do you love him?" After a long pause with no reply from Katherine, I repeated, "Well, do you?"

"I don't have to answer that."

"That's because you don't love him. If you did you would have said so and I probably would have stepped aside and left the two of you alone."

"Okay then, I *do* love him," she said, and I could tell that the lie didn't taste well to her.

"No, you don't. You just finally succumbed to the pressure from your father. Do you really want to spend the rest of your life with a man you don't love?"

"I suppose you think I should spend the rest of my life with a man that claims to mysteriously disappear?" she railed.

"Yes," I squawked back. Then, with as much tenderness as I could muster I added, "Yes, I do. If there is one thing I've figured out from my situation it's that you don't get to choose who you love. Love chooses you."

She said nothing, either finding my words thought-provoking or perhaps absurd. She broke the silence with, "Father will be home soon, I have to go."

"Please don't hang up! Please!" I pleaded.

"Don't try to see me, Joseph. It's for the best ... Goodbye." She didn't wait for me to say anything. She just hung up.

***

"C'mon, Joseph, we're not missing this fight. Get off your keister and let's go!"

"What's the point, Harry? Go by yourself," I said, as I lay down on my makeshift bed in Harry's bedroom.

"Look, see, I'm not gonna let you sit here and stew in your own gloom all night. We're goin' to the fight together and we're gonna have a ball and win some dough, and I won't take no for an answer."

I knew Harry was right, but I simply didn't feel like doing anything. All I wanted to do was lie in bed. The thought of time-slipping home and not returning to 1935 no longer scared me. I was so distraught over Katherine that I may have even welcomed the idea. If Katherine and I were not going to be together, then what was the point of me being in 1935 anyway?

Trying to get past my self-pity, I glanced over at the man who would one day be my grandfather and decided to enjoy the moments we had left together, moments we could no longer have in my own time. "Okay, get my hat ... I'll go."

I was surprised that Harry was driving; I thought we would be taking a train into Manhattan. When I mentioned this to him he laughed, "We're not goin' to Madison Square Garden Arena. We're goin' to the Madison Square Garden Bowl in Long Island City, you sap." He explained further that it was a large outdoor stadium. I had never heard of such a place and was pretty sure it didn't exist in my time.

While enduring Harry's daredevil driving act on the way to the stadium, I realized that I hadn't time-slipped since the previous night. I wondered if that part of my adventure was as over as my relationship with Katherine seemed to be. At that moment, the idea of not having to worry about time-slipping any longer actually gave me some comfort. It was nice to feel that I might actually stay still in time for a while, even if it was going to be without the love of my life.

With no straight south-to-north route, it took longer than expected to get to the stadium. Harry's wreck of a car delayed us further when we had to pull over and change one of its tires.

When we finally arrived at the Madison Square Garden Bowl, I got to see a collection of classic cars, the likes of which no one in my time had ever seen. There were classic Fords, Chevys, Dodges and Buicks all over the non-paved parking lot and many of them appeared to be brand new. I even saw, to my surprise, a few foreign made cars (a Volvo and a BMW).

The stadium was a massive and impersonal chunk of wood that rivaled the capacity of mega-stadiums from my own time. Harry and I met up with his bookie friend, the man we would be placing our bets with, outside the stadium. I was ready to hand all of my money over to the bookie when Harry reminded me that we still had to buy our tickets. Tickets for the bout were two, five, or ten dollars. Ringside seats cost twenty dollars which I thought was fairly reasonable when I considered what those seats would go for in my time. I saved a fiver for my ticket and gave the rest to the bookie. Harry had his money hidden around his waist in a money pouch. He removed the pouch and quickly counted out his cash, which, at a glance, appeared to be over eight hundred dollars. He removed what he needed for his ticket, but before he handed the rest of the bundle to the bookie he looked at me and said, "Are you sure?"

I replied, "I'm as sure as I'll ever be," and it was good enough for Harry. Every two cents he ever rubbed together was riding on James J. Braddock to win the heavyweight championship of the world. With the odds 10 to 1 against Braddock, we were in position to go home with a ton of money — me with about one thousand dollars and Harry with about eight thousand dollars. I just hoped and prayed that I remembered the outcome of the fight correctly. I also hoped and prayed that Harry's bookie would be able to pay up at the end.

When we entered the enormous stadium, an undercard bout was already under way. All of the seats were made of wood and had no cushioning of any kind. I was pretty sure that Braddock was going to win, but I had no idea how long the fight would last. For my rear end's sake, I hoped it was the next fight on the card and that it would be over quickly.

The stadium's seats did not go up on as much of an incline as they would in stadiums of similar capacity in my time. In future mega-stadiums, this was done to maximize the number of seats with a good view. The seats at Madison Square Garden Bowl just kept going back and back and back with little to no difference in height. The only real height differential was between the floor seats and the three different sections. How anyone sitting in the back row of the last section could actually see anything, I don't know. We settled in to our seats, about midway up the stadium, and I was surprised to see that the place was less than half full. I expected a much larger crowd for such a big event. I surmised that a good percentage of the population had not recovered enough from the depression to be willing to spend money on something as frivolous as a prize fight. I mentioned this to Harry and he said, "What are you talking about? There are over thirty thousand people here."

A cloud of smoke hovered over the stadium from all of the cigarettes and cigars the patrons smoked. The man seated to my right was smoking a real cheap-smelling stogie that had started to turn my stomach, but there was nothing I could do about it. The undercard bout ended, but, to my dismay, there was to be yet another match before the main event. A pugilist named Eddie Hogan was going to take on a boxer named Jack McCarthy. I paid very little attention to the six-round affair that Hogan won by split decision.

My butt was starting to feel very sore, so I decided to stand up for a while. The rest of the crowd stood with me when they saw the boxers for the main event enter the ring from their respective locker rooms.

To my surprise, the champion, Max Baer, was introduced first and with little fanfare. There were no series of nicknames used to announce him, as they would have done in my time, just his name and place of origin. He was wearing red trunks adorned with a rather large Star of David on the left side. There was a fair amount of applause for the champion, and he seemed to have just as many female fans as he did male ones.

James J. Braddock, the Cinderella Man, was introduced next and with more hoopla. The man wearing the plain dark trunks was announced as "The man who in the last year made the greatest comeback in ring history ... James J. Braddock of Jersey City". The fans erupted with applause and it was clear that Braddock was the crowd favorite.

The weights were announced next with Baer at 209 ½ pounds and the shorter and smaller Braddock at 191 ¾ pounds. Baer was considerably younger than Braddock and a much better boxing specimen. It was easy to understand why Baer was so heavily favored and why he boldly predicted a knockout in the first round. If I didn't know better, I would have placed all my money on the imposing Baer. The judges, timekeepers, and referee were announced and the bell rang to signify the start of the fifteen-round bout.

Braddock threw the first punch of the match, but it was Baer who landed the first good blow, an uppercut that stung his opponent. Figuring to be in for an easy night, Baer began to clown around and pretended to adjust his trunks.

The action was very slow, but I was entertained by what I considered to be the comical boxing style of the time. I couldn't imagine either one of those men lasting more than a round against one of the pumped up heavyweights from my time. I turned to my left toward Harry and was going to comment on my observations but thought better of it. Harry was already deeply into the fight and erupted with the rest of the crowd when Braddock landed a good right to the side of Baer's face. It didn't appear to hurt Baer and he stood in the same spot with his guard down daring Braddock to try and hit him again. Both boxers were very slow moving, especially the bigger Baer, and neither of them used a lot of fancy footwork. Baer tried to get inside on Braddock to hit him with his notorious uppercut, but the Cinderella Man blocked the advance and countered with a good combination of rights to the delight of the crowd. The match was just starting to have some good action when the bell sounded to end the round which prompted boos from the stands.

Harry looked over at me with a wide smile and said, "Some fight, huh? Our guy is gonna win, right?"

"Man, I hope so," I replied, which in turn gave Harry a sour face. "Don't worry, Harry, Braddock will win," I reassured.

The second round began with Baer doing more clowning around while Braddock continued with the business at hand, eventually landing some punches square in Baer's face. It was becoming more and more clear that Braddock was in control of the fight.

In the third round, Baer finally started to land a few punches and got visibly angry when the serious Braddock countered with effective punches of his own. In the fourth round, Baer tried to push Braddock down to the canvas and was cautioned by the referee. This dirty move prompted a cascade of boos from the crowd and Baer mockingly saluted them.

The lack of action in round five caused my mind to wander. Why was I still here, I thought, and could I possibly have been sent here for some other reason than to be with Katherine? As if on cue, the frosty feeling came rushing upon me and I knew what would happen next. I had not time-slipped since the previous night and thought that perhaps I was finished with that problem, but it was back and it was going to happen in front of thirty thousand screaming people. I was cold and numb and then suddenly my surroundings became very still and extremely quiet. I opened my eyes to see that I was sitting inside a car that was in a parking lot filled with other automobiles from my own time. I thawed very quickly, much more rapidly than in any of my previous time-slips, and I was able to turn my head almost as soon as I arrived. To my left and right I could see brand new cars and trucks with the sticker price still in the window. Yet, when I looked straight ahead,

I could still see the boxing match. Being able to view two time periods at once was not something that I had experienced before. If I hadn't been so terrified, I might have enjoyed the fact that I was able to watch the match from a more comfortable seat. Then, as if choreographed with each landed punch, I started to move back and forth between the two time periods at a dizzying pace. Nobody sitting near me in 1935 showed any signs of shock, so I figured my body did not disappear. I assumed the same held true in my own time, but there wasn't anyone around to witness anything anyway. The auto-mall must have been closed for the night.

I wasn't sure how much time, if any, elapsed between each time-slip, but it felt like each slip forward and back lasted less than a minute. I no longer knew what round the fight was in, as my brain had grown weary from trying to process new information at such a torrid pace. One minute I would be looking to Harry for help that I knew he couldn't give, and the next I would be looking at the sticker price of a brand new Chevy pickup truck. In one moment I saw Max Baer complaining to the referee about some unknown incident and the next I found myself staring through the windshield of a Saab Aero.

From what I was able to comprehend of the match, Baer had started to wear down and appeared much more fatigued than Braddock. Each time I glanced over at Harry, his expression of excitement grew and he probably never noticed the growing fear that my face must have projected. I believed that the tug of war between the two time periods I was experiencing signified the end of something, but I didn't know if it was going to be the end of my time-traveling days or the conclusion of my pathetic life. I continued to whirlwind back and forth between each time until finally, I blacked out.

When I regained self-awareness, I found myself floating in space in the same manner as I had just prior to my arrival in 1935. I witnessed the birth and death of stars, planets, and other heavenly bodies, and, just as before, my physical body had not come along for the ride. I was either going back to my own time permanently or I had really reached the end of my days. After moving slowly in space for what seemed like eons, I stopped dead still. I was at this standstill in space for another long period of time and wondered if whoever was in control of this operation had fallen asleep at the switch. Suddenly, I began to free-fall at an incredible rate of speed and, not wanting to see the horror of it all, I closed my eyes. It didn't matter to me if I landed on a tall building or in the ocean, I did not want to see it. Even though I knew that I wouldn't have actually seen anything with my own real set of eyes, I didn't want to open them just the same. I felt some sense of relief when my free-falling pace slowed and changed into more of a hover, but I still chose to keep my mind's eye closed. As I drifted down, I reflected on the mess I had made out of my life and realized that it didn't matter if I landed in my time, 1935, or the year 2525, there would be no one to hold me when I got there.

I then felt the jarring impact of being reconnected to my body. Completely frozen, I was unable to move or even open my eyes, but I was able to hear the muted sound of people murmuring. After a short while, I managed to open my eyes slightly, but my vision was not yet clear. Through a haze, I could see that there were people standing over me, but I didn't know why. My senses slowly began to return and I could feel that my landing spot was made up of cold and hard cement. Had I landed on a road? Was I badly hurt, maybe even hit by a car, and the people standing over me were on watch until an ambulance arrived? One of these people knew my name and with a familiar male voice said, "Joseph, are you all right? Joseph?" My eyes were then able to focus better and I could see that the haze I had been looking through was from the cigar smoke manufactured by some of the people standing over me. The young face of my grandfather smiled with relief when I gave him a look of recognition. I had not traveled back to my own time after all. I was still in 1935 and at the Madison Square Garden Bowl. With the assistance of Harry and another man, I was able to get up off of the concrete. "Are you gonna be okay?" Harry asked repeatedly after helping me to my seat.

"Yeah, I'm okay."

"What the heck happened to you? One second you're sitting in your seat and the next I find you on the floor."

Without wanting to give a real explanation I said, "I don't know, I just slipped out of my seat, I guess."

Harry didn't buy it and scrunched his face in a manner which told me that he knew I was keeping something from him. To his credit he didn't pursue the matter and said in a very clear manner, "Are you sure you're okay?"

"Yeah, I think so," I replied, though I was still somewhat dazed and confused. Surprised that there were still so many spectators in the stadium, I asked, "Is the fight still going on?"

"Yeah, they're gonna start the fifteenth any second now. If Braddock doesn't get knocked out, I think we're gonna win!"

"The fifteenth?" I asked, and smiled when I realized that my most recent experience had only lasted a little more than a half-hour of real time.

The bell rang to signal the start of the fifteenth and final round and almost immediately Max Baer complained to the referee about something that I either didn't see or didn't comprehend. Both men were physically exhausted after fourteen grueling rounds and they were barely holding on. At one point in the final round, both boxers had their heads down and were seemingly locked at the shoulders using each other for support. Each of them still managed to attempt punches in the direction of the other, but, since they were both in such an odd position, none of the wild punches made any contact. If one man had fallen down, the other would surely have landed right on top of him. Most of the crowd booed the lack of action, but I was impressed with the resolve of both men to refuse to give up and go down. Suddenly, Baer found a small amount of energy in his reserve and came close to the knockout blow, but James J. Braddock put his head down, squared his shoulders, and continued on. A split second before the bell rang to end the fight, Baer had just missed with his last ditch effort, a vicious uppercut that would have likely knocked Braddock out had it connected. With the epic battle over, the two combatants embraced each other and awaited the official outcome.

After a few minutes, the ring announcer entered the ring to relay the judges' decision. "The winner and *new* heavyweight champion …" The announcer either stopped speaking into the microphone or his amplified voice was rendered inaudible by the raucous crowd. His proclamation of "new heavyweight champion" meant that Braddock had won and was the new heavyweight champion of the world. As I had remembered from the movie, the Cinderella Man won the title and, in turn, a ton of money for both Harry and me.

Harry had a difficult time finding his bookie friend after the fight, and when he did, his friend was somewhat reluctant to pay up. After Harry and I did a little *persuading*, his friend was then only too happy to cough up the cash.

On the drive back, Harry was gushing and glowing. "I can't believe it. Look at all this loot!" he said, as he fanned out his winnings with one hand and steered his jalopy with the other. "The first thing I'm gonna do is move out of my father's house. Hey, you wanna move in with me? Maybe we can get a nice apartment or even buy a house."

Without thinking I said, "Sure, that sounds like a good idea," but my mind was completely pre-occupied. I was in deep thought about James J. Braddock and how he was able to persevere despite the odds against him. I was truly inspired by the way he never gave up. Even though I had witnessed the fight without the dramatic Hollywood-style music in the background, it nonetheless encouraged me to keep on trying with

Katherine, and I vowed to never give up on my only chance to be truly happy in life. Braddock made me richer in more ways than one that night.

Thirteen

When I woke up for work the next morning, I realized that I had slept completely through the night. I had no recollection of time-slipping to the factory, nor did I remember having any dreams. Despite the fact that he was up very late with me at his favorite watering hole celebrating our good fortune, Harry's bed was empty. When I entered the kitchen, Mrs. Dempsey informed me that Harry had already left for work. That surprised me, especially since he had raised a toast the previous night to, "Quitting my job and living off my winnings."

It was a lovely cool and dry Friday morning with few clouds in the sky and I thoroughly enjoyed my walk to work. I exchanged pleasantries with people along the way, people that I was getting used to seeing every day. I wasn't sure why, but I experienced a sense of stability that had never been present in me before at any point in my life. I felt as though I was permanently attached to that time and its people. I had previously been under the impression that the only way I would ever be able to feel that kind of permanence would be to bury the 1935 penny. Maybe there had been no need to worry about burying that stupid penny after all.

I arrived at Smith and Cooper Casualty and Life Insurance Company and checked in with Mr. Potato

Head. He was not very happy to see me and I surmised it was due to his perceived loss of one hundred dollars on Max Baer. "I have something for you, Mr. Pottershed," I said, and tried very hard to pronounce his name properly.

He didn't notice that my hand was in my pocket ready to pull out and return his money to him. With a sour face and a sad voice he said, "Joseph, I'm afraid I have some bad news for you."

"What is it?" I inquired and kept the cash in my pocket.

He handed me an envelope and said, "I'm afraid you've been terminated."

I opened the envelope and saw that it contained a check for five dollars, my salary for the week. "You're firing me?"

"Well, it's not me. I think you have some real talent. No, this order came straight down from Mr. Whitney. Unfortunately, I have to ask you to leave … now."

"Oh," I said, acting surprised, but I knew there was a good chance my employment at the company was coming to an end, especially considering I was supposed to have already left town. I took an empty hand out of my pocket and said softly, "I guess I'll go then. Thanks for everything, sir." I shook his hand and started to walk out of his office but stopped to add, "Hey, say goodbye to Sam Lerner for me, okay?"

"Okay, Joseph, I will." Then he looked me in the eyes and with true sincerity said, "Good luck to you, son."

He was such a nice man and he handled my firing with such dignity and respect that I knew what I had to do. "Oh, I almost forgot. Here," I reached into my pocket, walked back toward him, and handed him his one hundred dollars. "I never made it to the fight last night," I lied. "Good thing, huh?"

"Yes," he said with astonished relief. "Yes, a very good thing indeed."

I left the building and, even though I was unemployed again, I had confidence that I would land on my feet. I even stopped at the Valley View Savings and Loan to open an account and deposit my five-dollar paycheck and six hundred dollars in cash.

Shortly after leaving the bank, I heard the sound of a car slowly approaching behind me as I walked along the street. The car's engine sounded as if it was either brand new or just very well cared for. Expecting that Freddie and his band of brutes were following me, I readied myself for yet another battle with the town jerk.

I turned around quickly, hoping to take them by surprise, but the surprise was on me when I saw it was Harry who was following me and he was behind the wheel of a brand new Ford two-door sedan. The car was nearly jet black and it sparkled in the sun. With its front grille in the shape of a giant smile containing five rows of teeth, the car projected a grin almost as big as Harry's. He was gleaming from ear to ear when he asked, "Need a ride?"

I hopped into his new car and complimented him on his choice, but at the same time warned, "What are you going to tell your mother? If she finds out this was from gambling winnings she'll send you to a monastery for repentance."

He didn't seem worried and replied, "She doesn't have to know it's from the fight. I've been saving my dough for a long time you know."

"So where's your old car? Did you trade it in?"

"Trade it in? It's parked at the shop where I bought this baby. In fact, I was hoping I could drop you off there and you could drive it back home for me."

"Yeah, no problem. I got fired today anyway so I've got nothing else better to do. So, what are you going to do with the old jalopy?"

"Well, I thought I would try and sell it."

"How much?" I inquired.

"*You* want to buy it?" he said, and I shook my head in the affirmative. "Are you sure?"

"Yeah, if the price is right. How much do you want for it?"

"I don't know. I was going to ask for fifty, but for you ... I guess twenty-five clams would do."

"Sold!" I quickly counted out the money and handed it to him. My plan to eventually buy a bicycle was still intact, but I knew I needed some kind of vehicle for longer trips. I figured between the bike and the jalopy I would be set for transportation for a while.

He took the money and said, "What are you gonna do when she breaks down? You're not exactly good with a wrench you know."

"Well, if I have problems I'll call you and you'll help me. You will help me, right?"

Harry winked and his eye had that familiar sparkle to it. "Yeah, I'll help you. Maybe I could even teach you a thing or two." His words saddened me as I couldn't help but think that if he had lived long enough to teach me a thing or two about life, I might have become a much better person. God knows I never received any life lessons from my own father.

After seeing my face go from happy to sad, Harry changed the subject. "Have you thought any more about getting an apartment or a house together?"

"I don't know, Harry. A house is just too much of a commitment for me. I would say it's okay to start looking for an apartment, but I really don't know what I'm going to do or where I should live. I think for now I should just stay in your parents' house as long as they'll still have me. Is that okay with you?"

"Yeah, don't sweat it. I can manage on my own. If you change your mind, I'll make room for you."

I knew that his gambling winning streak wasn't going to last forever and I worried about him living alone in a very harsh and cruel world. I tried to offer up some advice. "Please don't lose all you've gained on more gambling. Just do me a favor and only bet when I say it's okay."

"You want me to clear all of my bets with you? What are you my old lady?"

I insisted, "Please?"

His expression told me that he thought I was being ridiculous. With sarcasm he said, "Okay, Joseph. I won't make any more bets unless you say so." I knew he wasn't taking me seriously, but I hoped that he would, at the very least, think twice about placing any bets on his own. Maybe just that second thought alone would keep him from entering the darkest part of his life and be enough to save him from himself. If that didn't work, then I vowed that I would try to be there to help him in any way that I could. I knew that, had he lived long enough, he would have been there for me during my dark years.

Harry dropped me off and there it was — my very own car. It needed a paint job and a ton of work to run better, but it was mine! I knew the ten-year-old Honda Civic that I left behind in the future was a much better car, but I never felt such pride in owning something in my whole life. I started up the jalopy, jumped in the driver's seat, and just sat there for a while reveling in the glory of being an automobile owner. The realization soon came over me that the jalopy ran about as well as the car I bought when I was just seventeen, a 1980 Pontiac Sunbird that had blown shocks and burned a quart of oil daily. It was as if I was given a fresh start in this time. Everything old was new again.

***

I knew I was supposed to stay away from the Whitney house, but my conscience kept telling me that I had to return the money I borrowed from Katherine's mother. I pulled up in front of the house and knocked on the door. Mrs. Whitney answered looking completely disheveled. She was wearing an old gray dress and her hair was partially falling out of her tightly wrapped bun. Beads of sweat were present on her brow, and she was huffing and puffing like an out-of-shape jogger. The look of surprise on her face told me that I was definitely unexpected.

"Joseph? You can't be here!" She opened the door and craned her head toward the York house. "Quickly, come in before someone sees you." I entered the house and I could see why she was so exhausted. She was preparing the house for Katherine and Freddy's engagement party for later that night. Her broom was at the ready as it leaned on the living room wall and her dustpan sat dutifully close at hand on the floor. A nearby pail of water with a mop soaking in it was still in the process of settling which gave me the impression that she was preparing to use it on her floor when I knocked on the door. A long sign which said *Congratulations Freddy and Katherine* sat on the couch waiting to be displayed on the wall. It pained me just to look at it.

"Mrs. Whitney, I won't be long. I just wanted to give you back the twenty dollars I borrowed." I extended the money from my hand, but she refused to take it.

"Keep the money, Joseph," she sighed. "Katherine tried to explain to me why you did what you did, though I don't think she really quite understood it herself. After all that you've been through, I wouldn't feel right taking the money back from you. Take it back home with you to Philadelphia. It might come in handy."

"Well, ma'am, just between you and me, I don't think I'll be going home. For now at least, I plan to stay here in Valley View."

"But, Joseph, you must leave. If my husband finds you anywhere near here he will be furious. And if Freddy sees you there's no telling what he may do."

"I'm not afraid of Freddy. He's nothing without his friends around to back him up. Your husband on the other hand ..." I looked down at my shoes and lied,

"Well, it doesn't really matter anyway. Katherine has chosen Freddy over me and that's that."

Her face expressed genuine sympathy for me. "I know she has more affection for you than she does for Freddy, but, and please don't take offense to this, Freddy's prospects seem so much brighter than yours. We only want what is best for our daughter, I'm sure you can appreciate that. I'm confident that in time he will make her very happy." Freddy and Jack Whitney must have done some major campaigning to get Katherine's mother on their side.

In an effort to undo what they may have done, I replied, "No disrespect, ma'am, but she would have been happier with me. I'm certain of it. I've seen what our future together would have looked like and it was a picture of love and respect, and respect is something she will never find with Freddy." I left the money on the floor near the front door and walked out of the house.

I headed to my car and started up the engine. As the engine turned over, Katherine pulled up beside me on her bicycle. Before she could say a word I grabbed her in my arms and kissed her. It was a long, passionate kiss and shortly into it I could feel her knees buckle in submission. It was the last ditch effort of a scorned man. I didn't really think of it as a goodbye kiss, more of a *good luck finding this kind of passion with Freddy* kiss. I was in love, but I was also angry and I didn't care who saw us kissing or what the consequences might have been for either of us. At that point it didn't matter to me if I ended up in jail or got jumped by Freddy and his friends.

When I finally released her, I could see that she was stunned and possibly outraged by my sudden display of affection. I got into my car and as I drove away I could see that her expression of astonishment was replaced by the look of love. I wanted to stop and tell her how much I loved her and how much she meant to me. I wanted to try once again to make her understand how far I had to come to be with her. I wanted to, but I didn't. Instead, I just kept driving.

Driving around the town of Valley View; that was how I spent the rest of that day. It truly was a wonderful place and I finally understood why my mother had remembered it so fondly. It was this great little town that was only a short train ride away from the biggest town of all, New York City. In that respect, Valley View really could offer its residents the best of both worlds. The majority of the town's people were so friendly that their smiles were infectious. Not in a creepy way, but in a good old-fashioned American hometown way. Even though I lost the girl of my dreams, I still found myself smiling as I drove past those cheerful folks. I was sure that many of them lost a great deal during the Great Depression, but it didn't stop them from being good and kind neighbors. When I first arrived in 1935, I simply couldn't imagine anyone from my spoiled generation surviving in that time, yet there I was with a car and money in my pocket. I had the kind folks of 1935 to thank for my survival. Of course, without foreknowledge of the future, I don't know what really would have become of me.

After stopping at Aunt Shirley's for another fine and inexpensive meal, I drove the jalopy over to

Milligan's for a beer. I wasn't all that surprised to see Katherine's friends, Walter and Eddie, sitting at the bar.

Eddie spotted me first and yelled, "Hey Joe! What d'ya know? Sit down and I'll buy you one!" To the bartender he sharply said, "Barkeep?" and he pointed to the seat on his left.

I hopped up on the barstool that Eddie had pointed to and asked, "Are you guys always here?"

Eddie responded with an affirmative, "Since they repealed Prohibition," and I didn't think he was kidding.

Walter, who sat to the right of Eddie, leaned in toward the bar so that he could see me and said, "I'm sorry about Katherine. I really thought that you two were right for each other."

Eddie chimed in, "What happened anyway? She didn't tell us anything. The next thing we knew she was engaged to that horse's ass."

"It's a long story, guys, but in the end she simply chose him over me. Aren't you going to the engagement party?"

Walter replied with a concise, "No."

Eddie elaborated a bit more. "What makes you think we would be invited to her party? Her parents don't even know we exist. I guess we don't have enough salad to be invited to the big wingding."

"Hey, it's not her fault," Walter said in Katherine's defense, "It's her parents. They watch her like a hawk and want her to marry some kind of king or something."

I laughed, "A king? Freddy's no royalty, that's for sure. I don't even know what he does to earn his money, do you?"

Eddie replied, "I don't know, but he sure has a sweet set of wheels. He must have brought home some pretty good bacon to afford that."

"Do you think maybe his parents gave it to him?" I questioned.

Eddie cut off Walter and clamored, "I don't think so. York's father works at the rubber factory. I think he's some kind of boss, but I doubt he could afford to buy his son a car like that. Maybe York works for gangsters? He probably worked for them during Prohibition and bought a shiny new tin can with the dough he made." Eddie drank a slug of beer, belched, and continued, "Maybe he still works for them and bumps people off for a living." Eddie and Walter both laughed, but I didn't join them. I doubted it was true, but if it was, then Katherine could be in danger.

Walter saw the worried look on my face and appeased me with, "I heard that he had a string of luck with the horses, that's all. Joseph, you saw him at the track. He goes there all the time. I think he just hit it big once and bought the car with the loot. Ever since then he's been driving around town like he's the big cheese."

That made me feel better and I said, "Yeah, that's probably more like it."

To comfort me further, Eddie added, "How much money could he make anyway?" He took a drag on a cheap-smelling cigar and added, "He lives with his old man and old lady. If he were really some rich goon he'd at least have his own place to live, wouldn't he? I never heard of a gangster who lives with his mommy." We all laughed which prompted Eddie to toast, "To living with your mommy!" and we all clinked glasses.

After five mugs of beer, I started to feel a little buzzed. The alcohol content of the beer on tap in Milligan's must have been greater than that of the bottled beer of my time. The mixture of the alcohol's effects and the testosterone in the atmosphere gave me a little courage. "Hey, guys, why don't we crash the party?"

Eddie liked the idea and said, "I'd love to see the look on York's face! And Katherine's father would probably cast a kitten!"

"Let's do it! C'mon, what do you think?" the words came directly from my own mouth. I hadn't heard that kind of alcoholic insanity in my own voice for quite a while and it scared me a little.

Walter, being the voice of reason, tried to calm me down with, "Joseph, if you show up there you'll be right back in jail a second later. And if the police don't get you, Freddy and Katherine's father will."

After taking Walter's words to heart, I tweaked my idea a little. "What about you guys? You two could go to give your regards to the future Mrs. York and tell me all about it." I really wanted to know if Katherine was enjoying being engaged to that blowhard and I secretly hoped she would send her affections to me through Walter or Eddie.

Eddie was on board, "We could do that! What do you think, Wally? What's the worst that could happen?" He then slugged down the rest of his beer and slammed his mug down on the bar to get the bartender's attention.

Walter replied, "I don't know, Eddie. I mean, I would love to give our dear Katherine our warmest regards, but York and his pals might have something to say about it."

"So what?" Eddie said, beating me to the punch. "What are they gonna do? If they try and start something we'll just leave, though I wouldn't mind taking a shot at Freddy's ugly mug. Let's do it for our new pal Joe, huh?" He gave Walter a friendly elbow to try and convince him further. The piano player had arrived and started playing *When Irish Eyes are Smiling*. Eddie started singing along, grossly out of tune.

Walter hesitated, but then interrupted Eddie's singing and conceded, "All right. But *I* do all the talking, see. And if you throw a single punch at anyone, I'll knock you down myself."

"All right, all right," Eddie wavered. "Let's go!"

"Can I go too? I'll wait in the car, I promise," I said.

Walter sighed and then relented. "Okay, Joseph. But don't start any trouble. I can't afford to bail you out of jail."

The three of us left Milligan's and piled into Walter's big green Oldsmobile. I had offered the use of my car, but Walter thought that my noisy vehicle would tip off the hosts that I was there. Walter parked his car two houses down from Katherine's and I sat in the back seat as he and Eddie entered the Whitney house. They had only been gone for a few minutes when they arrived back at the car.

"That didn't take long. What happened?" I asked as they opened the car doors.

"She's not there, Joseph," Walter said somberly.

"What do you mean she's not there?"

Eddie interjected, "She never arrived to her own party. The girl is missing."

"Missing?"

"Yes. Her parents were so worried about her that they didn't even notice that we were uninvited guests," Walter said. "Freddy and his friends are out looking for her."

"Oh," I said, and I realized that there was a good chance that she had cold feet and perhaps it meant that she would reconsider me. "I think I know where she might be."

"Where?" Eddie said.

"Well, I'm not supposed to tell anyone. She has a special place where she goes when she wants to be alone. She told me about it on our first date, but swore me to secrecy. I guess it would still be a secret if I don't tell you exactly where it is." I told Walter to drop me off at the movie theater and wait for me there. I would go the rest of the way on foot.

I walked along the path at the back of the movie theater that led to the woods that hid the pond where I suspected Katherine would be. Just as I did with Katherine a week earlier, I found the unmarked path near the big tree stump. It was a little difficult to maneuver my way through the woods without Katherine as a guide, but my memory didn't fail me and I found my way with the aid of a particularly bright moon. More than once I walked right smack into a branch, but I kept on going until I saw the pond. As I got closer, I could see the silhouette of a woman in the moonlight sitting near the water's edge with her knees bent and her feet flat on the ground. I called out,

"Katherine? Is that you?" The woman turned to see who it was and she seemed a little startled at first. "It's Joseph, Joseph Eaton," I said and I approached with caution just in case it turned out to be someone else entirely. The woman buried her head into her knees and as I got closer I could hear that she was crying. There was no longer any doubt; it was definitely Katherine. I crouched down next to her and asked, "Are you okay?" even though it was pretty obvious that she wasn't.

"How did you know I was here?" she said through sniffles.

"You said this was your place, the place you go when you need to think. Where else would you be?"

She laughed a little then sniffed again. "Well, have you time-slid since last night?"

I was taken aback by her question. "You mean time-slipped?"

"Yes. Have you done it since last night?" She took her head off of her knees and looked over at me. Her eyes were so sad and it pained me to know that I was at least part of the reason why they cried.

"No. As a matter of fact, I haven't."

"I buried it last night," she said very casually to her knees.

"What?"

She looked up and said, "Alice told me that she saw you disappear. She told me and I believed her. So, I buried a 1935 penny in a mason jar near the big oak tree in my backyard. Alice kept watch while I shoveled. Wasn't that what you were trying to do?"

I was shocked. I got out of my crouched position and sat down Indian-style on the ground. I sat

there with my jaw hanging open for a long time before
I said, "Yes, that's exactly what I was trying to do.
Why didn't you tell me about this earlier today?"

"You didn't exactly give me a chance to say
much of anything, did you?" she replied, referring to
our passionate kiss in front of her house.

"No, I guess I didn't." Still bewildered I said, "I
can't believe that *you* buried the penny."

"And you haven't time-slipped since last night?"

"No. I guess it worked. I thought I was
traveling back to my own time for good last night when
something seemed to snap me back. It must have been
you burying the penny ... That's great!"

She was still fighting tears and didn't agree.
"What's so great?" she asked.

"We can be together now! I won't time-slip
anymore! I'm here to stay and we can be together
forever!"

She didn't share my exuberance. "I can't,
Joseph. I made a promise to Freddy. I have to marry
him." She then started crying all over again.

I couldn't believe that she was still willing to go
forward with her plans. "If you don't love him, you
can't marry him." I turned toward her and placed her
head in my hand. "Look, I'm not exactly a fan of
Freddy's, but even *he* deserves to be with someone who
loves him. I know you don't love him ... I know you
love me."

"I *do* love you," she said, but sounded as if she
wished she didn't. "But how can I tell him that I don't
want to marry him after I told him I would?"

I thought about her predicament then said, "You don't!" I sprang up off of the ground, reached for her hand and continued, "You run away with me!"

"Run away? Where would we go?"

"Does it matter? We'll go where the wind takes us. I came into a little money last night and I bought Harry's car. We can leave tonight! What do you say?"

"We can't. My father would kill you," she said and she wasn't exaggerating.

"We can call your parents and tell them you're okay when we're far enough away, someplace where your father can't find us. Eventually he'll calm down or your mother will make him. C'mon, Katherine, let's do it!"

She didn't answer, so I got down on my knees and begged. "Katherine, run away with me. I swear I will make you happy, in fact I know I will." I kissed her hand gently and said, "We need to be together!"

She looked directly into my eyes, but didn't say a word. It was as if she physically couldn't speak. Finally, she gave me a wry smile and said softly, "But, it's crazy." She may have said it was crazy, but the expression on her face told me that she was ready to be crazy with me.

"Then you'll do it? You'll run away with me?"

"Yes." She smiled wide and repeated, "Yes!" She lunged toward me for a big hug and almost tackled me to the ground. We then kissed each other tenderly for as long as time would allow and we loved each other until time no longer mattered.

A MESSAGE FROM THE AUTHOR

I met Joseph Eaton in the mid-1980s at the nursing home where he lived while I was performing community service to atone for some youthful mistakes. He was in his late seventies and in failing health. I was assigned to keep him company and assumed I would be spending that time playing checkers with an old man. He had entirely different plans for me instead.

The moment after our introduction he asked me if I was a good writer. When I told him that I wasn't, he said I would have to do anyway. He handed me a notebook and a pen and instructed me to write down every word he said from that point on. When I asked him why he couldn't write for himself, he wrung his hands together and replied, "Arthritis."

Over the next three weeks he told me the incredible story of how he met the love of his life and demanded that I take notes on every detail. The story I was told in that three-week span has been presented here and the majority of it is in Joseph Eaton's own words. Of course, being the young delinquent that I was, I gave him as much grief and difficulty as I possibly could, especially when he dictated something completely unbelievable. Each time that I would stop him and cast doubt about his account he would ignore me and continue on telling his story, but it was clear that he resented the interruptions. Whenever I would get cranky and complain of writer's cramp or some other ailment, he would insist that I do as he asked and continue taking down his thoughts. For those three weeks, Joseph Eaton was my task master.

When I arrived at the nursing home for the fourth and final week of my sentence, I was told that I would be assigned to a different resident. When I asked the staff why I was no longer with Mr. Eaton, I was told that he had died over the weekend. I was saddened to hear about his demise, but at the same time I was glad that my last week would be spent doing something easier than writing for hours and hours on end.

After I finished my community service, I didn't give much thought at all to the story Joseph Eaton told. He had never given me any instructions as to what I was supposed to do with his account, and my notebook from those three weeks was thrown in the back of my bedroom closet not to be opened again for another twenty years.

In July of 2007, a planned major relocation prompted me to go through all of my things from clothes to personal papers and discard whatever wasn't absolutely necessary to keep. It was then when I rediscovered the notebook which contained Joseph Eaton's story. I viewed each page and was shocked after reading some of the passages, especially the notes where he talked about the Internet and cell phones. To my knowledge, the Internet did not exist when I took down those notes and cell phones were extremely large and used only by wealthy people.

Although he never told me exactly what "his time" was, I figured his time-travel adventure began in either 2006 or 2007. I became intrigued by the possibilities and began making phone calls. I found that a Margo Eaton actually existed in the town of Valley View and I called her after obtaining her telephone number through a private detective agency.

She was taken by surprise by what I told her of her brother, but corroborated much of the story in the early chapters of this book. Joseph's visit from Philadelphia to Valley View had been very recent and it was all very fresh in her mind. Months later when I decided to start transcribing the notes into a book, I received Margo's permission, but only if I would change her family name and the name of the town in which she lived.

After doing intensive research on the life of Joseph Eaton, I found that he and Katherine married and settled in a small town on the north shore of eastern Long Island. They lived in a modest house by a small lake and did not have any children. Joseph, in a twist of fate, worked for the local telephone company for over thirty-five years and retired in 1974, shortly after Katherine died of cancer. By all appearances, they had a wonderful life together.

It was never made quite clear to me how Freddy York was able to figure out that he had lost his fiancée to a time traveler, but he must have at least suspected that was the case to spend all of his money on the Whitney house and give Chuck Manning such particular instructions on who could live there. Perhaps Alice, his younger sister, told him about

Joseph's *disappearing act,* but even if she had, I doubt he would have believed her.

I had hoped that Chuck Manning would fill in some of the blanks, but he refused to meet with me or even speak to me on the phone. In response, I shipped him a case of Life Savers with explicit instructions that he bring them to his mother Alice. The card that I taped to the top of the box read: *To my Dear Friend Alice: See you in 1935, Love Joseph.*

I was also not quite sure how the trunk with the telephone ended up in the Whitneys' attic. It may have been done by Freddy York himself after buying the Whitney house. He may have inadvertently started the whole chain of events that eventually led to his own devastation. It may also have been possible that Joseph and Katherine snuck into the house and managed to set-up the trunk to look exactly the way Joseph and his sister Margo would find it all of those many years later.

I was only able to contact two staff members from the nursing home where Joseph died. One had no recollection of him at all, but the other remembered that Joseph spent as much time as he could playing the piano for the other residents when he wasn't pained by his arthritis. This staff member remembered Joseph because she found it so very odd that a man of his age enjoyed playing the music that was popular at the time with people in their teens, twenties or thirties. She went on to say that when the residents complained about his choice of music, he would play some of the songs that they enjoyed instead. There was one particular tune he would play for them over and over, but the former staff member didn't remember the name of the song or how the melody went. I'd like to think it was *Dream a Little Dream of Me*, the song he and Katherine played together at Milligan's bar shortly after they first met.

Joseph may have planned to tell me more about that week in 1935 before he died. He might have even wanted to give me more information about how their lives turned out after that week, but I'll never know. I just hope he is happy and with the love of his life wherever or whenever he is.

Acknowledgments:

I would like to extend a world of thanks to my dear aunt, Jane Archbold, for her support and invaluable knowledge about life in a small Long Island town in the 1930s and 1940s. I wouldn't have been able to construct the town of Valley View without her assistance.

A special thank you to Lucy Lupo Huttle for all of her help in navigating that minefield called the English language.

I would also like to thank the following people for their encouragement and support:

Jackie Yazzie
Jill and Martin Majka
Ida Ferrari
Bette Gilliom
Steve Smith
Timmy Bhagwandin
Ron Grage
Keith Thompson
David Morris

And last, but definitely not least, thank you to my dear husband John for continuing to put up with all of my time-travel fantasies.

www.ingramcontent.com/pod-product-compliance
Lightning Source LLC
Chambersburg PA
CBHW071239170626
46809CB00001B/11